El Chancho

by

Christopher L. Reilly

Christopher L. Reilly

EL Chancho

chrislreilly6@icloud.com

Case # 1-14815622221

Table of Contents

Prologue	5
Chapter 1	9
Chapter 2	18
Chapter 3	21
Chapter 4	25
Chapter 5	31
Chapter 6	44
Chapter 7	51
Chapter 8	57
Chapter 9	63
Chapter 10	69
Chapter 11	78
Chapter 12	82
Chapter 13	88
Chapter 14	91
Chapter 15	98
Chapter 16	106
Chapter 17	108
Chapter 18	116
Chapter 19	122
Chapter 20	129
Chapter 21	134
Chapter 22	138
Chapter 23	141
Chapter 24	145
Chapter 25	155

Chapter 26   158
Chapter 27   161
Chapter 28   168
Chapter 29   173
Chapter 30   185
Chapter 31   190
Chapter 32   192
Chapter 33   201
Chapter 34   205
Chapter 35   213
Chapter 36   220
Chapter 37   224
Chapter 38   227
Chapter 39   230
Chapter 40   238
Chapter 41   242
Chapter 42   247
Chapter 43   250
Chapter 44   258
Chapter 45   261
Chapter 46   264
Chapter 47   268
Chapter 48   273
Chapter 49   275

Prologue

Juan sat in his blacked-out Chrysler 300 as Conchita paced back and forth on the corner. He reached under his seat and felt for the bag of methamphetamines he'd purchased earlier in the day, just in case one of his customers wanted to pay a little extra for a good time. He then slid his hand over and felt for his Glock, just in case the good time got a bit out of control.

He reclined his seat and closed his eyes. August nights in Houston were sweltering. He knew business would be slow. No games in town, and the mosquitos were thick and vicious. He'd parked in the dark shadow of a streetlight with the engine running and the air conditioning on max.

Every half hour or so, Conchita made her way back to the car. "I need *agua*."

Juan passed a bottle of water out through a crack in the window.

"Can I please sit in the car for a while? I'm so hot."

Juan rolled up the tinted window without responding. He watched as she made her way back to her corner to wait. Time to get someone new. She was getting old.

He started to feel his luck changing when he noticed a car coming down the street. Conchita stepped off the curb and waved. The car crept slowly by but didn't stop.

"He'll be back around," he whispered. "They always come back around." He closed his eyes and smiled as he thought about the new wheels he'd just bought for the car. Twenty-one-inch high-gloss chrome beauties.

He was starting to doze when he noticed a light tapping by his left ear. At first he thought it was nothing, maybe a bug bouncing off the window. Houston nights were thick with bugs. June bugs, cicadas, wood roaches, you name it. He cracked his eyes and saw Conchita still standing on the corner, but she had a strange look on her face. Her mouth was half-open as if she wanted to say something but couldn't.

Tap, tap, tap. Tap, tap, tap.

Juan looked to his left. All he could see in the darkness was the tip of a baseball bat gently rapping on the glass. "What the hell!" He sat up and reached under the seat for his gun.

Crash!

The glass exploded as the bat barely missed the side of his head. Before he could find the gun, a pair of hands came through the window and grabbed him around the neck, choking him as his body was dragged across the broken glass and out the window. His head hit hard against the ground. When he opened his eyes, he saw towering over him a large man in a T-shirt, jeans, and wearing a pig mask. A baseball bat dangled from his right hand.

The man straddled Juan and bent down close to his face. "I don't like guys like you. I don't like guys who sell women and push that shit you have stashed in your car."

Juan lay frozen. He knew no one would be coming down that dark back lane to save him. He knew his time was up.

The man raised the bat high over his head as Juan screamed and covered his face. Suddenly he felt excruciating pain in his ankle as the bat connected with bone.

"Don't let me find you again. Get out of the business and get a real job."

Juan rolled around on the sidewalk in agony. He watched as the man reached into the car and opened the door. The man pulled the gun and the bag of meth out from under the seat. He tucked the gun in his pants, then emptied the drugs into the sewer.

"Nice car, by the way." The man made his way around the car, using the bat to smash every window. He put a big dent in the front hood, then broke the taillights. "Looks better now. You better call 911 and get that ankle taken care of." He walked off into the darkness.

Conchita rushed over to Juan once she was sure the masked assailant was gone. "*Estas bien?*"

"Shut the hell up and call an ambulance!"

Chapter 1

Max Donovan stood at the scrub sink, inspecting his hands. Blood was caked between his fingers where his surgical gloves had failed him. He reached up and grabbed a scrub brush from the shelf and began scrubbing vigorously, attacking the blood on his skin as if it were a cancer. He rinsed in the soothing hot water, then grabbed another brush and started washing again, each time staring at his hands to see if every last drop of blood was gone.

When he was convinced that he was clean, he dried himself, then returned to the operating room and poked his head inside. "Any family, Macie?"

"Just a girlfriend, Dr. Donovan. She's out in the waiting room."

"How old was he again?"

"Twenty-three."

Max winced. "Okay, thanks." He stood in the doorway for a few more minutes, quietly watching as Nick Jernigan, the anesthesiologist, turned off the ventilator and the monitors. The hot overhead surgical lamps he'd been standing under for hours had been shut off, and the room was now bathed in a dull, anticlimactic, sterile white light. The staff moved about quietly as if they'd been holding their collective breaths, only to have exhaled when defeat was eventually realized. Several cleaning staff were already in the room mopping up the pools of blood that were splattered about the floor. A pile of bloody towels lay in a corner. A nurse appeared from a side room with a clean sheet and placed it over the cold, naked body.

"Reminds you of Afghanistan, doesn't it, Max?" Dr. Jernigan cheerfully shouted from the far side of the room.

Max's face was expressionless as he looked across at Jernigan fiddling with his machine just beyond the head of the dead young man. His stomach twisted in a knot. The callous joyfulness with which some trauma physicians coped with the horror of their job always made him feel uneasy. Jernigan was one of them. Always joking when death was just around the corner. Never gave Max the impression he gave a damn. Just wanted to get done and get the hell home.

Jernigan had been tall once, but the years hadn't been good to him. His back was arched high up—not exactly a hunch, but just enough to make it difficult for him to look straight up. He had the habit of turning his body slightly to the side if he was to look you in the eye. His gray, unkempt hair sprawled out the sides of his faded burnt-orange UT Longhorns surgical cap. His reading glasses dangled on the tip of his nose.

"Let's go team. Clean this garbage up. I need my coffee," shouted Jernigan as he jerked his ECG leads off the body.

Max bowed his head and said nothing as he slowly turned away. He walked down the long corridor that led from the operating room to the waiting area, hesitating briefly before entering. He looked through the glass and saw an attractive young woman sitting quietly in a corner, staring at the screen of her cell phone. She wore a tight-fitting red top and expensive-looking jeans. She looked as if she'd just put on makeup. Maybe she wanted to look her best when her boyfriend came around and saw her for the first time? Next to her was a clear plastic bag containing the victim's belongings. The ubiquitous coffee cup and bag of chips lay on a table by her side.

Max knew he was about to shatter her world. He took in a deep breath, then confidently strode into the room and sat down. "Hello, I'm Dr. Donovan, trauma surgeon. Are you here with Nate Garner?"

"Yes," she replied, barely looking up from her phone as she continued to text. "Are you done already?" She wiped her nose with the back of her hand. "When can I see him?"

Max paused before responding. She didn't notice him sigh as he turned his head to look around the sterile expanse of the waiting room. The worn tiled floor and battered metal chairs had seen thousands come and go, but now there were just two.

"I'm sorry. He didn't make it." Max watched as her nonchalant expression changed.

Her mouth began to quiver. Her eyes filled with tears. "What do you mean? When they called me, they said he was fine! I want to see him. I want to see him now!"

For a brief moment, Max thought of trying to explain what had happened as if telling her how they'd used the massive transfusion protocols he'd become so familiar with in Afghanistan would've made a difference in how she felt. How Nate came into the emergency room alert and shouting about how he was going to get the guy who'd shot him and to let him go but suddenly arrested. How they'd barely gotten him to the operating room at all.

"I'm sorry." He slowly rose to his feet as her cell phone slid from her hand and crashed to the floor unnoticed. He gently touched her on the shoulder. "A nurse will be out here soon to help direct you in what needs to be done next. I'm truly sorry for your loss."

Max turned and walked out of the room. From behind, he could hear her burst into tears. "You could've saved him!" he heard her shout as the door slowly closed. "If he was rich, you could've saved him, you bastard!"

Max hesitated, then slowly walked down the long, sterile corridor back to the locker room. He'd never gotten used to the sickly-sweet smell of the antiseptic cleaning fluid that permeated the place. Now, as his aching body told him to take a break, it seemed to nauseate him.

He kicked open the locker-room door and headed straight to the bathroom, where he stripped down to his underwear and tossed his sweat-drenched scrubs into a laundry bin. The water ran cold as he soaked his head in the sink. The chilly stimulation helped him block out all thoughts of his latest failure. When he was finished, he stroked back his graying black hair. His coal black eyes scanned his half-naked muscular frame in the mirror, his handsome, chiseled features expressionless.

"You're a goddamn pretty bastard, aren't you," he whispered sarcastically as he slowly rubbed the large, jagged scars on his chest. *A few centimeters higher and you wouldn't have been able to be a surgeon*, he thought. *A few lower and you'd have been dead.*

He walked to the rack of clean scrubs positioned between old steel lockers painted pale beige and covered with patches of rust. He grabbed his size and quickly dressed. He spun in the combination to the padlock on his locker and tried to pull open the door, but it jammed.

"Damn piece of shit!" he shouted as he kicked the locker hard with his foot. The door swung open. *Trauma surgeon and all the county can get is surplus high school lockers!*

Max reached deep inside his locker and pulled from behind a heavy lead radiation vest a Beretta in a small-of-the-back holster and clipped it onto the back of his scrub pants. He reached in again and pulled out a fixed-blade commando knife and strapped it to his ankle. He took a Rolex off the top shelf and slipped it on. *Need a little walkabout.* He slammed the locker shut and turned toward the locker-room door.

BANG!

Max fell to his knees, pressing hard against the lockers as he shielded himself from the door. He held the Beretta close to his chest and waited. He closed his eyes for only a second, but in that second, he swore he could smell burning flesh and dirt. When he opened his eyes, he was still alone. There were no noises coming from the hallway. The only sounds he could hear were his own heavy breathing and the pounding of his heartbeat in his ears.

Max rose to his feet as he holstered his gun and walked to the door. He paused briefly, then cracked the door, only to see that a large cleaning cart had slammed into it, blocking his way.

A petite cleaning woman looked up at him in surprise. "Sorry for the noise, Doc. Kind of got away from me." She smiled as she struggled to move the cart to the side.

"No problem."

Max squeezed past the cart and headed down the stairs and across the first floor toward the emergency room exit.

"How ya doing, Slim?" Max said to the guard. He liked Slim. Ex-military. Took guarding the back door seriously. *What a crazy nickname,* he thought, as he smiled at the huge man. He wasn't quite fat, just big. Big enough to stop a running back dead in his tracks. Big enough to stop someone coming through the back door uninvited. And that was important. Drive-bys didn't always end on the street. Sometimes bangers tried to bust into the emergency room to finish the job. That was where Slim came in.

"Good, Dr. Donovan. Going for another walk?" Slim leaned across the guard desk, resting on his hands as he shrugged his shoulders. "You know this ain't the best time of night to be out there wandering about."

"I know, but I've got to get some fresh air."

"Fresh air!" Slim laughed as he thumped his meaty fist on the desk. "It's midnight in Houston, in August. It's still ninety-five outside and probably ninety-five percent humidity!"

"I know, but I've gotta get out. You remember how it was over there. Too damn claustrophobic in the tents." Max wiped the sweat from his forehead. "Same with this place. Been here already seventeen hours and got seven to go." He walked past Slim and through the metal detector.

Slim straightened up as the alarm started chirping. "Hey, Doc . . ."

Max waved his wrist in the air, flashing his big watch. "Does it every time."

He heard Slim grumble as he sat back in his seat. "Damn fool gonna get himself killed out there this time of night."

The sliding doors opened, and Max walked out of the emergency department of Harris County Hospital and into the parking lot. It was lit by floodlights raised high up on poles, but still there were plenty of shadows, and those shadows were teeming with people. Some were lying against the walls sleeping. Others in small groups leaned against cars. A taco truck sat parked on the far side of the lot under a solitary light. A long line of customers trailed away from the pickup window and into the darkness. In the distance, someone in a car had Tejano music playing which added an undercurrent of joviality to the muffled hum of the crowd.

Max could almost see the air; it was so thick with humidity and the smell of sweat. His shirt clung to his torso to the point where simply walking across the lot was an effort.

Across from the hospital was a large park and adjacent zoo. He had a favorite bench he liked to go to when he was particularly stressed. It was next to a pond and near enough to the zoo that he could hear the animals making grunting noises as they moved about in their enclosures. The homeless usually stayed closer to the covered benches near the playground and for the most part left him alone.

Max tried not to make any eye contact as he crossed the lot. Nevertheless, out of the corner of his eye, he noticed a woman stand up from leaning on the hood of a car. She stepped out of the shadows and stopped right in front of him. She was young, very young. Maybe seventeen? Her small breasts pushed up high and tight. She wore a short pink skirt and uncomfortable looking matching stilettos. She had on no makeup. Wouldn't last long in this humidity anyway, he thought. Her black hair pulled back exposing her high cheekbones. Definitely Mexican, he figured. More native than Spanish. Max paused and stared into her eyes. There he saw a deep sadness hiding behind a forced smile.

He generally knew her history. Like so many other girls passing through the human trafficking capital of the US, she probably crossed the border illegally looking for a better life. Or maybe she is one of the thousands that just disappear regularly from their small villages south of the border and ended up here. The ER was full of them on any given night. Battered by their pimps or roughed up by their Johns. Scared, aggressively defensive. Caught in a world that didn't seem to really care.

"Need some relaxation, Doc?"

"No thanks darlin. Why don't you get out of those stupid shoes and go home."

"Please," she asked desperately. Her voice quivering as Max turned to go.

She turned her head slightly to the side and looked over her shoulder. A man opened the door of the car she'd been leaning against and stepped out. As he slowly sauntered over in their direction, he noticed the young girl's eyes starting to water. When the man was within earshot, she shouted at Max. "Fuck you pendejo, you no dick hijo de puta!" then turned and walked back into the darkness.

Max's hands slowly clenched and unclenched as he glared at the approaching man. He'd seen plenty of guys like this one. The bandana. The wife-beater shirt covered with stains and sweat. Pants hanging low. Arms sporting gang tattoos.

"Waz up, Doc? Shouldn't you be inside?"

Max smiled and stepped around him.

"Yo, Doc. Nice Rolex. Would look good on me."

Max said nothing as he continued toward the park.

"I'll give you cash for that watch. Thousand, two thousand? What you want?"

"What the hell are you talking about?" Max turned and went back to the harasser. "You have that kind of money?"

"Yeah, I got that kind of money, motherfucker." The man produced a large roll of cash and flashed it in Max's face.

"So, you must be the man around here then." Max inched closer, seething with rage. "Keep everyone supplied while they wait for their families, that it?"

"Name's Angel." The man slid his hands under his armpits and leaned back. "You should remember that." He smirked. "I got a business. So what?"

"Know about Nate? Boy shot out here few hours back."

"Heard something about some punk-ass dude wanting to start his own business. Nothing else."

Max turned and gave him a sideways glance. "I hate businessmen like you." He jiggled the Rolex in Angel's face. "I wouldn't sell this to you for a million bucks. You know why? Because I don't like you."

"I'm just supplying where there's a need." Angel slid in closer to Max, grabbing him by the arm, and whispered in his ear. "You know what? I think I'm going to have that watch for nothing 'cause I don't like fuckers like you. Coming out into my world with all your fancy shit and judging me. Got your fancy cars and big-ass houses, but you no better than me. You be in my situation, you'd do the same. Fact, people like you not in my situation do much worse."

Max jerked his arm away and stepped back. "I've been working hard all day, and I think I'm going to go into the park and rest for a while." He turned away from Angel and didn't look back. He walked across the lot and along the empty street that ran beside the hospital. He passed under the spreading boughs of live oak and pecan trees that scattered the light from the streetlamps into bright claws that seemed to cling to the pavement. He crossed over and into the peaceful darkness of his favorite park, where he found his bench and sat down. The lights from the hospital were just a glow off to his right. To his left, complete darkness. Above him, he could see the stars as they peeked through the old trees. Before him, a hedge grove covered a large fence that separated the park from the zoo. All he could hear was the buzz of cicadas and the calling of frogs mixed with the grunt and shuffle of large beasts trying to settle themselves in the stifling heat.

As Max spread his arms across the back of the bench, he turned and saw the dark silhouette of a man cross the street to his right and head toward him. The park became silent. Nothing moved. Nothing breathed.

"Doc. You got my watch? Give it to me."

Max stood. He could only make out Angel's silhouette, his features shrouded in darkness as the distant light from the hospital outlined his frame. "Come and take it, you son of a bitch."

Without another word, Angel swung a roundhouse punch straight for the left side of Max's head. Max reflexively pulled his left hand up and grabbed his own neck, blocking the punch. He then spun his left arm around, catching Angel above the elbow and wrenched it backward. Max squatted down and pulled out his knife from his ankle sheath and brought it up into Angel's abdomen. He pushed it in hard and to the left.

Angel let out a scream as Max held him fast by his broken elbow.

"Good thing you screwed with a surgeon, you bastard," he whispered in his ear. "You're going to limp away with only a bag to shit in, unlike poor Nate." Max pulled out the knife and stuck it into his ankle, slicing Angel's Achilles tendon. He then wiped the blade clean on Angel's shirt as he let him drop to the ground. "I assume you have a cell phone. Better call 911. You don't want to be here too long; the ants will get to you."

Max stood and slowly walked back toward the hospital. He took a right along the road and avoided crossing the parking lot. He skirted the edge of the building and walked out of the darkness immediately in front of the emergency room door.

"Good walk, Dr. Donovan?" Slim asked. "Must be hotter than I thought. You're soaked through."

"Yep. Pretty damn hot out there. Need to take a shower."

The metal detector chirped again as Max passed through. He just waved his watch and kept walking.

Chapter 2

Max scrubbed himself so hard that red streaks started appearing across his torso. Once he'd rinsed the soap off, he started all over again, never feeling quite clean enough. Finally, he stepped from the shower and put on a new pair of clean scrubs.

He hurried out of the locker room and down the hallway to his call room. He turned on the light, pausing momentarily before entering. *Not much bigger than a prison cell*, he thought. There was a twin bed crammed against one wall. Beside it stood a bedside table with a phone and a solitary light with a battered shade. The room was barely wide enough for him to walk around the bed. How many years had he spent alone working to near complete exhaustion only to come back to a small, empty space like this and collapse? He closed and locked the door, then hung his coat on a hook. He slipped out of his surgical clogs and neatly aligned them by the door, then fell onto his bed and waited.

When his phone rang, he saw that it was from his chief resident. His sweaty hand trembled as he held the phone up to his ear. "Donovan," he barked.

"Dr. Donovan, Nigel here."

"What's going on?"

"I've got a twenty-seven-year-old Hispanic male who stumbled into the ER from across the street. Man, someone really did a job on him! Stab wound to the abdomen, laceration to the right Achilles tendon, and fracture dislocation of the right elbow."

"How's he doing?"

"He's very stable, except maybe a little delusional. Doing a drug screen on him now." Max heard him chuckle. "Kind of funny. Screaming that some surgeon did this to him. Cops were here and seemed to know him really well. They took his story, but to be honest with you, boss, they said there were no witnesses and kind of felt he deserved it. Don't think they're going to try too hard to find the guy that did this."

"All right then. I'll pop my head in when you're underway. Thanks." Max tried to slow his breathing. He felt his muscles finally starting to relax as he sunk into the worn old mattress. He closed his eyes and drifted off to sleep.

Rat, tat, tat. Whoomph. Rat, tat, tat. Rat, tat, tat.

Donovan! Help, we need you right away! Blood on the walls. Bodies in the hallway.

Max sat bolt upright and stared into the darkness. Silence. Sweat had soaked through his scrubs. He turned on the light and slipped into his clogs. He puffed his cheeks and exhaled as he threw his worn white coat over his shoulders, and headed down the long, empty hallway toward the operating rooms. He walked silently through the swinging electric doors that opened into the operating room complex. He passed multiple empty rooms until he reached the operating room reserved for late-night traumas. He hung his coat on a hook then grabbed a facemask from a box over the scrub sink and tied the strings securely around his head. He paused briefly and looked through the glass of the operating room door.

Nigel, his chief resident, was leaning his lanky frame over the operating room table as he held up segments of intestine to the light, his red hair creeping out from under the edges of his surgeon's cap. Sweat glistened on the back of his freckled neck.

Max thrust open the operating-room door and strode up to the side of the table. "What've you got?" He leaned in and looked over the chief resident's shoulder.

"Pretty amazing." Nigel flipped the colon back and forth for Max to see. "Knife wound through the colon. Spilled a lot of stool, but nothing else hit. Because of the contamination, I'm going to give him a colostomy. Otherwise, he's good."

"How about orthopedics?"

"They're coming in next to do something about the elbow. Doesn't seem to have a vascular injury. They're going to wash out his ankle and pretty much leave it alone for now."

"Good work." Max turned to leave. "He's your private patient. I think you're up to it. I won't need to see him unless you have a problem."

"Thank you, Dr. Donovan."

Max left the operating room and nodded to Damien, the anesthesia tech, on his way out the door. He was a good tech. Worked his ass off. His thin, muscular frame never seemed to tire.

"Don't you sleep, Dr. Donovan? Every time I'm here, you're here."

"No, Damien. Never sleep anymore."

Chapter 3

The town of Nuevo Laredo sits on the south side of the Rio Grande connected to her American cousin, Laredo, by five bridges.

Several miles from the border, in a one-story cinder-block house with a strangely out-of-place orange front door, sat Rosa. She leaned over her papers and stared at the list of English vocabulary words her high school teacher had assigned to be memorized before class the following day. She was good in English, and that made her parents proud. They knew that if she was going to get a good job one day, maybe in a hotel like her father, then she would need to be fluent.

Her mother, Juanita, was in the kitchen cooking. The aroma of tortillas warming on the grill filled the house. Rosa could hear the crackle of the chicken as her mother mixed it with peppers and onions. She would mix in a good helping of jalapeños because she knew she liked it hot. The warm steam from the kitchen wrapped her in a blanket of smells and comfort. Her brother, Miguel, played with a toy car on the floor and kept running it into the leg of her chair.

"Miguel, stop! I need to get this done before tomorrow."

"Rosita, you're no fun anymore since you started high school. They make you work too hard."

"Don't be silly." She looked lovingly at her younger brother. He'd come along late and was a surprise to Rosa's parents and was just starting elementary school. "One day, you'll have to do this too if you want to make anything of yourself."

"You don't have time to play. Why would I want to do that?" He crashed his toy car back into the leg of her chair.

"Stop! I need to work." She placed her pencil down in exasperation. "Mama!"

Her mother came into the room with two plates of food and placed them down on the table. "Enough for now. You both need to eat." She went back into the kitchen and returned with some apple juice for the two children, then sat at the head of the small dining room table.

Rosa pulled her long black hair back and tied it with an elastic band. She glanced sideways at Miguel as he was about to put a piece of chicken in his mouth. "Eh? Say your prayers." Rosa looked up at her mother with a smile as they all bowed their heads and said grace.

Rosa ate quietly. She looked around her small dining room and was content. There was nothing fancy about it. It was painted in a pale blue, its walls covered with pictures of the family. A brown credenza along the opposite wall from the kitchen had several painted plates on top surrounded by pictures of her parents and grandparents. It was a good home and sitting there quietly with her mother and brother made her happy.

"Aren't you going to eat, Mama?" asked Miguel.

"No, dear, I'm going to wait for your father. He's working late tonight."

Her mother reached across and gently grabbed Rosa by the forearm. "It's your sixteenth birthday tomorrow. For dinner, I'm going to make pork with mole poblano for you."

Rosa smiled, her mouth still full of chicken. She loved her mother's cooking.

After dinner, she helped clean up, then sat back down to complete her studies. It was late when she finally finished and crawled into bed. Just as she turned the light out, her father came through the front door. She could hear him talking quietly to her mother before coming into the room she shared with Miguel. She acted as if she were asleep as he kissed her and Miguel on the foreheads before quietly closing the door and going back to the kitchen.

When Rosa woke the next day, there was a small package on her bedside table with a bow around it.

Miguel woke and rolled over. "*Feliz cumpleaños*, Rosita. What did you get?"

Rosa carefully unwrapped the present. Inside was a small jewelry box.

"Oh, it looks expensive!" Miguel squealed.

Rosa slowly opened it. Inside the felt-lined box was a small silver heart-shaped locket and chain. She carefully opened it and smiled. Inside was a picture of the four of them standing in front of the orange front door. She remembered when Uncle Carlos had come last year to visit. He'd insisted that they stand in front of the house to get a picture.

"That's me!" Miguel exclaimed. "Now you'll always have me around!"

Rosa gently unbuckled the clasp. She pulled her long black hair to the side and placed the locket around her neck. She climbed out of bed and stood in front of her small vanity mirror. She knew she was pretty. She was tall for her age, and her light brown skin had never suffered the blemishes other teenagers often had to endure. Her clear almond eyes crinkled around the edges as she smiled. "It's beautiful," she whispered. She didn't have much jewelry and having something that was so beautiful and also contained her family was perfect.

Rosa ran from her room and into the kitchen, where her mother was already cooking her favorite breakfast, chilaquiles with green sauce. She grabbed her around the waist and buried her head in her back.

"Be careful, silly. You're going to make me burn myself." Rosa's mother turned and gave her a kiss. "Feliz cumpleaños, my big girl." She prepared two plates and carried them into the dining room. "Hurry up and eat or you're going to be late. Your papa will be home early from work today so we can have a nice dinner together."

When Rosa finished her breakfast, she tucked her locket inside her shirt, then swung her backpack over her shoulder. She kissed her mother goodbye.

"You are getting so big. I can't believe how fast you've grown."

"Mama, I can't find my shoe," Rosa heard Miguel shout from the bedroom.

"Hurry along, Rosa. I'll see you when you get home." Rosa watched her mother move into the bedroom as she turned and locked the front door.

She walked briskly along the sidewalk down the two blocks to her school, where she saw her friends waiting by the entrance. She liked to get to school early so they could talk a little before going in. Louisa had a crush on one of the boys in the class and couldn't stop talking about how good-looking he was. Rosa smiled as she thought about boys. She wasn't going to have a boyfriend until she had finished university. She wanted to be able to support herself first before starting a family. Maybe one day she would move away from all the gang violence that plagued Nuevo Laredo. Maybe a nice place in Mexico City.

As she got closer, she waved to Louisa. Louisa waved back, then turned away as the boy she liked came up and started talking to her.

A white panel van seemed to appear from nowhere and came to a screeching halt next to Rosa. She paused and stared, confused as to why it had stopped so close to the curb. The side door slid open, and a man jumped out. He grabbed Rosa around the waist with one arm and covered her mouth with the other. He picked her off her feet as she thrashed about trying to free herself. Within a few seconds, she had disappeared inside. The door slammed shut as the van pulled away and vanished down a side street.

Chapter 4

"**G**ood morning, Doctor."

"Good morning, Max. Have a seat."

"Do you mind if I call you Jack, Dr. Simkins?"

"I think it's better that you call me Dr. Simkins. Are you okay with that?"

"Sure, of course." Max paused as he looked the doctor over, not knowing what to make of him. He seemed strangely familiar. He was stocky, but his hands were unusually thin and spiderlike. Wire-rimmed glasses wrapped around ears that looked too big for his balding head. His thin, pale skin made the blue vessels of his forehead appear unusually prominent. Max couldn't decide if he looked grotesque or unusually handsome.

Reluctantly, he lay back on the overstuffed couch and wiggled to get comfortable on the well-worn leather. He looked around the room and noticed that there was nothing there. Sure, to his right was a shelf full of unreadable medical texts, journals, the usual professional decorations. He noticed the degrees. The desk with well-aligned stacks of rubbish. But no family photos. No pictures of the kids in baseball uniforms. No loving wife leaning in for a picture in front of the Eiffel Tower. No ring on Simkins' finger. Truly a psychiatrist's office. Nothing personal on display.

"Now I understand you asked a mutual colleague of ours, Dr. Jernigan, about seeing someone, and he referred you to me. Apparently, you both go way back."

"Yeah, you can say that." Max could hear the rustle of pages turning and the scribble of a pen off to the side and out of his line of sight.

"What seems to be bothering you, Max?"

"Just feeling a little stressed, that's all."

"Have you spoken to anyone before about your stress?"

"Not really." Max shifted uncomfortably. He didn't like having someone behind him.

"I understand you saw someone at the VA in the past."

"That was more of a debriefing than anything else. Nothing more."

Silence.

Dr. Simkins turned a page. "What seems to be causing you stress?"

"Well, you know what I do. It's stressful."

"Is there anything going on in your life right now that's making things more stressful than normal?"

"Always something going on. Some days more than others."

"How are you sleeping, Max?"

Max stared at the ceiling. He couldn't remember the last time he'd slept more than two hours at a stretch. "Not too bad. I don't usually sleep much."

"Why is that?"

"Oh, you know. I'm always up late at night. Been a habit I guess I got used to."

"Any nightmares, dreams that keep bothering you?"

"No, pretty dead to the world. When I'm out, I'm out."

Dr. Simkins sighed. He turned another page. "Why didn't you go back to your doctor at the VA? I have your file here. It says you were quite the hero."

Now it was Max's turn to let out a sigh. "There were no heroes, Doc."

"What do you want, Max? Why did you come to see me?"

"Any ideas on meditation? Some way to relax at work? You know, any *Reader's Digest* suggestions on how to make my workday less stressful?"

"I see that you're a twin."

Max sat up and swung his legs off the couch and planted them solidly on the floor. He turned and looked sideways at Dr. Simkins. "Maybe you could give me some sleeping pills or something to help when I'm off duty. You know I can't write them for myself. Can you do that, Jack? I think that would be a great help right now."

Dr. Simkins folded his notebook. "I can do that. But you must come back and see me next week and tell me how you're sleeping. Deal?"

"Deal."

Dr. Simkins stood and went to his desk and sat down on his large wraparound leather chair. Max sat leaning forward with his elbows on his knees as he watched Simkins pull a pad from his top drawer and scribble out the sleeping pill prescription.

"You know this better than anyone, but don't take with alcohol or any other sedative. And for God's sake, don't operate if you've taken this."

Max stood and snatched the script from Simkins' hand.

"I need to see you next week, agreed?"

"Yes, I'll see you next week. Same time and place." Max turned and left the oak-paneled office, barely acknowledging the secretary as he headed out into the hallway. He shoved the prescription into his pocket and hurried to the pharmacy located on the ground floor of the professional building and picked up his pills. He headed to the parking lot, anxious to get home and hopefully get some sleep. He'd gone straight from working at Harris County to the appointment and now had that sick, nauseated feeling one gets when sleep-deprived but too tired, or too overstimulated, to rest. He hated shrinks, but something had to give. He knew he had a serious problem, and it was only getting worse.

Max lowered himself into his supercharged 1967 Chevy Nova and started the engine. The growl of the big V8 brought a smile to his face, and for a moment, he forgot about what had happened the night before. Squealing tires announced his departure before he raced down through the garage and out into the bright sunshine. He put on his sunglasses as he turned down Rice Boulevard and headed toward his home in the village of West University. Having a house only ten minutes from the hospital made sneaking home every now and again easy. As a bonus, he always found the drive beneath the canopy of giant live oaks relaxing. He jealously watched the Rice University students enjoy the day as they jogged around the outside of campus.

Max cut across several side streets and soon was home. Given that he wasn't into gates and pretentious McMansions, he liked the fact that his place was an unassuming single-story traditional. He'd always just wanted a quiet home, and when he'd moved back to Houston to take this job, he was happy to have found this fully furnished rental. It was small. One bedroom with attached bath, a living room, and a dining room. The kitchen looked out on a small patch of grass that passed as a back yard. There was a small front porch just big enough for a loveseat. A rose trellis clung to one side by the front door. The house was dark green. He liked the color. When he'd seen it for the first time, he thought it looked warm and calming. Just what he needed to come back to at the end of a shift.

He pulled into the driveway and pressed the garage-door opener for the detached garage and slid the Nova gently in. The old garage was a tight fit, and he squeezed out of the Nova trying not to bang the door on the wall. He slowly walked around the back and smiled as he rubbed a smudge off the SS logo. He looked up at the sky and saw a wall of dark clouds rolling in from the west.

Going to be a good one, he thought.

Max closed the garage and walked in through the back door and into his living room. Suddenly, he was overcome with fatigue. He staggered to the sofa and dove onto it face first. Within minutes, he was sound asleep.

~~~
~~~

BOOM!

The house shook. Max awoke, startled, and slid off the couch and under the edge of the coffee table. He reached around for his gun but noticed that it had fallen to the floor beside him.

BOOM, BOOM!

Lightning flashed across the darkened room. Rain started falling heavily on the old roof, drowning out all other noises.

Max rolled onto his back and stared at the underside of the coffee table that took up much of the center of the small room. "Damn fool," he mumbled. He was angry with himself for not having removed his gun before diving onto the sofa.

He closed his eyes and listened to the rhythmic patter of the rain. The hardwood floor felt good under his back. He shifted his hips and stretched his arms above his head. The rain started to fall harder, and he wondered if it would last all day. The house had never flooded, but street flooding around his neighborhood could force him to stay in. He remembered times when he'd left the hospital after being cloistered there for thirty-six hours, only to find that half the city was underwater. The Gulf Coast was that way. Hot as hell one minute, underwater the next.

Max rose from the floor and flopped onto the sofa. Despite it now being midday, it had grown dark outside. Gray-green light filtered in through the front windows and cast the room in an eerie glow. He sat with his hands folded on his lap. Across from him, standing between two windows, was a large dark wooden credenza. A dozen or so pictures with an eclectic mixture of ornate and simple frames were arranged along its top. Suspended on the wall between the two windows was a simple shelf. On it rested a triangular box containing a folded American flag.

Max focused on a picture of two young boys, soaking wet in their swim shorts, arms wrapped over each other's shoulders. Between them was a large Texas redfish they could barely hold up for the photographer. The corner of Max's lip quivered. The rain continued to beat on the roof, its intensity rising and falling as the wind rushed around the wood-framed house. The loose gutters rattled, and the rose trellis near the front door made an unsettling scraping noise.

"That was a good day," he whispered.

Max stood and crossed the room and picked up the photo. He pulled the picture to his chest and rubbed the dust off the glass with his scrub top and placed it gently back in its place. He glanced across at a photo of an attractive young woman, smiling, holding a stuffed elephant. Dust had accumulated on the frame. As he reached for it, he felt a heaviness descend upon him as if the storm had entered his living room. He left the photo where it was and turned away.

He went into his bedroom and pulled out the bottle of sleeping pills and took one, washing it down with a bottle of water. He stripped down to his shorts and fell onto his bed and closed his eyes. He tried to remember. To remember what it was like before it all went to hell.

Chapter 5

2003

Max squirmed in his seat as he stared at the clock, waiting for the final bell to ring. His football jersey felt scratchy, which just heightened his feelings of anxiety and excitement. He could hardly focus as Mr. Albertson finished the day's lesson.

"And finally, there'll be no homework tonight. Last big game of the year and all." Mr. Albertson took off his thick glasses and rubbed them on the tail of his untucked shirt. "Let's all show up and support Max and the team." He placed his glasses back on his face and ran his fingers through his thinning gray hair. "Would be nice to get this win. Been a while since we beat West Side. Let's hope the class of 2003 can finally get the job done."

When the bell eventually rang, Max sprang to his feet, slung his backpack over his shoulder, and bolted for the door. As a high school senior, Max was already several inches taller than his teacher and most of the other kids in class. Mr. Albertson patted him on the back as he maneuvered his large, graceful frame out the door.

Max smiled when he looked up and saw a tall, scrawny kid leaning against the lockers, his dark hair ruffled, his clear dark eyes a mirror to Max's own.

"Come on, Max. Not going to be the big hero today if you keep moving that slowly."

Max placed his arm around his brother. "Don't worry, Sam. I can handle whatever West Side has to offer." He smiled and took his brother's backpack and slung it over his own. He then grabbed him by the right arm and pulled him down the hallway.

"Whoa, big boy. I know you're excited, but the old leg will only go so fast."

Max paused and looked down at his brother. Sweat beads had started to form on his forehead. His stiff-pointed left leg had almost lost its shoe, and his cocked left arm was starting to quiver.

Max was mortified. "Sorry, Sammy." Max placed the backpacks on the floor, then knelt and replaced the oddly worn shoe and laced it up tightly. "Need to tell Mom to get you some new shoes. The side of this one is almost worn through."

Sam took several deep breaths. "Go, already. I'll catch up."

Max paused. "You sure?"

"Yeah, you need to get there and get ready. You need to beat those guys today. I'll be in the stands."

Max hesitated, then looked down the long hallway in the direction of the lockers. "Okay, see you in a bit." He turned and jogged away.

"Remember, you said I could drive home if you won!"

Max smiled and shouted over his shoulder: "You got it!"

He passed quickly through the brick-lined hallways of Katy Lakes High School. His thoughts were about Sam and whether he was going to be able to get to the game safely or not. It made him uneasy when he had to leave him on his own. He'd always been there when Sam needed him. To pick him up when he fell in the mud, fix his clothes, everything. Ever since they'd shared the same womb together, he'd been there to make sure Sam was okay.

Max's head cleared as he entered the locker room. The familiar stale sweaty smell of excited young men readying for battle erased thoughts of anything other than football. It was game day. A really big game day at that, and he was ready. He knew he was the best. Had it ingrained in his head from coaches all the way down to the janitor in the hallway who gave him the "go get 'em, big guy" as he jogged past. He felt good, and on that day, he was determined to show the little world of Katy, Texas, that there was no one better.

~ ~ ~

Sam reached down and grabbed his bag, twisting his torso as he slung it over his shoulder. With a well-learned contortion, he was able to work his left arm through the strap. "Come on, lefty," he whispered as he twisted his hips and swung his left leg around, pivoted on the extended left foot, then swung it around again. Usually, he was quite good at keeping up with Max when walking at normal speeds, but today, his brother was in a different world. Senior quarterback. He understood. They both understood. They'd always had that connection.

The hallways had cleared unusually quickly, which made it easier for Sam to navigate the often chaotic after-school rush. Everyone wanted to get to the game. The hallways were empty except for those who, like himself, were a little on the misfit spectrum of the class.

As Sam passed the men's room, he had the sudden urge to go. *God, why now?* He hated to go to the bathroom at school. He looked up and down the hallway and saw no one. He'd not soiled himself in public in years, and he was determined not to do so today. He knew it was a long walk from the stadium bleachers to the bathroom, so now was as good a time as any. He grabbed the door handle and pulled it partially open, then wedged his shoulder into the door to allow himself to get his left leg in. His heart sank as the door slammed behind him. Two boys were sitting on the counter by the sink, smoking and blowing large clouds across the room.

"Well, look who it is, Mike. The brother of mister big fucking quarterback."

"Rob, I just got to take a piss and go."

Rob stood up from the counter. His shredded jeans caught an edge and tore. "Shit, these are brand new!"

Sam couldn't help but smirk at the irony. He knew them both well. Rob was short and stocky. Had patches of hair on his face in a poor attempt to grow a beard. He'd played football in junior high and had been a star. Then he stopped growing. Mike had always been his skinny sidekick. Never did anything that anyone would remember him for except getting suspended once for hiding out in the stall of the girls' bathroom.

"Mike, I think this freak is laughing at me," Rob said as he snuffed out his cigarette on the counter and moved around behind Sam.

Mike slid off the counter and adjusted his fake brown leather jacket and walked up to Sam. "What are you laughing at?"

Sam's heart was pounding. "Come on, guys. Give me a break. Just got to piss, all right."

"Piss? Okay, piss then." Mike gave him a little shove.

"Yeah, piss, you freak," Rob said with another little push from behind.

Sam struggled to maintain his balance. He dropped his bag to the floor and staggered to his left.

Rob grinned. "Where's the big jock now to save you?"

Sam pivoted on his left leg as his face slammed into the towel dispenser. As he straightened himself up with his right arm, he felt the warm sensation of urine running down his leg.

"Oh shit, he did piss himself!" Rob laughed as he slapped Mike on the shoulder. "Oh, shit!"

Sam stood with his head bowed as his pants turned darker and it started to run into his shoes.

"You're one piece of shit, Sam." Mike gave him another tap on the shoulder and watched him struggle to stay upright. "Damn." Both boys stood for a few more seconds, just staring, then turned and left without another word.

Sam stood alone looking at the bathroom's tiled floor, tears streaming down his face. Eventually, he bent down and picked up his bag. He placed it on the counter and reached into one of the pockets and pulled out his cell phone. "Mom, can you bring me some pants?"

"Sam, what happened?" a sweet voice asked.

Sam could sense a hint of panic.

"I thought you were going to the game."

"I had an accident. Pants are all wet."

"Oh, sweetheart! Do you want to come home?"

"No, just some pants. I'm in the bathroom just off the main hallway by the entrance. Can you come in and help me please?"

"Of course. I'll be right there."

Sam hung up and waited. He was glad that no one else came in. Within a few minutes, his mother burst into the restroom. She gave him a big hug, then they began. She quickly removed his shoes. He placed his good arm on her back. They maneuvered together in a well-choreographed dance that they'd been practicing for the past eighteen years. She took a paper towel and washed his legs and feet. Before long, he was in a clean pair of jeans and socks.

"Need new shoes, Mom."

"I know. Let's do that this weekend. You know it's been hard to do anything during the week. Since your father deployed, it's been difficult getting anything done."

"Why did Dad have to go?"

"You know why, honey. We've been over it a thousand times. The army paid for his schooling, and he owes it to them. At least as a nurse, he should be safe in a hospital."

"Whatever." Sam handed his backpack to his mother. "Can you take this home, please?"

"What? You're still going to the game?"

"Max expects me there. You know he can't throw worth a damn if I'm not there," he added with a twinkle in his eye.

"You boys." She gently shook his head between her hands and kissed him on the forehead. "I don't care what you say, I'm walking with you to the stadium. I need to get home, though, to get to work later."

They slowly walked down the empty hallway. Sam didn't rush this time. He knew he was safe, and the game would still be going when he got there. He looked at the lines on his mother's face. With Dad gone off to war and with Sam's cerebral palsy, he could see the strain. Her blue work shirt was ruffled and hung loosely on her tall, thin frame. Her *Welcome to Walmart, Sally* tag was twisted sideways. Gray showed along the roots of her bleached blond hair that hung loosely around her shoulders. It had been black once. That was where his dad said he and Max got their hair from, but you'd never know it. It had always been blond as far back as he could remember. "Gonna get my hair done before your father gets back," she was often heard saying when she looked in the mirror. But there had been no time—at least no time when she didn't appear overwhelmed taking care of him and Max. And with his disability, he knew it made things all that much harder for everyone. She always tried hard to put on a smile, but they would often hear her crying in the kitchen late at night.

"I'm going to be a famous doctor one day," Sam would hear Max whisper as they squirmed to find extra room in the double bed they shared. "Gonna take care of you and Mom."

As they approached the stadium, the thump of the drums from the marching band rattled Sam's insides. Football in Texas was a religion, and the massive stadiums their cathedrals. The ten-thousand-seat Katy Lakes stadium was near capacity with past and present students and their families. All there to see the age-old rivalry between Katy Lakes and West Side play out before their eyes.

"This is so exciting!" His mother truly looked happy. She took five dollars from her purse and handed it to the student at the ticket booth, who proceeded to tear off an orange paper ticket and hand it to her. Sam noticed the sideways glance the student gave him as he stood by her shoulder.

"Here you go, honey. Enjoy."

"What? Aren't you going to come in for a while? This is Max's last big game."

For a moment, she stood perfectly still, a smile on her face as if she were remembering better days. Sam watched her stare unblinkingly at the throng of excited students pouring into the stands.

He reached out and touched her on the elbow. "Mom, you're blocking the way."

His mother shuddered. She looked down into her empty purse, then at her watch. "No, honey. I've got to be off to work. Can't be late." She leaned over and kissed him on the cheek. "You okay getting to your seat?"

"Sure, I got this."

Sam swung his left leg around and started into the crowd. After he'd made it about ten yards, he turned to see her still standing there. She wasn't looking at him. She was just looking at all the excitement. He took another few steps and turned again. This time, she was gone.

Sam made his way to the stands. His friends Maria and Logan had already saved his favorite spot on the lowest bench by the stairs and were waiting for him.

"Your brother is on fire tonight!" Maria slid a padded pillow with their high school logo on it underneath Sam as he sat down. "Where've you been, anyway? They're about to score."

"Got harassed by Mike and Rob in the bathroom."

Maria put her arm around him and gave him a squeeze.

"God, I hate having to go to the bathroom at school," Logan replied.

Sam liked Logan. He was super skinny and covered with terrible acne, but he was loyal and never mentioned Sam's cerebral palsy. They'd been in school together since first grade when he'd moved to Katy, a suburb of Houston, from Killeen. Other than Max and Maria, he was his closest friend. Sam remembered once finding Logan in the bathroom alone, staring at the mirror, gently rubbing soap on a particularly painful-looking boil. The acne had come on suddenly with his adolescent growth spurt, and he'd gone from a cute, pudgy, clean-faced kid that no one paid much attention to, to a gangly, six-foot-tall pus-face that everyone made fun of.

"Sam, I finally know how you feel," he'd said as he slowly rubbed the soap on the wound. They didn't have to say much more.

Maria. Well, she was something else altogether.

"Damn, what an arm he has!" Logan shoved a hot dog into his mouth. Max threw the ball into the end zone for their first touchdown. Bits of bread went flying all over the bench as Logan stood and screamed.

Sam sat as the crowd stood and went wild. The smile on his face hurt all the way up to his ears. As Max jogged to the sideline, he took off his helmet and pointed to Sam and gave him a big wink. Logan leaned over and slapped him on the back. "That was for you, Sam. I knew it. Max did that for you!"

Maria leaned in silently and squeezed Sam's bad arm tightly against her chest. Sam sat quietly, his eyes watering over with pride.

~~~

Max didn't know why he felt so good that day. The smell of the fresh-cut grass. The feel of the ball in his hand. The roar of the crowd. It was one of those rare moments in an athlete's career when everything seemed to mesh. Maybe because his father was away, he wanted it that much more. Maybe because it was his last game and Sam, his other half, was there with him. Whatever it was, he was fluid. No one could touch him, and in the end, it was a rout. West Side had never suffered such a humiliation.
~~~

When it was all done, he jumped over the team bench and ran up to Sam and gave him a high five. He then picked him up and dragged him down to the field. "We did it, buddy. What'd you think of that?"

Sam laughed as Max finally put him down. "Not too bad. You missed a few passes, but not too bad."

Logan ogled him as if he were a conquering warrior. Maria stepped out of the stands and wrapped her arms around his neck and gave him a big kiss.

Max and another teammate lifted Sam up on their shoulders and carried him into the locker room and sat him on his usual chair in a corner near Max's locker. No one dared to bother him when Max was around. Several of the players saw him almost as a lucky mascot and exuberantly slapped him on the shoulder in celebration. Max watched him out of the corner of his eye as he changed. He could see the look of envy and contentment on his face. At least he could be here with him while they all celebrated.

When Max was finished, he turned to Sam and helped him to his feet. Sam held out his hand. Max looked at him curiously. "What?"

"The car keys, please. Remember?"

Max smiled. "Okay. But you better not screw up and wreck her, promise?"

"What? I'm a better driver than you, you big meathead jock."

Maria was waiting outside the locker room. "You guys are taking me home, right?"

Sam seemed to hesitate when he saw Maria.

"Come on, bro," Max snapped. "You said you wanted to drive. Don't just stand there. Let's go."

The three slowly made their way out to the parking lot. Max walked on one side of Maria and Sam on the other. The sun was setting in the west, and the parking lot was bathed in red and orange. Parked off in a corner away from any potential door dings sat their car, a '67 Chevy

Nova. Together they'd lowered it and put fat tires on the back. Adding a supercharger had been their crowning achievement.

"The green metallic paint we did looks awesome in this light."

"Yeah, but you better not scratch it on anything or there'll be hell to pay." Max went around to the passenger side and opened the door for Maria. She pulled the seat forward and slid gracefully into the back.

Max watched over the top of the car as Sam pulled the door open with his right arm, pivoted on his left leg, and dexterously slid behind the wheel. When he was sure Sam had made it into the driver's seat, Max slid into the passenger seat and closed the door. He held his breath as he watched Sam work through all the movements they'd rehearsed over and over again in the driveway. Sam reached across with his right arm and pulled the door closed. He shifted his body so that his left leg stayed away from the pedals and his left arm was comfortable. Max smiled as he looked at Sam's stern face as he put the key in the ignition. When the engine rumbled to life, Sam's expression turned to one of joy.

Max turned around to Maria and gave her a wink. She stared back at him with her midnight-black eyes, her long black hair falling gently across her shoulders. She flashed him with her perfect smile as she reached across the seat back and gave him an approving pat on the shoulder.

Max had taught Sam how to drive a manual transmission with one functioning leg. Sam revved the engine several times before pressing the clutch with his right foot and shifting into first gear.

"Remember to get on the gas as soon as you let up the clutch, Sam."

Sam released the clutch, and the car jerked violently forward. He quickly stepped on the accelerator pedal and gave the engine more gas just before it could stall. The jerking stopped, and soon they were slowly driving down through the row of parked cars and out onto the main road. Max watched as Sam listened intently to the sound of the engine. When the revolutions were just right, he quickly clutched, gently moved the gear shifter into the right gear, then moved his foot back to the gas, all without stalling. Max watched with pride as his brother cautiously maneuvered the Nova along in traffic as the long line of cars slowly meandered away from the stadium. Soon they were free of the crowd and heading down Route 90, a dead straight road leading out into the Katy prairie.

By now, the sun had set. Max noticed Sam staring unblinkingly at the straight-as-an-arrow road before him, his hand tightly gripping the wheel. He knew what was going through his head. "You better the hell not!" he shouted.

Sam looked over his shoulder at Maria, who was clinging to the back of Max's seat. "No, Sam. Don't!"

"Oh, hell yeah!" Sam grinned as he pressed his right foot to the floor. Their heads snapped back. Maria let go of Max's seat and fell backward. The Nova spun its fat rear wheels and screeched forward.

Max gripped the armrest tightly. "Last time! Last damn time I let you drive!"

The prairie grass and telephone poles became a blur in the headlights as Sam rocked back and forth in his seat, laughing uncontrollably. As the speedometer roared past one hundred, Sam's expression suddenly changed.

Max spun his head around only to see the red-and-white lights of a police car rapidly approaching from behind. "Now you've done it!" Max thumped the armrest with his fist. "How the hell we gonna pay for a ticket?"

"Sam, what were you thinking?" Maria snapped from the back seat as she sat bolt upright and adjusted her seat belt.

Sam pulled over onto the gravel shoulder. The floodlights from the patrol car filled the Nova with blinding white light. Max watched Sam twist his body to hide his deformity as much as he could as they all sat silently and waited.

The officer eventually got out of his car and came up to Sam's window. He glanced back at Maria. "Miss, you all right back there?"

"Yes, officer, I'm okay."

"What the hell was that, boys?" he asked, clearly annoyed.

"Sorry, sir," Max replied.

Sam sat frozen with fear.

"You know I got all kinds of dumb fools driving around and getting into accidents after the game. Why do you two have to make my work any harder? Let me see both your licenses."

Sam fumbled around in his pocket and finally pulled out his wallet and removed his learner's permit. Max slapped his license on top and reached across and handed them to the officer. He walked back to his patrol car as Max and Sam sat motionless in the blinding glow of the police car's light.

"We're screwed," Sam whispered.

Maria slumped down in the back seat and glared at him.

"Yup. Damn learner's permit and doing over a hundred," Max grumbled.

Rings of sweat formed under Sam's arms when they heard the crunch of gravel under the officer's boots as he approached.

The officer took off his hat and leaned in the window once again. "You Max Donovan? Quarterback for Katy Lakes?"

"Yes, officer."

He rested his forearms on the door and scratched his shaved head. "You boys' daddy work up the road here at the General in the emergency room?"

"Yes, sir," Sam mumbled.

"Damn it, boys! I should lock you up. Especially with a damn learner's permit doing this kind of foolishness." He shook his head. "Max, get behind the wheel and get your ass home and don't let me catch you and your brother doing this ever again."

"Yes, sir," Max replied as he swung his door open and sprang from his seat.

The officer stood, replaced his hat, then took a few steps back as Max opened the door and practically threw Sam from the car. The headlights illuminated Sam's contorted frame as he did his best to move around the front of the car. The officer just stood and shook his head as the two scrambled into their seats.

The officer once again leaned in the window. "I've known your daddy for as long as I can remember." He paused and shifted his chew wad in his cheek, then spat on the ground. "He's a fine man. And I hear you played a damn good game tonight. But one more stunt like that and you'll be in a hell of a lot of trouble, you hear?"

"Yes, sir," they both mumbled as they looked down at their feet.

"Miss, keep these two in line before they do something really stupid."

"I will, sir."

"Get out of here and get straight home."

Max slowly pulled away from the shoulder and headed down the road toward home. They could finally breathe once they saw the flashing lights turn off.

Sam was the first to start laughing. Then Maria.

Finally, Max cracked. "You son of a bitch," he said with a big smile. "Son of a bitch."

Chapter 6

The Present

Max's alarm went off at 5:30 a.m. He sat up and was happy that the sleeping pills had actually worked. He stood and stretched his aching arms above his head and winced as he heard his back crack. He quickly showered, shaved, and put on a clean pair of scrubs before heading back to the hospital. As he drove the empty oak-lined boulevards back to County, he thought about how peaceful it was. How tranquil and empty. Even the birds hadn't yet started to chirp.

As he approached the parking garage, he heard the harsh roar of the trauma helicopter's turbines as it passed overhead and started to make its descent onto the helipad.

"Good morning, Houston," he whispered as he peered out the window to get a better look.

His shift didn't start until seven, but he always got in early to scope out the problems he was going to face over the next twenty-four hours. By the time he made it to the emergency room, the new arrival had been unloaded and transported from the helipad to the trauma bay.

Max walked in to find Nigel, his chief resident, standing by the new arrival in a plastic gown and gloves.

"Thoracotomy tray, stat!" Nigel barked.

Max's morning calm was shattered. The bright lights reflected off the blood as it dripped down the side of the stretcher. The staff were frantically moving about as Max maneuvered his way up to the bedside.

The high-pitched monotone of the heart rate monitor reading nothing screeched in his ears.

He frowned as he looked down at the motionless young man. "Nigel, what the hell's going on?"

Nigel proceeded to pour betadine across the victim's chest. "Drug deal gone bad somewhere up in the Heights. Guy's got a massive hole through the abdomen. Goddamn bastard must've shot him with a cannon, by the looks of it!" Nigel took a large scalpel and cut a deep incision in the patient's left chest, starting at the sternum, and continuing all the way down to the stretcher. "Can't believe he even made it here with a heartbeat. Lost his pulse just as you were walking in."

Max put on a pair of sterile gloves. He leaned over and watched as Nigel sliced open the sac surrounding the heart and exposed the aorta. "Here you go." He passed Nigel a large, curved aortic cross clamp and watched approvingly as Nigel clamped the aorta. He stepped away as Nigel proceeded to place a catheter in the heart.

"Blood!" Nigel said. "Where's the blood?"

Max looked around and grabbed a unit of blood from a nurse and connected it to Nigel's newly placed catheter and began squeezing blood directly into the victim's heart.

Silence fell across the room as they all watched the motionless heart and blood pressure monitors.

"Epinephrine and shock. Let's go, Nigel!"

The resident injected epinephrine directly into the heart. The heart started to quiver. He then took defibrillator paddles and placed them on either side of the heart. "Everybody clear!" He shocked the heart. It froze momentarily, then began to quiver again.

Max stepped up and placed his hands into the victim's chest and gently started squeezing the heart in an attempt to pump the medicine and the new blood around the body. He then stepped back as Nigel used the paddles to shock the heart again. They proceeded for over half an hour, trading places, Max pumping the new blood in and Nigel injecting medicine and shocking the dying heart.

Eventually, Max stood back and put his hand up in the air signaling Nigel to stop. He stared at the motionless, pale organ waiting for some kind of miracle, but nothing happened. Despite all the blood and drugs, the heart never responded. The blood dripping down the side of the stretcher was now a large pool covering a good part of the floor.

"Let's call it," Max pronounced. "Six forty-three a.m." He took off his gloves and threw them across the room and into the trash bin. He patted Nigel on the back. "Good job. He was dead before he got here."

Nigel looked dejectedly at his bloody feet. "Son of a bitch. This early in the morning too."

"The Heights, you said?"

"Yes, Dr. Donovan. Apparently by one of the warehouses off I-10."

"Same area the cops told us about last month?"

"Apparently so, sir. New group moving in, I guess."

Max knew the area. It had been a bad area since he was a kid. Despite gentrification, there were still pockets of gang violence and drugs. He went to the locker room and showered again. Seemed to him that he was always scrubbing someone's blood off of himself.

He went about the rest of the day and night as he usually did. Fortunately, that was the last of the deaths that day. He and the residents operated on several stabbings, two appendectomies, one stable gunshot wound to the belly, and pulled one foreign body out of a rectum. He'd slept very little. During his breaks between cases, he couldn't stop fixating on the gunshot wound death that had greeted him when he arrived.

"The Heights," he kept mumbling to himself as he tossed and turned in his call room bed.

When his shift ended, he drove straight home. He was so agitated that for a brief moment he considered calling Dr. Simkins, the psychiatrist, but he didn't. He stumbled into his house and glanced over at the folded

American flag and photographs on the credenza before heading to the bathroom. He quickly showered and slid into bed. He pulled the bottle of sleeping pills out of his side-table drawer and took one, washing it down with half a bottle of water.

"The Heights." Max shook his head. "Bastard blew the shit out of that boy!"

Max slept without dreaming. When he eventually woke, it was dark outside. The blankets were strewn across the floor and his bedsheets soaked with sweat. He sat up in the darkness.

"The Heights."

Max dressed in a pair of old jeans and a T-shirt. He slipped the Beretta in the small of his back and strapped his knife to his ankle. He knew he should have called someone, anyone. Definitely Dr. Simkins. But he didn't want to be stopped. He knew his agitation would only go away if he did something about it. And he didn't want that something to be anywhere where nice people would feel his wrath.

Max opened the garage door and rummaged around in the dark until he found what he was looking for. "Good old Louisville maple," he whispered as he gripped the baseball bat and gave it a few good shakes. He placed his hand deep inside a dark hole behind a pegboard that ran along the back wall. He grimaced as he pulled out an old rubber pig mask. *Was scary when we were younger. Scarier now.*

He slid behind the wheel of the Nova and gently placed the bat across the back seat with the mask. He backed out of the garage and drove through the quiet empty streets of West University and headed up Montrose Boulevard toward the north side of town. All the while, he kept looking down at his cell phone resting on the passenger seat, almost wishing someone would call. Anyone.

Max knew where his prey would be. It was just past midnight, and some of the dingier clubs always had a guy hanging out in the shadows. Max had ascertained from one of the police officers in the emergency room where the shooting had occurred. He thought it was unlikely that he would find the guy who did the deed, but he had to go look.

"Un-fucking-believable—they're still here," he whispered as he turned onto the street where the shooting had happened.

He could barely make out the silhouettes of at least two men standing in a corner wedged between a rusted chain-link fence and the crumbling wall of an abandoned warehouse. The light from a nearby streetlamp cast long shadows along the sidewalk. Giant oaks arched over the road.

Max drove slowly by the two men. They stepped into the light and came up close to the curb. They both wore loose jeans that showed their boxers. One had on an Astros jersey while the other had a knit hat and sleeveless white T-shirt.

"Yo, you want to buy something?"

Max cracked the tinted window to get a better look but said nothing and kept on slowly down the street until he got to the corner. He watched in his rearview mirror as they retreated back into the darkness. He waited for a moment longer to see if anyone else came out, but it was just the two of them. He turned the corner and parked out of sight under a giant live oak.

Max reached into the back seat and grabbed the bat and placed it on his lap. He reached for the mask and held it in his hands. He stared at its hollowed-out eyes and grotesque, fanged snout. Lifeless and empty. He sighed as he stretched the musty-smelling rubber over his head.

He took off his Beretta and held it in his shaking hand. He was terrified that he would be tempted to use it. "Better leave it here," he whispered as he slid it under the seat. He quickly got out of the car and jogged across the street. The heat and humidity were unbearable, and the mask only made it worse. Sweat dripped from his forehead and burned his eyes. He'd noticed as he drove by that there was an empty lot next to the warehouse. He scrambled over the chain-link fence and silently moved across the lot and came up behind the two men.

Max crouched in the darkness, trying to decide what would be his best approach when suddenly a car pulled up to the curb and rolled down its window. Max peered around the corner. The car was full of several young white kids.

The sunroof rolled back, and a pretty young girl still in her slinky nightclub dress popped her head through the roof. "Hey, we want to party!" she shouted.

"Good, good. We're the party kings." One of the dealers leaned into the car window as the other stayed back and looked up and down the street. The man at the car then walked back to the fence, holding a wad of cash in his hand. He proceeded to roll back a portion of the fencing right next to where Max was crouching. A hand came through the fence and felt around in the dirt until it settled on a plastic bag. The man pulled the bag through the fence and proceeded to remove several vials of pills and other assorted substances in lunch baggies. He had his partner check that he had the right stuff, then tossed the bag back through the fence, landing it at Max's feet.

When the transaction was completed, the girl poked her head out through the roof again. "We love you guys. You're the best!" With a screech of the tires, they were gone.

The two came back to their corner and waited in the dark for their next customer.

Max's rage grew uncontrollable as he looked down at the bag. *Hole the size of a cannonball through his belly*, he thought. *All for this shit. So party girl can get high with her boy toys.* Max grabbed the bag of drugs and tossed it over the fence, where it landed at the feet of the two men.

"What the fuck?" They both reflexively bent down and scrambled to collect the bottles and pills that spilled across the sidewalk.

Max grabbed the bat tightly and flew over the fence. He hit the first dealer across the jaw as he looked up to see what was happening. The blow spun him around as he fell face first to the sidewalk, unconscious. A pool of blood collected around his broken mouth. The second man had time to jump back as Max swung the bat again, this time only clipping him on the upper arm. Max could feel the arm snap through the bat as the blow connected. The man screamed in pain. Max spun the bat around again and hit him on the kneecap.

The man twisted violently as he fell to the ground. "Please don't kill me," he begged. "I got a kid."

"Did the boy who died here this morning beg?" Max shouted. "Did he have a kid?"

The man stared silently at Max as he slid onto his side next to his comrade. Max towered over the two, silently spinning the bat in his fingers. His face contorted in pain and rage behind the dead pig mask. Tears streamed down his face.

Finally, he turned away from his two victims. He took his foot and smashed the pills into the sidewalk and scattered the collection of assorted powders and plants into the gutter. He leaned over the unconscious man and checked his pulse, then moved him into a better position to breathe.

Without another word, he jumped back over the fence. He ran as fast as he could to the car, ripping off his mask as he jumped behind the wheel. He fumbled with the keys as he tried to steady his hands long enough to get the car started. He finally began to calm down once he heard the engine roar to life.

Within minutes, he was on Interstate 10. He first went east to the ship channel, then cut down south to the beltway, finally meandering across midtown and making his way back to West University. He gently squeezed the Nova into the garage, taking care not to scratch it against the wall. He grabbed the bat and mask as he slid out from behind the wheel. He placed the bat against the wall in a dark corner and the pig mask back in its hole behind the pegboard.

He showered and scrubbed himself raw. Finally, he felt he was clean enough and went back to bed. He lay staring at the ceiling, terrified by what he'd become.

"Maria, what happened to me? You could've stopped me."

He closed his eyes.

"Sam," he whispered as he fell off to sleep.

Chapter 7

2003

Max pulled up in front of Maria's house and smiled. She was sitting on her front step and sprang to her feet when he arrived. *How could I be so lucky?* he thought as he watched her walk up to the car. She was beautiful.

She flashed him her beautiful smile as she came up to the window and leaned in. "About time you showed up." She put her hand on his cheek and kissed him on the lips. "I don't like to be kept waiting."

The sweet, fruity smell of her perfume made him dizzy. He smiled. "Never again."

She walked around the front of the Nova. Max's varsity jacket hung loosely over her shoulders and extended below her slender hips. Her long black hair fell gracefully to the middle of her back, partially covering the outline of a Spartan helmet. Along the bottom in bold white letters read *Class of 2003*. She slid into the passenger seat, leaned over, and wrapped both arms around his neck and kissed him again.

"Nice to see you too," Max said as he tried to catch his breath.

"Let's get out of here. I want to have some fun."

Max gunned the engine and spun the Nova around 180 degrees, leaving a patch of rubber and smoke in front of Maria's house. Maria laughed as she leaned back and put on her sunglasses. They drove out of Katy and got on I-10 and headed east. Maria rolled down the window and let the cool autumn air blow back her hair. Max raced through traffic, no longer caring about tickets. He had Maria by his side, and all was good.

Maria turned on the radio and placed her feet up on the dash. Max leaned back, driving with one arm out the window. "How about the boardwalk?"

Maria touched him on the arm. "Sure. Better win me something."

They drove past the towering glass skyscrapers of downtown Houston and got onto I-45 south toward the coast. They slowly drove through the ever-present bumper-to-bumper traffic until Max turned off on NASA Route 1.

Maria sat up and looked at a pair of jets that were propped up on pedestals in front of the Johnson Space Center as they slowly drove past. "I should have dated an astronaut. I bet they know how to be on time."

Max laughed. "Maybe I should go into the Air Force. Don't see me fitting into one of those small cockpits though. But if that's what it takes to keep you happy."

"No." She leaned back in her seat as they continued down the road to the waterfront. "Don't want you out flying around. Damn well don't want to have to worry about you flying in a rocket." She pulled back the hair from her face. "Just want you always here by me."

They crossed the Kemah Bridge that passed high over a marina packed with boats and descended into the small town of Kemah on the edge of Galveston Bay. Its main attraction was an amusement park situated at the outlet of Clear Lake as it drained into the bay.

Max parked the Nova away from all the other cars at the far side of the parking lot.

"Honey, you've got to get over this car. No one is going to dent it. You always make me walk."

"Sam and I painted this, and I want to keep it nice as long as I can."

They walked along the boardwalk that skirted the outside of the park. Max placed his arm around her as they leaned against the rail and watched the pelicans dart and dive in search of a meal. Yacht after yacht slowly passed through the narrow channel to their left and sailed out of Clear Lake on their way to the Gulf of Mexico. The occasional cigarette boat would break the peaceful calm of the afternoon by gunning its engines just as it left the no-wake zone. Behind them, they could hear the sirens and bells of the rides. A Ferris wheel towered over their heads. Numerous restaurants faced the bay, their outdoor tables stalked by seagulls waiting to snatch an easy meal. The smell of fried seafood and alcohol gently blended in with the light salty breeze blowing in off the gulf. Children ran from ride to ride laughing that uninhibited laugh that is the blessing of youth.

"Feel up to a ride?"

"Okay," she replied apprehensively.

"The Bullet?"

Maria cringed as she pulled away. "You know how I hate roller coasters."

"Come on. You wanted to date an astronaut. Should be able to ride a roller coaster."

Maria straightened up. Her lips tightened into a snarl. "Sure. Not going to let you hold it over my head any longer. Let's do it."

Maria clung to Max's arm as they slowly followed the line to the ride, a towering wooden coaster perched on the edge of the water. When finally it was their turn to get on board Maria hesitated, her voice quivering. "Do we have to?"

Max laughed. "Yes. You can do it."

They squeezed into the car of the wooden roller coaster and clamped the safety bar tightly across their laps. Maria buried her head in his shoulder as the ride slowly climbed to the top and stopped. Max looked out across the bay. From their height, he could see all the way to the Gulf. Far below the people milling about looked small and artificial. To his left, the Ferris wheel with its lights flashing was slowly spinning at almost their height.

"Look, Maria. It's beautiful."

Maria lifted her head slightly to look just as the roller coaster started its descent. "Oh my God!" she screamed as she dug her fingers into Max's arm.

Max laughed as the wooden coaster rattled and clacked around corner after corner.

When they finally came to a stop, Maria let go of his arm, then punched it hard. "Never again." There were tears in her eyes. "You owe me now."

Max helped her off the ride and rested his arm around her shoulders. "Okay, what can I get you?"

As they walked through the midway, Maria stopped and pulled Max by the arm and up to a basketball toss game. She pointed toward an ugly pig mask that hung against the wall surrounded by large stuffed animals. "Win that for me."

"Really? That's so ugly." Max cringed at the sight of the horrific mask. It had a snarling snout with large fangs, sunken eyes, and an overhanging brow. "What the hell is that doing there anyway?" he asked the girl running the game.

"Oh that?" She placed her hands on her hips and stared at the mask. She spun her hat backward and chomped on chewing gum as she struggled to come up with an answer. "Left over from Halloween, I guess. No one wanted it."

"Get it for being so rotten and making me ride that ride," Maria said, poking his arm.

"I'll win you something, but not that." Max placed two dollars on the wooden barrier and looked up at the hoops along the wall. Behind each one was a spinning wheel. Stuffed animals tightly packed the small stall. Max tossed the basketball and easily made the shot. He repeated it two more times, a big smile on his face as he looked at the girl and asked for his prize.

"No one ever gets that many baskets, mister. Your pick. Whatever you like."

Max smiled at Maria. "I'll take that big elephant."

The girl pulled down a large green elephant off the wall. "Here you go."

Max turned and offered it to Maria. She glared at him. "I want the pig. I've told you how much I hate roller coasters, and you made me go anyway. And it was horrible."

"But the elephant is so much nicer."

Maria stepped up to the barrier and placed two dollars down. "Ball, please." She sank three baskets in quick succession.

"Damn, you two were made for each other." The girl manning the stall spun her hat back around so the peak lay low over her eyes. "That was amazing. What will it be?"

Maria glared at Max. "I'll take the pig, please."

"Sure." The girl reached up with a long wooden pole with a metal hook on the end and pulled the mask off the wall. "I know the boss will be glad to get rid of this ugly thing."

Maria took the pig mask and handed it to Max, then took the elephant from his hand. "Thank you for the elephant. I love it. But you are a pig for making me ride that ride."

Max laughed and kissed her. "Okay, you win. I'm sorry. Never again." They made their way to a photo booth and squeezed in together. Max put the mask on and raised his hands and growled. Maria smiled and held her now beloved elephant close to her face as the picture was taken. Max insisted that he get a picture of Maria by herself. Afterward he shoved the mask in his back pocket, where it dangled for the rest of the day.

The remainder of the afternoon was spent slowly walking around the park, arm in arm. No longer interested in riding, just walking under the stunning blue sky. The breeze gently blew Maria's hair back, her elephant tucked under Max's arm.

That evening, they ate fried catfish in a restaurant along the boardwalk, then went to the water's edge and watched the sun set. Max turned to Maria as the moon started to rise. Its reflection on the water set the few remaining boats returning for the day aglow. "I love you, Maria."

Maria touched him on the chin and kissed him. "I will always love you, Max."

Chapter 8

2003

Sam sat on his front porch swing and looked across the street at the community park. He loved where he lived, even if it was a little run-down. The house wasn't much to look at. A single-story ranch painted white with two bedrooms toward the back and a single bathroom. A living room and kitchen were toward the front. A wraparound counter separated the kitchen from the living room and a small dining room with an oval table just big enough to seat four. The living room and dining room had windows that looked out onto a covered front porch.

A gravel drive ran along the side of the house that led to a single-car garage packed to the roof with car parts and tools. That was where he and Max had spent most of their time before Maria came along. Tinkering with the Nova. Adding a supercharger. Dropping its suspension. All under the guidance of their father. It was their little special place where the three of them worked side by side. No mention of Sam's deformity. Just a peaceful space where they could sweat and bond.

The other houses running along the street facing the park were the same. They may have had their shutters painted differently or may have had slightly different landscaping for their small front yards, but other than that, they all looked alike. Small and comfortable. Towering old trees gave some degree of shade during the terribly hot, endless Texas summers.

Sam would sit there on the swing for hours, looking at the people playing in the park. Immediately across the street from the house was a large jungle gym where children with two good arms and legs climbed and laughed. In the distance, a baseball game was in session, and he would occasionally hear the crack of the bat as a ball was hit over the fence. He imagined himself running across the street to play a game of basketball. There was always a pickup game going on, and he envied those who could just get up and play anytime they liked.

He was starting to feel drowsy as the sun hung low in the west. An autumn breeze stirred the leaves as they clung to their branches, desperate to hold on just a little longer. As his head started to bob, he was startled awake by the squeal of brakes. He opened his eyes to see Maria slide from behind the wheel of her old Ford pickup and start up the sidewalk.

"Hi, Sam. Max around?"

"Hey, Maria. No. He's off doing some errands."

She sat on the swing next to him, placing her hand on his knee. "How you doing? Been out here all day?"

"You know me. Love watching people do what I can't."

"What do you mean? You can do anything."

"Not that," he replied, nodding in the direction of the basketball courts.

She grabbed his hand and stood up. "Let's go."

"What? I can't!"

"Oh, be quiet and just come on, you wuss."

Maria helped him to his feet. He was no longer sleepy, and the sensation of her warm hand in his made him feel alive. As they passed the back of her truck, she leaned into the bed and pulled out a basketball. "Bet you didn't see this happening today, did you?" she said with a giggle as she slowly walked with him across the road, all the time holding his hand.

The basketball courts were covered with a large roof but open on all sides. Two of the six courts were occupied, so she led him to one of the empty courts, far away from the other players.

As they slowly made their way to the far side, one of the players stopped and put his hands on his hips. His muscular arms flexed through his sleeveless T-shirt. He towered over Sam. A black dew rag covered his enormous head. "Oh, mama. You're one fine piece of merchandise."

Sam started to sweat profusely.

"Just ignore him, Sam. Keep walking."

"You going to play or what, Dwayne?" one of the players asked. "Come on, man. Leave them alone."

Dwayne turned back to his friends and continued with his game. Maria patiently walked by Sam's side as they made their way across the concrete. His left shoe scraped along the ground, making the hole in the side ever so slightly bigger with each step. Maria positioned him on the free throw line and tossed him the ball. He struggled to stay balanced as he dribbled. He took the ball in his right hand and tossed it toward the hoop. It fell about three feet short.

"Come on, what was that?"

She bounced the ball back to him, and he grabbed it with his good arm. This time, he aimed and gave it a heroic shove, twisting and pivoting like he'd had to do since birth to get anything done. The ball flew through the air and slammed off the backboard and straight into the basket.

"Yes!" he screamed.

Maria came over and gave him a high five. "See? Just try, and you can do anything. Let's play Around the World."

For the next few hours, Maria helped Sam move around the court shooting the ball from different positions. Each time he made a shot, they both screamed with joy. With each basket, Sam noticed Dwayne look over in their direction.

As his game broke up and his acquaintances started to disperse, Dwayne approached them. "Hey, baby, why you playing with this freak? You should be in the back of my car where I can let you be my freak."

Sam tried to move in front of Maria. "Don't talk to her like that," he stammered.

Dwayne pushed up on him. Sam looked around for help. The sun had set, and there was no one else around. The fluorescent lights from high up in the roof made the surrounding park appear pitch black.

"What you going to do, cripple? You've got a fine lady here, and I just want to show her some love. I know you won't mind." He pushed Sam hard on the shoulder.

Sam stumbled backward and fell to the ground. He struggled to get to his feet as Dwayne moved in closer to Maria. "Leave her alone!"

Maria stood frozen as Dwayne slithered up next to her. He reached out and stroked her breast. "Fine woman. No one around but the two of us and your pet."

Maria raised her hand and slapped him hard across the face. "The only pet here is you, bitch!"

~ ~ ~

Max pulled the Nova into the drive. He was tired, and the shorter autumn days made him depressed. He popped the trunk and gathered up the groceries in his arms and carried them around to the front of the house and up the porch steps. He was surprised that the house was dark. He struggled with the packages as he turned the handle and pushed open the front door.

"Sam? Get up and help sort out these groceries."

The house remained quiet. He turned on the kitchen light and started to unpack the bags and placed their contents on the counter.

"Sam, get your lazy ass up and help."

He turned around and looked at the empty living room.

"Sam?"

He walked down the short hallway and poked his head in the bedroom.

That's crazy. Where the hell could he be?

He checked the bathroom and his mother's room just in case he'd fallen and hurt himself. Max's mind flashed back to when Sam was nine and he had fallen in the shower and couldn't get himself up. Max had found him curled up crying, the hot water turning his skin red.

"Sam!" he shouted. "Where are you?"

Max hurried to the front door. His eyes scanned the porch and along the front bushes. Then he looked out across the park.

"What the hell?" he whispered as he saw Sam down on the ground struggling to get to his feet and some guy moving in close to Maria.

Max leapt off the porch and started to run across the street. The sight of Sam on the ground had him in a panic. Then he saw Maria raise her hand and strike the stranger across the face. The crack of the slap was loud enough to be heard halfway across the park.

Max's eyes narrowed to thin slits as his clenched teeth contorted his face into a terrifying grimace. He started to sprint. By the time Maria's assailant raised his hand to strike her back, Max was at full speed and in a mindless rage. He dove through the air as if diving into the end zone, only this time instead of landing on soft turf, he landed on Dwayne. Max struck him several times with his fist before standing up, panting, and covered in sweat.

He straddled the unconscious body as he turned to look at Sam and Maria. "You two okay?"

Sam finally made it to his feet and hobbled over to his brother and grabbed him by the arm. Maria wrapped her arms around his neck and wouldn't let go.

"What the hell!" Dwayne moaned as he slowly regained consciousness.

Max let them go and bent down close to his face. "You see these two," he said, grabbing him by the jaw and twisting his head in the direction of Sam and Maria. "Never even look at them again."

"Yeah, yeah, okay, fuck!"

Max let Dwayne's head fall back and stepped over him. He put his arms around Maria and Sam as they slowly made their way back across the park toward their house. He turned around as they walked up onto the porch and saw that Dwayne had gone.

Before entering the house, Maria paused. "I need to get home." She leaned over to Sam and gave him a kiss on the cheek. "Thanks for a fun afternoon." She turned to Max and wrapped him in her arms. "Thanks for saving us."

They both stood motionless as she turned and walked to her truck and drove off.

"She's killing me, bro," Sam said with a sigh.

Max put his arm on Sam's shoulder as he held open the front door and helped him inside. "I know what you mean."

Chapter 9

The Present

Rosa was bundled up in a blanket and carried into a warehouse close to the border. She kicked and tried to break free, but when her captor whispered in her ear, she went silent.

"We know where your family lives, little girl. That house with the nice orange door. Your mama. Cute little brother. Papa works at the hotel. They will all die if you don't stop fighting."

She tried to suppress her tears as she thought of her mother and baby brother, of her father coming home so tired each night. She knew they would be panicking when she didn't return home, but that wouldn't be for several hours. November first was supposed to be her great day. Her sixteenth birthday. Mama was to make mole poblano for her tonight. Now it was a nightmare, and all they knew was that she was at school and that everything was fine.

Two men carried her to a room in the back of the warehouse, which was stacked floor to ceiling with crates of car parts. It was cold, and when they left, they turned off the light, leaving her in complete darkness. She could hear a heavy bolt on the other side of the door slide into place and their muffled voices as they walked away. She wrapped her arms around her knees and pulled them close as she tried to stay warm.

Why are they doing this to me?

She placed her head on her knees and wept.

~ ~ ~

Rosa woke to the sound of footsteps coming toward the door. It seemed like hours had passed. She had cried herself to sleep, the stress having exhausted her.

She heard the scrape of the bolt, then the creaking of the large, heavy door as it slowly opened. She was temporarily blinded when the light was switched on. She tried to shield her eyes with her hand. Through her fingers, she saw two middle-aged men and a gray-haired woman standing in the doorway.

The woman was plump and wore her hair pulled back tightly behind her head in a long ponytail, revealing a sun-cracked brown face. She wore a large men's shirt that draped over her sagging breasts. Her jeans were dirty and worn. "Hold her down while I check her," she said. She scowled, revealing worn, broken teeth. "No point sending her north if she's already been with someone. The order is for a virgin."

Rosa screamed as both men held her down on a wooden crate.

The old woman pulled down her pants as she pried apart her legs with her elbows. She seemed remarkably strong and was probably younger than she looked. "Okay, we're good. She can be moved."

Rosa curled up in a ball and shook uncontrollably as the door slammed shut and once again, she was left in the dark. She kept rubbing the insides of her legs trying to rid herself of the sensation of that horrible woman's calloused hands. She was devastated. No one had ever touched her that way. So coldly. So much hatred. Why would anyone want to do this to her?

Soon, the woman and the two men returned. "You need to come with us," the old woman snapped. She grabbed Rosa by the shoulders and glared into her eyes. "I'm your grandmother. Remember that. Say anything and you'll never see your family alive again. Do you understand?"

Rosa nodded.

The two men grabbed her by the arms and led her to a large white box truck. One of the men slid in behind the wheel. Rosa was placed in the middle of the bench seat, then the old woman squeezed in tightly next to her. The second man rapped his hand against the side of the truck several times as the driver started up the engine and pulled away from the warehouse.

Within minutes, they were in the middle of a miles-long traffic jam to cross the Puente de Las Americas Bridge to the United States. They sat quietly. The old woman never looked down at Rosa. She kept her eyes forward as if she were trying to ignore the fact that Rosa was there at all.

The man was different. He seemed younger than the woman, but not by much. He kept looking down at her. Placing his hand down on his leg near her thigh. His body odor filled the cab, and Rosa crinkled her nose every time he shifted in his seat. He had on a long-sleeved flannel shirt, jeans, and boots. A two-day-old beard covered his sunbaked face. He wore a yellowed straw cowboy hat that was battered as if he'd been using it as a pillow.

When they finally reached the border, the old woman and man showed their papers.

"And what about her?" the border agent asked.

"She's my granddaughter. Just going across with us on this trip. Will be coming back this evening."

"That right, young lady?"

The old woman had her left hand under Rosa's thigh, and she squeezed hard. Rosa thought about what they'd said they would do to her family. "Yes, officer."

The office let his hand momentarily drop inside the window. The old woman slipped something into his hand and with a knowing nod, he waved them through.

"Good girl," the driver growled. "We'll let them know not to kill your mama today. But maybe tomorrow if you don't behave."

They drove in silence along Route 35, heading northeast until they reached the outskirts of San Antonio. They exited and eventually turned down an unpaved dirt road. They drove along in the dust between low-lying cactus and thick scrub for over half an hour before eventually coming to a cluster of small, whitewashed buildings in differing stages of decay. There was trash scattered across the dirt. Several large oaks spread their boughs over the old buildings, giving them some degree of shade.

The old woman opened the truck door and climbed down and started toward one of the buildings. "We'll stay in this colonia tonight." Without looking at Rosa, she snarled. "Don't try to run, little girl. There's nothing out there in the dark but rattlesnakes and coyotes. They'll eat you alive."

The driver got out and went around to the back of the truck. Rosa stepped down out of the cab and was immediately overwhelmed by the stench from the trash mixed with the unmistakable smell of human waste. She held her hand over her nose as she watched the driver pull a key from his pocket and insert it in a heavy padlock used to secure the rear doors of the truck. When the doors swung open, Rosa was shocked to see a dozen people stumble out. Several fell to the ground and had to be helped to their feet. Rosa rushed forward and helped lift up a woman who looked to be around her mother's age. Their eyes met, and Rosa saw in them only sorrow and pity. She started to follow her into the building when the old woman reappeared.

"No, you can't go with them. You need to come this way." She grabbed her by the arm and led her away from the others and into a small building toward the back of the compound. It was dark and musty, the floor nothing more than well-worn dirt. She marched Rosa through to a small room in the back. Crammed in one corner was a bucket. Along the floor was a mat with several bottles of water on it.

"That's your toilet," the old woman said, pointing with her nose at the bucket. "Don't make too much noise. We leave first thing in the morning." From a bag, she pulled out a sandwich and tossed it on the mat, then turned and closed the door. Rosa heard the lock snap, then the woman's footsteps receding.

The night was miserably hot. She tried to get comfortable, but she couldn't sleep. She could hear people walking around outside and speaking in muffled tones. Some were weeping. There were bars on her window, but no screen, and the mosquitos were merciless.

She lay awake staring at the ceiling as she clutched her locket. The light from a full moon played off the dirty white washed walls, filling the room with ghostly shadows. She remembered how her mother would always lie in bed with her on a night like this, when shadows were the only things to be afraid of. She would wrap a sheet around her tightly and whisper in her ear. "This is how I used to wrap you when you were a baby. Nice and tight. I would carry you all day like this. Don't worry there are no demons in this world that can harm you while I'm here."

It always made her feel safe, that nice tight wrap and Mama snuggled up next to her. Now the demons were real, and Mama was gone.

As the night drew on, the people outside her window stopped talking. She knew they were probably scattered around on the ground sleeping, trying to stay cool.

The constant buzz of cicadas concealed the creak of her door as it slowly opened. At first, she thought she was dreaming. She'd been staring into the dark nothingness for so long trying to fall asleep that she didn't immediately comprehend that there was someone in her room. She lay frozen as he approached.

A raspy voice broke the silence. "Think it's time someone broke you in."

Rosa screamed as he rushed across the room and fell on her. Suddenly, a light flashed on. She could clearly see it was the driver of the truck on top of her. His stench mixed with the smell of alcohol made her gag. In the doorway was the old woman. She had a thick stick in one hand and a large flashlight in the other. She came up behind the driver and started beating him hard over the head with the stick. He rolled off Rosa and onto his side as he tried to cover his face from the blows.

"What are you doing, *cabrón*? She's no good to us if you violate her!" She kept swinging and swinging as if glad for the excuse to hit him.

"*Ayee, perra!* You're hurting me! *Mierda!*"

He got on all fours and scurried from the room. The old woman chased him into the darkness and kept hitting him on the ankles until Rosa heard the front door slam and the sound of feet running away across the compound.

When the woman returned, her face was bright red and dripping with sweat. "Did he hurt you?"

"No."

"Go to sleep. We're going to Houston in the morning." She turned her flashlight away and locked the door once again leaving Rosa in darkness.

Chapter 10

The Present

Max crawled from bed and shuffled to the closet. He pulled a pair of well-worn sweatpants off the shelf and slipped them on. He put on a T-shirt, then headed to the kitchen and made himself a cup of coffee. He slowly poured milk into his cup and watched as the swirls of white slowly disappeared into the blackness.

He took his cup and moved into the living room and stood in front of the credenza. He looked up at the flag and gently picked the box off the shelf. He carefully carried it back to the sofa and sat down, placing it across his lap as he lay back into the pillows. He continued to slowly sip his coffee as he stared across at the credenza covered in pictures. His eyes focused on a photo of Sam and Maria smiling, sitting on the front porch of their old house.

~ ~ ~

2003

Autumn turned to winter, sending a foreboding chill into Sam. Football had long ended. His brother, Max, was ahead enough in his credits for graduation with the class of 2003 that he was able to get early dismissal. This allowed Max to come home from school most days at one-thirty. With his mother's help, he took a shift at Walmart. He was placed in the back storeroom, stacking and handling incoming shipments. Sam could only ever daydream about a job as physical as that.

Sam was a sophomore, even though they were twins. With all the surgeries and time in the hospital he'd had to endure as a child, he'd fallen behind. Now for the first time, he saw his brother starting to move away. They'd normally spent every lunch together and often passed each other in the hallway. Always with a high five or a touch on the back. Just enough to signal to each other that they were nearby. Now Sam maneuvered the afternoon hallways alone, his brother off stacking boxes, his mother manning a cash register and trying to make ends meet while their father was away.

Maria had got into the habit of bringing Sam home after school. She and Max had made their relationship official by being seen together out late at the local Whataburger. Now she came over after school most days and waited for Max to get off work.

"Drink?" Sam asked.

"Sure. Got a Coke?"

Sam pivoted and pulled the refrigerator door open with his right arm and leaned in. "Here you go." He grabbed a can and placed it on the kitchen counter, then went back and got himself one.

Sam sat down across from her at the dining room table and opened his chemistry textbook. Maria opened her biology text and started reading. They sat quietly. Occasionally, Sam would look up at her as she concentrated on her work, her long black hair resting gently across her shoulders, her light brown skin tight across her high cheekbones, her brow furrowed as she struggled to understand her lesson.

This time, Maria caught him. "What? What are you looking at?"

Sam blushed. He wanted to say something clever but couldn't find the words. He awkwardly looked away and out the front window. It was cold and raining. The park across the street was shrouded in mist, and water had begun to pond in the street.

Sam finally turned back to her. "Why are you here, Maria?"

"Huh?"

"Why don't you ever go home?" Sam leaned back in his chair. "I know we're friends and all, but why?"

This time, Maria blushed as she looked away. Sam could tell immediately that he'd said the wrong thing. They'd known each other for years, but only now that she was dating Max did he see her almost daily. It had never occurred to him that she could be running from something.

Maria sighed. "You know, Sam." She paused and looked down at her book. "There's a lot going on at home that I really don't want to be around right now."

Sam could see tears in her eyes. He wanted nothing more than to take her in his arms and console her. He realized that he was falling in love with her. Ever since that afternoon in the park, when it was just the two of them for hours playing basketball, he'd felt himself sliding out of control. Now she was with him almost daily, sitting in his dining room as she waited for his brother.

"Sorry. Didn't mean to get you upset."

"I'm not upset with you." She closed her book. "You won't understand. Your dad's great. He's home every night. He cares for you."

"Yeah, well, where is he now?"

"Do you think that's his fault?" she said, leaning across and grabbing him by the hand.

Sam's heart raced. "Well, he's not here. No one is here. I'm here alone." He bowed his head. "When I walk the hallways at school, Max used to be there. Now when I'm in trouble, there's no one. They all ignore me and keep moving. Bumping me. Watching me struggle."

"That's not true. I'm there. You have a good family. And hopefully your dad will be home soon." She let go of his hand. "Anyway, sometimes being alone is better than being in a bad situation."

"Maria, please tell me what's going on?"

Maria reached for a napkin and wiped a tear from her eye. "Sam, my stepdad drinks too much. And when he does, he can't keep his hands to himself, if you know what I mean."

Sam was mortified. "I'm sorry for asking."

"Don't be sorry. It is what it is. Next year, I'm moving out when I go to college."

Sam cringed. Next year. He would be a junior and Max would be in college somewhere. He'd already been getting calls from recruiters. Their mother had been hoping for scholarship money, and Max looked like he was going to get a free ride somewhere. Then they both would be gone, Max and Maria.

For the rest of the afternoon, they sat in relative silence. Sam stared at her now dreamily, not caring if she saw. His studying was done for the day.

~ ~ ~

Max had to admit that for a high school senior the Walmart job was a good one. He dragged a hydraulic hand dolly piled high with paper towels from the loading dock and placed it next to a nine-foot-tall stack of bottled water. He then headed back to get another. The place was massive. Rows and rows of shelves stacked twenty feet high with merchandise. Walking all day on the cold concrete floors hurt his knees, and the poor lighting made the place feel all the more oppressive. The routine was mind-numbing, but the paycheck was helping.

Out of the corner of his eye, he saw his supervisor walking in his direction. "Christ, what now?" he mumbled. He stopped and watched as the supervisor waddled his way around the stacks, his eyes trained on Max.

Sweat poured off his forehead. His untucked shirt was barely big enough to cover his bulging gut. "When I played defensive line at OU, we would eat guys like you for lunch, Donovan." He paused and took a gasp of air. "Know why? 'Cause you're too damn slow on your feet."

His supervisor stopped directly in front of him. Max tried not to breathe. The man's breath smelled like roadkill, and he found it hard not to gag.

"Goddamn, too slow. I told you to take that pile of boxes out to the dumpster thirty minutes ago."

"Yes, but this shipment just arrived and needed to be offloaded ASAP so the next truck could move in."

"You don't run the plays here, mister. You may have been a big man on campus when you played your sissy little high school ball, but I played with the big guys. I call the shots and run the plays from the sideline. Your job is just to run the plays I give you. Don't try to write your own playbook. Got it?"

"Yes, sir."

"Now stop what you're doing and get your ass over to the dumpster."

Max drooped his shoulders. "Yes, sir, right away." He left the hydraulic hand dolly where it was in the middle of the walkway and moved toward the back of the storeroom.

"Come on, Donovan. Too damn slow on your feet." The supervisor paused to catch his breath. "Surprised you won any games at all for Katy Lakes. We would have eaten you alive at OU."

Max just shrugged his shoulders and kept walking. He found the pile of discarded boxes and loaded them on a cart. He struggled to keep them all together as he pulled the cart through the plastic strip curtain that led to the back of the mall and the trash dumpster. It was cold, and the mist in the air chilled him to the bone. He tossed the boxes into the dumpster.

"Shit," he whispered as several slid off the top and fell to the ground along the far side near a high concrete retaining wall. Last thing he needed was coach sending him back out here to clean up around the dumpster. He walked around to the back but paused when he heard something move. *Not going back there if there're any damn rats.*

Suddenly, Logan stepped out from behind the dumpster.

Max jumped back in surprise. "Holy crap Logan, you scared the shit out of me. What the hell are you doing back there?" Max was shocked by his friend's appearance. He'd lost some weight, even though he'd always been skinny, and it looked like he'd been living rough. His hair was matted, and his clothes were covered in a layer of grime. Acne stood out starkly against the pale skin of his face.

"Sorry to scare you, Max."

"Damn man, you look like shit. Come on in here and get out of the cold." Max grabbed him by the arm and led him just inside the plastic strip curtain. He looked up and down the length of the storeroom, but his supervisor was nowhere to be seen. He tried to keep his voice down. He knew he could get in a lot of trouble if he got caught with a nonemployee in the back.

He turned to focus on Logan. "What's going on?"

Logan looked down at his feet. Max, still holding on to his arm, gave him a shake. "Come on, buddy, what's up?"

Logan looked up with desperation in his eyes. "Can I tell you something?"

"Sure."

"Been staying away from the house. Kinda shit at home."

"What?"

Logan crumpled to the ground. He pulled his legs up to his chest and started crying. Max looked around in a panic, expecting to see his supervisor appear at any minute. "Hey, keep quiet. You're not supposed to be back here." Max crouched down next to him, putting his arm around his shoulder. "Keep it together, will ya? I can't lose this job."

Logan stopped crying but couldn't stop shaking. "Dad's been a little crazy lately."

As Max gave him a gentle squeeze, he noticed Logan wince in pain. He could barely make out the shadow of a bruise on his neck.

"Telling me to get the hell out of the house. Telling me I'm not his kid."

That wasn't what Max had expected to hear. "Is that true, you're not his kid?"

"Don't know. He and my mom have been fighting a lot lately. Don't know if she said it just to make him mad, but since then, he's been beating the crap out of me."

"So you've been living out here?"

"Anywhere, really. Got a sleeping bag stuck up underneath the bridge in the neighborhood. I've been sneaking home when I know no one is there just to get changed and maybe a shower."

"Donovan!" Max heard the supervisor shout from across the cavernous storeroom.

Logan was shivering. Max knew it would take that old walking heart attack a few minutes to find him.

He looked around at the stacks of boxes piled high, rack after rack, all the way to the roof. "Sit here and don't make a sound."

Max stood and started running up and down through the stacks. His eyes scanned the labels as he pointed with his finger. *Where the hell did I see those boxes? There you are.* He grabbed a box off the shelf and ripped open the top. It was full of down coats, one of which he pulled out and dropped on the floor. He took a few more boxes off the shelf and shoved the damaged one all the way to the back before replacing the undamaged ones.

Satisfied that he had properly hidden the crime, he ran back to where Logan was sitting by the doorway. He helped him to his feet and placed the coat around his shoulders.

"Here you go. Ya gotta go now, though."

"Thanks, Max."

Max gently pushed him out through the plastic curtain. "My advice? Call the cops. Don't let anyone push you around."

"Sure, Max," he said with a half-smile as he pulled the coat in tighter around himself and wandered back out into the darkness.

"Poor kid," Max said as he shook his head.

When his shift ended, he met his mother by the time clock and walked her out to the car. They were both exhausted and didn't say much. They picked up a bucket of Popeyes fried chicken on the way home.

When they arrived, Max found Sam and Maria still sitting quietly around the dining room table. "Food's here," he shouted as he burst through the front door.

"Great, I'm starving," Sam replied.

Maria gave Max a hug and said nothing as she got plates and set the table for the four of them. Max couldn't stop ranting about his boss but left out any mention of Logan. He didn't know how to respond to what he'd been told and didn't want it to get around school that Logan was having trouble. He hoped Logan would take his advice and get some help. The cold, drizzly night seemed distant now. Max entertained them with one embellished story after another. It made him feel better, and soon he'd forgotten completely about Logan.

When they'd finished eating, Sam and his mother moved to the sofa.

"How have the spasms been, dear?" she asked.

"Today was pretty bad," he replied as she took his shirt off. He lay on his side, and she started to massage his back. "You know this cold weather always makes it worse."

She pulled out a bottle of lotion she always kept in a drawer by the sofa and slowly started to rub it along his curved spine. She turned the television to the local news and quietly hummed a tune from a product jingle as she pressed her hands deeper and deeper into his tight back. Max watched as Sam slowly relaxed, wondering how he was ever going to take care of himself whenever that inevitable day came when Mom was gone.

Max cleaned up the kitchen, then smiled at Maria. "Come on," he said with a wink. He grabbed her by the hand and led her toward his bedroom. The house was small. The cramped living room was just big enough to fit the sofa, a coffee table, side table, and a television. Not much room to be alone.

Max was confused by the look Maria shot Sam as he lay quietly on the sofa. *What's going on there? She's seen him get his back rubbed before.*

Sam must have fallen asleep on the sofa because it was late when he woke Max as he slid next to him into bed. Maria had long gone, but the smell of her perfume remained like a rose-scented ghost lying between the two of them. Sam seemed restless and spent the rest of the night tossing and turning in the spot where she'd been lying. Max kept poking him with his elbow, trying to get him to settle down but eventually fell asleep thinking about Logan and what the poor kid was going to do next.

Chapter 11

2003

Sam and Maria sat on the front porch swing. They said nothing as they enjoyed the late-afternoon spring sunshine. The park across the road was full of children playing. Off in the distance, the usual crowd was playing basketball. Maria had looked at him with a twinkle in her eyes as if to say, "How about a game?" but they both were so comfortable enjoying the beauty of the afternoon that she quickly looked away and just sat still, smiling.

Max had the day off, and he'd taken his mother out to shop for groceries. That was why he was gone when the letter arrived from the University of Texas at Austin. Sam and Maria were dying to know what was inside but didn't dare to open it without him. Sam was silently hoping Max wouldn't get accepted there and would have to go to school locally. He knew deep down, though, that he was going to go. He was too bright and talented. Everyone wanted a piece of him.

Sam didn't know what Maria was going to do next year either. They'd grown so comfortable together over the winter that he couldn't imagine her not being with him every afternoon. She never mentioned, at least in his presence, where she'd applied and what her plans were.

~ ~ ~

Max saw them there on the porch when he arrived with his mother. Even before he could get out of the car, though, Maria sprang to her feet and ran into the house, only to return waving a letter. "Got something for you!"

Max got out of the car and popped the trunk. He gathered up the bags of groceries and headed up the walk.

"Is that what I think it is?" his mother asked with a smile. "Envelope looks awfully thick."

Max went into the house and placed the groceries on the kitchen counter, then returned to the porch. "Give me that, please."

Maria held the envelope behind her back and tried to hide it.

Max laughed as he grabbed her and lifted her off her feet with his left arm and snatched the envelope with his right. "Okay now, let's see where I'm going to be next year."

Just as Max was about to tear open the envelope, a nondescript gray Ford Taurus pulled slowly up to the house and parked behind Max's Nova. They all stood silently watching as two army officers in dress uniform got out of the car and approached the porch. Max let the envelope slip from his fingers and fall to the floor.

"No," their mother whispered as she staggered backward and sat down on the porch swing. "No, no, NO!"

"Are you Mrs. Sally Donovan?"

"NO, NO, NO!" Sally was sobbing.

"What's happening, Max?" Sam asked, looking to his brother for answers.

"I'm Captain Lewis, and this is Captain Cooper."

"NO!" she shouted.

Tears started streaming down Maria's face.

Their mother rocked back and forth. "He's a nurse! He's safe in a hospital!"

Max moved between Sam and Maria and grabbed them both in his arms, pulling them close to his chest.

"I'm sorry to inform you that your husband, Luther Donovan, was killed while honorably serving his country in Afghanistan."

Sam's good leg buckled, but Max held him tight. "It's going to be okay, brother," he whispered.

Their mother sat slowly rocking, her face buried in her hands. Tears dripped through her fingers and formed little spots on the dusty floor of the porch. "He's a nurse," she whispered. "He told me he'd be safe."

They all stood silently as she rocked, slowly growing quieter as the new reality set in.

As the sun started to dip toward the horizon, they all moved into the living room. Max pulled chairs in from the kitchen and placed them around the sofa. Max and Sam sat on the sofa on either side of their mother.

Max's voice cracked. "What happened to our father?"

"Your father was a brave man," Officer Cooper began.

Officer Lewis cleared his throat. A bead of sweat formed on his forehead. "He went with a team of combat medics to a forward operating base and was helping transport several severely injured soldiers back to a MASH unit when their ambulance was struck by an IED."

"He was in a large, safe hospital," their mother mumbled. "He told me that just last week when we talked."

"Unfortunately, no one survived."

"Why was he out near the front lines, Captain?" asked Sam.

"Young man, your father was part of a rapid response group that went to the front lines to help transport and stabilize the injured when the choppers couldn't get to them. He helped pilot the project in his unit to get more skilled people to the front lines and faster care for the injured."

Max put his arm around his mother.

"He was supposed to be safe in a hospital," she sobbed.

The officers sat awkwardly for another half hour. Max realized nothing else really needed to be said. Their father was dead and was never coming home. He stood, thanked both men, and showed them to the door. Then he returned and sat by Sam and their mother for what seemed an eternity. No one wanted to move.

Maria finally stood up. "I'm so sorry, Mrs. Donovan." She leaned over and gave her a hug. She kissed Max and squeezed Sam's hand, then quietly left and headed home.

Max and Sam took their mother by the arm and led her to her room where they laid her down in her bed, still dressed, and pulled a blanket over her. She buried her head in the pillow and wept quietly.

By now, it had grown late. Max lay quietly staring at the ceiling as Sam slid into bed next to him. He eventually rolled over and put his arm around Sam and started to cry. He'd never cried in front of Sam before. Even when he'd broken his leg as a kid jumping into a canyon pool up in the hill country, he hadn't shed a tear. He felt he needed to be strong for his brother. Sam was the one who had to suffer every day. Had to deal with constant pain and frustration. But now Max couldn't control himself. Their father was gone, and that was something he wasn't prepared for.

Sam grabbed Max's arm and pulled him closer. "It will be okay, brother."

Chapter 12

2003

The funeral for Luther Donovan was a large community affair. He'd been a staple at the local hospital, and with his son being the star quarterback, everyone in little Katy, Texas, either knew him or knew of his death. The chairs supplied by the funeral home were full, and surrounding the grave site, mourners stood several rows deep, their heads bowed. The occasional muffled weeping competed with the chirping of birds watching from the overhanging trees. Katy people were hardworking folk. They stood in their coveralls and boots, shorts, and T-shirts. They came with whatever they had on knowing that showing up was the most important thing. Some were even in their hospital scrubs, leaving work briefly just to show their respect for one of their own.

Max held his mother's arm as they slowly approached the edge of the grave. A canopy covered the burial plot, shielding them from the blisteringly bright spring sun. He stared down at the cold steel box suspended over the pit, his face drawn tight in grief.

His mother bent down and touched the casket tenderly with her hand, then grabbed a handful of brown Katy clay and sprinkled it across the top. She stood for a few more seconds staring in disbelief. A gentle breeze blew her hair across her face. She wiped a tear from her cheek with the back of her hand as she staggered backward. Max grabbed her by the arm and steadied her. Eventually, they turned away from the grave and slowly returned to their seats.

When she'd settled herself, an honor guard presented her with a carefully folded flag, which she placed across her lap.

Max sat quietly and stared at the lines on her face. He'd not seen her cry since that first night. She'd made the arrangements for the funeral, signed up for more hours at work, and applied for all the veterans' benefits that she could.

He'd caught her many times staring at Sam since the soldiers had ascended their front steps. He knew what she was worried about. Their father had been the solid foundation of the family, and Sam had always relied on him being there. Sure, Max was his twin, his comrade in arms, but Dad was the anchor. He had never let Sam feel sorry for himself. When chores needed doing, their father had made sure that Max didn't do them all and that Sam did his fair share.

Max closed his eyes as the priest said some last words before they lowered Luther Donovan, army nurse and local hero, into the ground, never to be seen again. He took a deep breath and imagined he could smell the sweet, salty air of Galveston. He remembered the time they'd caught that giant whale of a fish when they were little. When their father had let he and Sam fight the fish for what felt like an eternity. His skinny arms intertwined with Sam's one good arm. Sam's leg wrapped tightly around a pole lest he get pulled overboard. Their father had had a tremendous smile on his face as he watched his boys struggle. Max thought at the time that they'd fought the monster for hours, but now in his wise teen years, he realized it was probably no more than a few minutes.

When the redfish had finally been landed, their father had come up and given them a good shake on the shoulders. "That's my boys," he'd said over and over again. Max remembered the look of pride on his face as they held up the fish for the camera. They'd filleted it and grilled it over an open fire at a camp they'd made on the beach. Max could almost taste it, the tender white meat, the smell of the smoldering wood, the gentle sea breeze.

"Time to go, Max."

Max opened his eyes to find Sam standing over him. He looked around and realized that most of the guests had already left. Sam handed Max the flag. One of the officers came up and handed him a triangular wooden box, and they carefully placed the flag inside. They slowly returned to the Nova, Maria walking arm in arm with their mother a few paces ahead.

Max held the door for Sam as he slid into the passenger seat. He looked across at Maria. She gave him a sorrowful glance as she helped his mother into her truck. He moved around the front of the car and slid behind the wheel.

Max was silent for the first half of the drive home. Finally, he turned to Sam. "I joined up."

Sam's brow furrowed in momentary confusion. "Joined up what?"

"Joined up, joined up. I enlisted in the army. Going to be a combat medic."

Sam looked wildly about the car. "Oh God!" He started to hyperventilate.

Max quickly pulled off the road and onto the shoulder. "Okay. Slow, deep breaths." He put his arm around Sam and slowly stroked his back until his breathing settled.

"You're leaving? What are we going to do? We need you!"

"I've got to do it. They killed Dad. I've got to go back and finish what he was doing."

"Max! I need you!"

"I'll be able to send money home. That will help with the bills. Can't make any money just sitting around in college."

Sam suddenly pushed the car door open and began to vomit onto the side of the road. Max jumped out and ran around to hold his head. Once again, he started to hyperventilate. Max was afraid he was going to pass out. He looked in the back seat and found an old Whataburger bag. He grabbed it and placed it over Sam's face until he calmed down.

Sam leaned back against the seat. "Have you told Mom yet?"

Max shook his head.

"Maria?"

"No."

"Have you thought this out? You can't do this to us."

Max went around the car and slid back behind the wheel. "It's done. I've got to do it, and that's that."

They drove the rest of the way home in silence. When they arrived at the house, they found a dozen or so neighbors scattered about eating deli sandwiches and drinking beer. Sam and Max smiled and accepted their condolences, but they couldn't look at each other. The sun had long set when the last sandwich had been eaten, and the house was silent once again.

"Mom, my back is really bad. Please can you rub it?"

Their mother smiled for the first time that day. She had a purpose, and it was to take care of her baby. "Of course. Take off your good clothes and come lie on the sofa."

Max came up behind Maria and put his hands around her waist. He tenderly kissed her on the neck, then took her by the hand and led her out to the front porch. He put his arm around her as she snuggled in close by his side as they gently rocked on the swing. She was warm, and the smell of her body close to his made him feel light-headed.

For a brief moment, he considered not telling her. Not leaving at all. Just staying like this forever. Her intoxicating body close to his. Forever on a swing enjoying a beautiful spring evening.

"Maria," he whispered.

"Yes, sweetheart?"

"You know how hard this is."

"I know. I loved your dad. I'm so glad so many people showed up today."

"No, I mean what I have to tell you is hard."

Maria sat up and stopped the swing from rocking. "What, Max?"

"I joined the army."

"What?"

"Going to be a combat medic. Going to go do some of the stuff Dad did."

"What!" She stood up and placed her hands on her hips. "You're kidding, right?"

"No. I decided a few days ago. I went and saw the recruiter and signed up. I'll be leaving in a few weeks."

Maria turned her back to him and stared out into the darkness. "I thought you were going to go to college."

"I can do that when I'm done."

"I thought you were . . ." She turned to face him. Tears streamed down her face.

Max stood up. "Have to do it."

"I thought you were going to be around for me. I thought you loved me!"

"I do."

Maria turned her back to Max, then violently spun around again and started hitting him across the chest with both fists. "What about me?" she screamed. "What about Sam? Your mother? What about us?"

Max grabbed her around the shoulders and pulled her in tightly, smothering her blows. "I'll be back. It won't be that bad."

"No!" she shouted as she broke free from his grasp. "No, it will be that bad! We need you. I need you!"

Max looked down at his feet. "I'm sorry. It's done. I have to do this."

"You have not thought this through, Max. You're being impulsive. You've always been that way. It may be okay for deciding to do something crazy on the football field, but this is life. You can't just decide one day that you're going to up and leave without considering what it's going to do to the rest of us. Think!"

Max remained silent. He knew she was probably right, but he felt he needed to do it anyway, and that was that.

"Well?"

He looked up. Her beautiful face was swollen from crying. Her mascara streaked around her eyes. He said nothing. She stepped up to him and slapped him hard across the face. Still he remained silent. He didn't know what to say. His mind was settled. He'd signed the papers and was set to go. Maria trembled as she stood before him waiting for an answer. Finally, she simply turned and stormed off the porch. She spun the wheels of her truck as she sped away. Gravel from the drive scattered across the porch and landed at his feet. When the taillights of her truck finally disappeared in the distance, Max turned and walked into the house. He didn't acknowledge Sam or their mother as he went straight into his room. He spent the rest of the night pacing the floor, wondering if he hadn't just made the biggest mistake of his life.

Chapter 13

The Present

Rosa woke to the sound of shouting outside her window.

"Wake up, *hijos de putas*. Time to move."

She could hear an engine start up and the muffled groans of the passengers as they loaded into the back of the truck.

"Time to go, *niñita*," the old woman said as she burst into the room. "Better grab a bottle of water. We're not stopping until we get to Houston."

She led Rosa back to the truck and placed her in the middle of the bench seat, once again pressed up against the man. This time, he kept his eyes forward and wouldn't look at Rosa. She could see bruises on the side of his head where the old woman had hit him with the stick.

The three-hour drive from San Antonio to Houston was spent in silence. Rosa quietly sipped on her water bottle as her stomach cramped with hunger. When she started to see the city rising up before her, she noticed the old woman take an envelope from the glove compartment. She ripped it open and removed a letter, then started reading it. Rosa watched her moving her lips as she slowly made her way to the bottom of the page.

"Says to get off at the next exit." She proceeded to read turn-by-turn directions until finally they turned down a quiet side street and came to a stop. The old woman pulled out a burner phone and began texting. When she was done, she shot a glance at the man, then sat silently and waited.

Within a few minutes, an old green car came screeching around the corner and stopped directly in front of the truck. A man jumped out and ran up to the driver's side door and pulled it open. Rosa could see that he was slightly hunched and looked at the driver sideways. She could just make out the shape of a gun in the man's hand over the belly of the driver. The driver was startled and started to tremble as he was pulled from his seat.

"Are you Rosa?" the man with the gun shouted.

She nodded.

"I'm here to save you. Move quickly."

Rosa slid from her seat as he continued to hold up the pistol, waving it between the old man and the woman still seated in the cab.

"Get in the back seat of my car and keep your head down."

Rosa ran to the car and turned just in time to see the man tuck the gun in his pants and toss something into the cab of the truck. He ran toward her and jumped behind the wheel.

"Stay down."

Rosa lay across the back seat as he gunned the engine. The tires squealed as they raced down the quiet street and onto a busy thoroughfare.

"Are you okay?" the man asked, looking over his shoulder. He smiled a kindly smile. "They didn't hurt you, did they?"

Rosa looked up at him from the back seat. "No."

"Good. I guess I saved you just in time then."

"Where are you taking me?"

"You must be hungry. I'll take you back to my house, where you can have a bite to eat while we wait for the police to come get you."

Rosa could see out the windows that they were driving down a street lined with large oaks that arched over the road. She sat up a little more, and over the edge of the door, she saw that they were driving through a beautiful neighborhood with well-groomed lawns and large houses.

Soon they turned into the drive of one of those houses.

"Come on, Rosa. Let's get you something to eat."

They walked into a big kitchen. In its center was a dark, thick wooden table. Dark wooden cabinets lined the walls. The floor was cold gray stone.

"Come sit." He pulled out a chair for her. There was jam and bread already spread out on the table. He got some milk out of the refrigerator and poured her a glass. "Eat up. I'm just going to go into the next room and call the police while you eat."

Rosa grabbed the bread and smothered it in jam. She shoved one piece after another into her mouth, then drank the entire glass of milk without stopping. She hadn't realized how hungry she was until then. When she'd finished, her belly hurt.

She leaned back in her chair and took a deep breath. Finally, her nightmare was coming to an end. Soon the police would be here, and they would tell her family that she was okay and send her back home.

She closed her eyes and lowered her exhausted head to the table.

Chapter 14

The Present

"How've you been, Max? Those sleeping pills helping?"

Max's butt made squeaking noises as he squirmed on the leather couch. He imagined all the scribbling and turning of pages just behind his head were notes about his appearance, demeanor, or possibly just writing checks to pay bills. He did look a bit disheveled. Up all night again. No night prowling, though, since his little adventure up in the Heights. *Boy, wouldn't he like to hear about that?* he mused. *He could write a book on me.*

"Sleeping better? Yes, definitely sleeping better." Max reached down to rub his left knee. It had started to swell a little after that night. He didn't remember hurting himself, but he must have landed wrong jumping over the fence.

"Since your last visit, I've had a chance to delve a little more into your records from the VA."

Max felt rings of perspiration start to form under his arms.

"Says here you joined up and worked as a combat medic. That right?"

"Yeah, that's right. What does that have to do with my sleeping issues?"

"Nothing really. Just want to get a better picture of who you are and what may be bothering you."

Max winced as he heard another page turn.

"So what was it like over there, and why did you decide to go? Must have been quite a culture shock. First time really away from home. From family."

"Yeah, it was different." Max pulled his white coat tighter across his chest. "The why? Well, that was just a part of my impulsive mentality that I've never really outgrown."

~~~

2004

Max lay on his cot shirtless. Afghanistan in July was hot. An electric fan placed precariously on a small shelf over his head made a comforting whirring sound as it slowly rotated back and forth.

There were six men in his tent. They were good guys, kept the place neat. Three beds along each wall. They each had their own shelf above their bunk and a locker at their feet. Theirs was the closest sleeping area to the operating-room modules, and often, when things got really bad, the staff would roll out of the operating rooms and use their space as a sleeping area. They would hot-bunk there until things got a little more under control. His MASH unit had seen a lot of casualties recently. He started every shift sorting through bloodied and broken young bodies. Processing them. Readying them for surgery. Cleaning up the mess, then receiving another group. They all looked like him. Fit. Young. Invincible.

He tried to close his eyes, but he kept seeing visions of a patient from the night before. Triage had already been crammed wall to wall with young men in varying degrees of distress. The smell of urine and feces mixed with the stale metallic smell of blood filled the poorly ventilated room. A forest of IV poles with bags of blood and saline surrounded the stretchers.
~~~

Max had already cut the clothes off two young men and started their IVs when they brought him in. He'd been no older than Max. They'd rushed him into triage, bypassing the more stable patients, and placed him on a stretcher right outside the operating-room door. A table in the operating room had just cleared, and they were momentarily stopping in triage as it was being cleaned. He was hysterical. Two medics had to hold him down as he screamed.

"Oh my God! Help me!"

Max pulled off the blanket covering the lower half of the boy's body, only to find two bloody stumps. Double tourniquets were cinched tightly around both upper thighs. Below them lay two jagged bones surrounded by shredded flesh.

The boy looked down at his lower half, his eyes wild with pain. "Where are my legs? Someone get my legs!"

He had never known doubt before. Never questioned his potential. His future. Now he saw himself everyday bleeding, crying, dying.

Max opened his eyes. The fan was doing little to stop him from sweating. On his chest lay several letters from Maria. He'd read them a dozen times. Each time, he was determined to write something back, but he couldn't. The letters had sustained him. He looked forward to them, anxiously tore them open when they arrived, and scoured them for news of home, of Sam, of Katy. But he couldn't write back. He'd become incapable of putting his feelings down on paper. He'd realized that it took a certain amount of calm and self-control to sit quietly and compose something meaningful. He'd tried, desperately tried, to let Maria know how the high desert was killing the old Max. How he felt it must have affected his father. But he was silent. Trying to write Sam was even harder. He received but could not give.

Max sat up and took the letters off his chest and placed them with the others in his locker. He stood and stretched. Several of the other medics were still sleeping in their bunks. He quietly moved around them, slipped on a shirt, and stepped outside.

The sun was rising in the east. A haze along the horizon made the early morning light seem even more orange than normal. The mobile field hospital was a maze of interconnecting tents surrounding and feeding into several large steel modular units that housed the operating rooms and diagnostic equipment. The tan canvas of the tents rippled in the hot breeze. He looked to the perimeter. The village lying a thousand meters beyond the barbed wire seemed peaceful. Its high mud walls sprawled across the arid plateau, sheltering its inhabitants from the outside world. Several dogs scurried about, nosing through trash. A chicken stood on a wall. Nothing particular about the scene would reveal why a boy from Katy was halfway around the world standing in that spot at that moment.

"Good morning, Private Donovan."

Max jumped a little as he turned to see one of the Afghan sentries standing behind him. He was much shorter than Max. His tan uniform was covered with dust but well kept, a carbine slung over his shoulder.

"Sorry, sir. I didn't mean to startle you."

"No, you're fine, Asadi," he said with a smile. He liked Asadi. "Just didn't hear you come up behind me. You're too quiet."

That elicited a faint smile. "It's good for a guard to be quiet, eh?"

"Yeah, I guess so."

Asadi turned and looked out across the barbed wire. "Not much of a village. Probably nothing like the town you're from in Texas."

Max scratched an insect bite on the side of his scalp. "Asadi, there're lots of towns in America that are as small and isolated as this one."

"I like my village. You may look at it and see only some mud buildings, but it's home."

"I think everyone has some feelings for where they were raised. Good or bad, those feelings are hard to erase."

Asadi sighed. He stroked his dark beard as he looked lovingly at his home. His cracked brown face resembled its ancient mud walls. "I have only good memories as a child." He raised his hand and pointed to a patch of dirt just to the west of the village. "We used to play football there when I was young. I was the best in the village."

"I used to play American football when I was younger. Pretty good too."

"Off to the side, just beyond that ditch, we used to fly kites. The children can't play there now because it's mined."

"Do you have many relatives in town?"

Asadi smiled a big, toothless smile. "All of them are relatives. Cousins, brothers, uncles. My family has lived here for generations."

"What do they think of you working here?"

Asadi straightened up a little. His chest pushed out as if he'd been asked to stand to attention. "They're proud of me. To be in a place with so many educated people, with such high-tech equipment. We've never seen this before. Even when the Russians were in the region, they never were this close to our village."

"I *bet* your family is proud."

"They treat me differently now. My opinion means something."

"And it should. You do a good job, and you deserve their respect."

"Thank you, Private." Asadi nodded and flashed his toothless smile once again. "I hope you have a good day, sir. I must finish making my rounds now." He turned and started walking a slow, steady soldier's walk around the perimeter of the compound.

Max stared at him as he walked away. *Probably not much younger than my dad was*, he thought. *Has a family, kids maybe. Look at me. Impulsively following after dad, who'd never said he wanted me over here.*

Max decided to make the most of his morning by visiting the triage tent attached to one of the operating-room modules. He wanted to sort out the triage area and make sure all the supplies were stocked before the next big wave of casualties arrived.

He pulled open the metal door that separated the dusty, primitive Afghan desert from the high-tech world of an American MASH unit and entered the triage area. The large, open room was quiet now. The blood had been cleaned off the floor, and the smells and screams from the night before were just more bad memories permanently seared into Max's brain.

As he loaded a cabinet with fresh towels, he thought he heard a noise coming from one of the operating rooms. *Who the hell would be here now but me?*

He walked down the short, canvas-covered hallway to the main operating-room area and slowly pushed open the door. When he looked inside, he was surprised to find Dr. Nick Jernigan, the anesthesiologist, shuffling through a medicine cabinet next to a large metal anesthesia machine. "Good morning, Captain."

Dr. Jernigan seemed surprised to see anyone there that early in the morning. "Oh, hello, Private. Just checking on supplies to make sure we have everything for the day."

"Sorry to bother you. Was thinking of doing the same thing. Hate to get caught off guard and not have something when you need it."

Dr. Jernigan sat down on a chair in front of the cabinet. He turned his head slightly to the side so he could look directly at Max. "How are you holding up, Private? I know this place can really wear on you."

"Okay, I guess, sir."

"Well, I can tell you, this is my third tour, and it certainly has worn me out."

"Sir?"

"I had a nice practice going back at home. Every time I got it up and running, they called me back." He sighed as he took a checklist off the shelf and started writing on it. "They paid for all my schooling, so I definitely owe it to them, but never thought I was going to have to start over so many times."

"Must be difficult."

"It's Max, right?" He placed the checklist on his lap. "Did you sell your soul to the army, Max? Owe anything?"

"No, sir."

"Well, good for you. To be honest, I can't imagine what would make a good-looking young man like yourself sign up for this shit. I lost a wife and all my money running back and forth to this godforsaken place. Can't even get laid over here with all their rules about women. Wouldn't mind seeing a little local leg every now and again. Know what I mean?"

Max didn't know how to respond and simply shrugged.

"Well, you must have a good woman at home then. For me, this is torture."

Max just stood and stared. He did have a good woman at home. At least he thought he did. He'd been reading her letters over and over again all morning and was starting to get a sense that he may be losing her. His inability to write. His total involvement in the day-to-day, so distant from Texas. As for why he'd signed up? Well, he was starting to ask himself the same question.

"Carry on, Private. Don't let me stop you. I know you have a lot to do."

"Thank you, sir."

Max decided to come back later. Having the captain there made him uncomfortable. He looked in the cabinet to make sure there were enough bandages, checked the storage area for bags of saline, then quickly left.

Max stepped out into the bright sunshine. He had to shield his eyes as he looked across the compound at Asadi's village. It was definitely no Katy. *Really, why the hell am I over here?*

Chapter 15

The Present

Max pulled his white coat tightly across his shoulders as he darted past Simkins's secretary and out of the office. He'd spent the past fifteen years trying to forget what it was like over there and what he'd done when he got back. The heat, the loneliness, the trauma. And to think after all he'd endured, he ended up as a trauma surgeon. With Dr. Jack slowly ripping the bandage off, the wounds were starting to feel raw all over again. Maybe it was part of his self-imposed penance for his own sins that he faced every day the horror of what man can do to his fellow man. Maybe he was just too screwed up in the head for even Simkins to figure out and all his rationalizations were just crap.

He went straight to his car and drove home. He shuffled in from the driveway and shot a sideways glance at the credenza as he made his way to the front door. A pile of mail had accumulated on the floor in front of the mail slot. He scooped it up and plopped the stack down on the dining-room table.

"Bills, bills, bills . . ."

Suddenly something caught his eye. Poking out from underneath a stack of advertisements was a letter. He pulled it out and went around the corner and sat on the living room sofa.

Huh, no return address.

The writing on the front was in a beautifully fluid script. He gently tore it open and unfolded the letter. It was handwritten on thick, cream-colored stationery.

Peace be on your victims and the mercy and blessings of Allah.

Max turned the letter over several times, each time expecting something different. A signature, a mark, fingerprint, something. But it was blank except for a faint watermark that looked like a brand symbol of some kind.

"Must have been sent to the wrong address," he mumbled as he walked back to the dining room and tossed it on the stack of junk mail. *Don't know who would send me something like that. But definitely need to find some peace of my own.*

Max went to his room, showered, then dove into bed. He'd promised a colleague that he would cover him for a few hours that afternoon, and he needed to get some sleep before heading back.

When he woke later that day, he swung his legs over the side of the bed and winced as his feet hit the floor. He placed both hands on his left knee and gently rubbed it.

Must have really strained it.

He stood and gently walked to the bathroom and took an anti-inflammatory. He dressed and headed back to County, where he went straight to the operating rooms to see if there was anything interesting going on.

As he walked through the swinging electric doors, he heard the PA system crackle to life. "Code Blue, surgical staff locker room! Code Blue, surgical staff locker room!"

Max made a quick detour to the locker room. The door was being held open by a surgical tech.

"What happened?"

"Dr. Donovan, it's Damien. We found him on the floor in the bathroom stall."

Max pushed through the onlookers and moved into the bathroom. He opened the stall door, only to find the anesthesia tech crammed between the toilet and the wall. Fully clothed. His face blue. A needle on the floor.

"Help me get him out from behind here!" Max shouted to one of the onlookers.

They grabbed his feet and pulled him to the middle of the bathroom floor. Max knelt next to the limp body and gave it a good shake. "Damien! Damien!" He grabbed his wrist and could barely feel a pulse.

The code team arrived and squeezed the resuscitation cart into the room. Max closed his eyes for a brief moment. Damien's blue face. His deathlike appearance. The people gathered in the room couldn't see that Max was trembling. Couldn't see that it was taking all his willpower to control his breathing, to stop himself from running from the scene screaming. They didn't know his history.

Max stood and ripped open the top drawer of the resuscitation cart and pulled out a syringe of Narcan. "Looks like a drug overdose," he said to the on-call cardiac arrest resident. Max strapped a tourniquet around Damien's arm and injected the syringe of Narcan into a bulging vein.

Within seconds, Damien showed signs of life. His eyes opened as he took a big gasp of air. He lifted his head and looked around the room, trying to comprehend what had happened.

"Let's get him down to the emergency room where we can assess him better."

Several of the staff dead-lifted Damien up and out into the hallway, where a stretcher was waiting. Max stood and watched as they rolled him away.

"Wow. Was that Damien?"

Max turned to see Nick Jernigan standing behind him. "Yeah, one of your anesthesia techs, Nick. Looks like an overdose."

"Gonna be okay?"

"Probably. Don't know how long he was down, but he came right back with some Narcan."

They walked down the corridor toward the operating rooms. "Crazy profession, Max. They've got a lot of exposure to drugs here in the hospital. I guess he just got hooked on some."

Max stopped and shook his left leg. Kneeling in the cramped bathroom had made it ache even more than before.

"Got a problem with the knees?"

"Oh, I think I just sprained it the other day, that's all."

"You should get that looked at. If you want, swing by my clinic this afternoon. I can shoot a quick x-ray."

Max clicked his knee back and forth a few more times. "All right. Probably a good idea, just to be on the safe side. You have a clinic around here?"

"Just over in the Fifth Ward. Not much, but I have an x-ray machine. Swing by this afternoon."

He took down the address. "Thanks. I'll see you this afternoon when I get off."

Max watched Jernigan as he walked back toward the operating room. He'd aged since he'd known him in Afghanistan. It had been nice seeing a familiar face when they reconnected all these years later. It had also been helpful that he'd recommended his good friend, Dr. Simkins. As much as Max hated going to a psychiatrist, he did feel it was helping a little.

Max swung by the emergency room that afternoon once the surgeon he was covering came back on duty. Damien was still in one of the rooms with an IV in his arm.

"How ya doing, Damien?"

"Fine," he replied as he looked away.

"Very close call today. Almost didn't make it."

"Thanks for saving me."

"Anytime." Max walked around the stretcher. "This ever happened before?"

"No," Damien replied immediately.

"What was it, fentanyl?"

Damien nodded slowly.

"Where'd ya get it from?"

Damien looked Max in the eyes but said nothing. Max could tell that he was still a little shaken by what had happened but also scared to say anything more.

"All right then." He patted him on the shoulder. "You get better. Rehab is a great thing. I'd hate to be a few minutes too late next time."

Max walked out of the emergency room and went to his car. He plugged the address to Dr. Jernigan's clinic into his phone, then headed out of the hospital parking garage. He drove around the park where he'd had his encounter with Angel, then meandered past a public golf course situated across the street from the zoo. He envied those who were out in the middle of the day playing. *Must be nice to have nothing important to do but play all day in the sunshine.* He eventually made his way over to Route 59, then northeast toward the Fifth.

Max pulled off the main road and followed the voice prompts directing him down the old narrow streets of the Fifth. It had come a long way since he was a kid, but the improvements were still a work in progress. He'd taken care of a lot of the victims of urban violence from this part of town.

"You have arrived at your destination," chirped the sweet voice of his phone's navigation system.

Max was surprised. The clinic was in a run-down strip mall. The parking lot out front was full, and several people were pacing in front of the door.

He made sure that he locked the Nova but was not so sure it would be there when he came out. He gently brushed the bump in the small of his back to reassure himself that he had his Beretta on board.

When he entered the clinic, he was overwhelmed by the number of people crammed into the front office. It was small, and the ceiling-to-floor window glass in front of the clinic was greasy as if it had once been part of an old fried food restaurant. Covering it was a broken venetian blind, its thin metal slats bent in varying directions. The floor was cracked linoleum. Old, battered office chairs were lined up in rows facing a door that Max assumed led to the doctor. The receptionist sat behind a wall with a frosted sliding-glass window cracked open just enough to see what was happening in the room.

Max squeezed his way up to the window. "Dr. Donovan here to see Dr. Jernigan."

The receptionist barely looked up. "Through the door on your right."

Max passed through the door and into a corridor also jam-packed with patients, some sitting on the floor, others on plastic chairs. He eventually found Nick Jernigan at his desk at the far end of the hallway. A stack of charts was piled high in front of him.

"Hey, Max. Glad you could make it." He got up from behind his desk. "Come on down the hallway and let's look at that knee."

As they walked down a long, narrow corridor, Nick stopped momentarily in front of a patient who was sitting on the floor leaning up against a door. "Hey, you!" he snapped as he pointed to a big red sign on the door.

DO NOT ENTER. NO SITTING IN FRONT OF DOOR.

"Can't you read? Get the hell away from the door!"

Max was surprised at how aggressive he was with the patient. "What was that all about?"

"Oh, there's a storeroom in there, and the fire marshal says they can't block the door. Drives me crazy. How big a sign do I have to make, for God's sake?"

They moved to a small exam room that had supplies piled high along the walls. To Max, it looked more like a storeroom than a room anyone could do a decent examination in. He sat on a table shoved up against the wall.

"Okay now, let's see what we have here."

Max rolled up his pant leg. The knee was slightly swollen. Dr. Jernigan's examination was cursory at best. "Okay, let's get an x-ray, shall we?" They moved to an adjoining room centered by an antiquated-looking x-ray machine.

"Haven't seen one like this in ages," Max said.

"Well, I can't really afford a new one. Anyway, it gets the job done." Nick placed a plate under Max's knee. "Don't move."

Nick stepped from the room. The machine came to life and made several unsettling noises before he returned to take the plate. "Be right back, Max."

Max sat alone in the room for several minutes as Dr. Jernigan went off to develop the film. *What a pit*, he thought as he looked around at the peeling paint and the rusted pipes poking through gaps in the drop ceiling.

"All good. Nothing broken."

"Didn't think so."

"A good dose of steroids should do the trick."

Before Max could object, Dr. Jernigan had whipped out an alcohol swab and a syringe and stuck Max in the knee, injecting the steroid deep into the joint.

"What the . . ."

"Trust me, you'll thank me tomorrow." Dr. Jernigan pulled out a thick pad from his pocket and scribbled a prescription on it and handed it to Max. "Okay, buddy, you're all fixed up." He slapped him on the shoulder. "See you at County. Got to run now. Way behind, as you can see."

Max sat and watched as Nick scurried from the room. He gently placed his feet on the floor and made his way down the corridor toward the front of the clinic. On his way, he saw a new patient sitting on the floor in front of the door with the big red sign.

Max noticed that his knee was feeling a little better as he limped across the parking lot. *Huh, maybe the pain was more psychosomatic than anything else. Medicine can't work that fast.*

His heart sank when he saw several brawny young men leaning on the back of his car. One of them was taking a selfie. "Hey, guys. Do you mind not leaning on the car?"

"Yo, this your car?" one of them asked as they all stood up from leaning on the rear deck.

"Yeah."

"Damn. You a doctor too, like Doc Jernigan?"

"Kinda, but not the same."

One of the men swaggered up to Max and leaned in. "Can you cut me a deal? I got me a real bad back and could use some Oxy."

"Sorry, but you need to be evaluated by the doc. Can't do that."

The man gave Max a sideways glance. "I got cash."

Max opened the door and slid behind the wheel. "Sorry, can't help you," he said as he closed the door. The men stepped away from the car and slowly returned to the front of the clinic. Max sat behind the wheel for a few seconds and pulled the prescription from his pocket and looked at it as the engine warmed up. Oxycontin, two-hundred tabs. One refill.

Chapter 16

The Present

When Rosa woke, she found herself lying in a bed under a pile of blankets. She poked her head out and saw that she was in a large white room. There was a simple white vanity pressed up against a wall and two overstuffed chairs situated on either side of a window near the foot of the bed. Heavy drapes extended from the high ceiling to the floor. The room was warm but the décor cold, and it reminded her of a doctor's examination room.

She swung her feet onto the floor and wiggled her toes in the soft plush carpet. She stood and walked to the window. It appeared as if the window had been blacked out, and not even a speck of light could be seen. She walked to the door and tried the handle, but it was locked from the outside.

"Hola! Anyone there?"

She rattled the handle and kicked the door several times, but there was no response. She walked over to the vanity and sat down.

"Oh, my *madre* would be so upset with my messy hair," she whispered.

She opened the drawer and found a brush and proceeded to untangle her hair. As she stared into the mirror, she noticed that every time she moved her head to the side, the reflection distorted ever so slightly.

That's strange, she thought. She pressed her face up close to the glass and squinted. *Just an old broken mirror, I guess.* She continued to brush her hair. *I wonder when the police are going to get here.*

When she finished, she placed the brush back in the drawer and walked across the room and found that there was an attached bathroom. She hadn't washed in days, and the thought of a nice hot shower was appealing. She didn't want to be filthy when the police came.

She undressed in front of a large mirror that covered most of the wall behind a double sink, then stepped into the shower. The water felt good as the grime and sweat slowly washed away. She thought of the good story she was going to have to tell when she got home and how lucky she was to have been saved. She toweled off quickly and put her clothes back on. She hated dressing in dirty clothes after showering, but that was all she could do until she got back home.

When she walked back into the bedroom, she saw that there was a tray of food on her bed and some clean clothes in her size.

That's strange, she thought.

She moved the tray to the side so she could sit down without disturbing the folded clothes. She saw the edge of a photograph poking out from underneath. She slid her hand under the tray and pulled it out.

"*Ay, Dios!*" she screamed as she knocked the tray onto the floor.

Her hands trembled as she held up a picture of the front of her house. She remembered what one of her captors had whispered in her ear: "We know where your family lives, little girl. That house with the nice orange door." They would kill her family if she didn't behave.

She now realized that she had not been rescued. The threat was the same.

Better behave. We know where you live.

The nice man who brought her to his house was the one that had ordered her kidnapped in the first place!

Rosa slid to the floor and started to shake uncontrollably.

What do I do now?

Chapter 17

The Present

"**G**ood morning, Max. All quiet in the hospital last night?"

"All the same, Dr. Simkins. You know it never changes." He lowered himself onto the couch and got comfortable. "Man is destined to slaughter his fellow man. It seems to be in our nature. I guess it's my fate to try and put all the pieces back together again."

After a momentary pause and the usual shuffle of papers, Dr. Simkins asked the question Max knew was coming. In a way, he was surprised it'd taken so many sessions to get to the question. "Max, can you tell me what happened that night?"

"What night?" He started to gently rub his chest with his left hand. "There were lots of nights over in Afghanistan. Hot nights. Damn freezing nights."

"Max, stop avoiding the subject. *The* night. The night you earned your Purple Heart."

Max relaxed into the couch. He closed his eyes and took a deep breath. "You know he was a friend of mine."

~ ~ ~

2004

Max strolled across the compound, having just left the mess hall. Lunch was the same. The heat and dust of the August afternoon were the same. The war had been going on for three years and was just the same. He hoped to get a few hours of sleep before he worked the night shift. They were expecting a lot of casualties to be transferred in that evening.

"Hello, Asadi," he said to his favorite Afghan sentry as he walked in the direction of his tent.

"Hello, Private Donovan."

Max always liked talking with Asadi. Their exchanges about their homes and families seemed surprisingly similar despite growing up half a world apart. Max admired how cool and relaxed Asadi could be when all hell was breaking loose. Just what you wanted in a soldier.

"I'm glad I ran into you." Asadi looked at his feet uncomfortably. "Things are changing for the better in my country. Better at least for my family."

"Yes, that's what we're hoping for."

"Well, I never thought my daughter had a chance to be anything before, but now that's changing." He shuffled back and forth not able to make eye contact. "You've always been nice to me. Would it be possible for you to show her around? I want her to see what a woman can be." He dug the toe of his boot in the dirt. "I see lots of women officers in the hospital. Maybe she can be a doctor one day."

"Sure, Asadi. If I get some sleep tonight, then you can bring her around first thing in the morning and I'll give her a tour. That okay?"

Asadi looked up from the ground and into Max's eyes. His toothless smile was so big it caused his beard to curl up under his chin. "Thank you, Mr. Donovan. You'll make me and my wife very proud. Our daughter is sixteen. We were never able to have any other children. She's all we have. I'd like her to think she has a future."

Surprisingly, that night was quiet, and first thing the next morning, Asadi was outside his tent patiently waiting.

"Sir, this is my daughter, Asalah."

Max stood momentarily stunned. He'd expected a small child, but before him stood a tall, beautiful woman. She had light skin and green eyes. Her auburn hair just peeked out from underneath her headscarf.

Max extended his hand, but she kept her hands folded and shot a panicked glance at her father.

"It is okay, Asalah."

She timidly held out her hand and took hold of Max's. "Nice to meet you."

"So, I understand you're interested in medicine?"

She smiled, her perfect teeth such a contrast from her father's. The sparkle in her eyes made Max feel flush, and he quickly turned away and started walking toward the medical structures.

Asadi and his daughter followed close behind as they made the short walk across the dusty compound to the triage tent. Max pulled the metal door open and held it for them so they could enter. The large, open triage room was quiet now. No screaming. No smells. The stretchers lined up against the walls were spotless.

Asalah turned slowly in the middle of the room, gazing in wonderment at all the tech. Max watched her examine the monitors stacked near the stretchers.

She placed her hand on top of one. "Is this how you watch their hearts?"

Max was surprised. He knew she lived just across the barbed wire in a building made of mud centuries ago. "Why, yes, that is a heart monitor."

She smiled as she slowly walked along the line of stretchers, her fingers gently massaging the clean white linen. She turned to Max, her bright green eyes looking directly into his. "Can we see where they do the operations?"

"Sure, just this way."

They walked down the canvas-covered hallway to the metal prefab operating-room unit. When they entered the first operating theater, Max found Dr. Jernigan once again checking the anesthesia machine.

"Excuse me, Captain. We didn't mean to bother you. I was just showing Asadi and his daughter around. Hoping maybe she can become a doctor one day."

Max looked around and saw that Asadi had stayed in the doorway, a look of panic in his eyes.

"Not a problem, Private." Jernigan stood up from his chair and walked over to Asalah. "My, what a beautiful woman you are." He looked over at Asadi, who'd not budged from his spot by the entrance. "Asadi, you never told me you had a daughter."

Asadi finally moved from the doorway and stood between Asalah and Dr. Jernigan. "She's my only child. I want her to be something special one day."

Jernigan kept staring at Asalah. "Oh, I'm sure she will be. If she ever wants to come and see us in action, just let me know and I'll show her around."

Asadi turned to Max. "Her mother will be getting worried," he stammered. "She has a lot of work to do today. We must be going. Thank you very much for the tour."

Asalah looked down at her feet and followed close behind as her father hurried out of the room.

Max watched as Jernigan's eyes latched onto Asalah and tracked her.

"Well, Private. Maybe you made a doctor today. We shall see what becomes of that beauty." He kept staring at the door long after she'd left.

"Yes, sir, that really would be something."

Jernigan seemed to snap out of his trance at the sound of Max's voice. "Good work, Private. Keep the locals on our side." He turned and sat back down at his machine. "Carry on. I have a lot of work to do."

"Yes, sir." Max turned and left. *That was really strange*, he thought as he headed across the compound toward the mess hall. But he had to admit she truly was a beautiful breath of fresh air in this dusty hellhole.

Max was so involved in the day-to-day intensity of his job that before he knew it, it was already October. The cooler weather saw a decrease in the daily number of wounded as the offensive missions in the area began winding down. One or two wounded straggled in each day, but none of the volume they had experienced in the past. There had even been talk of packing up and moving.

That evening, Max lay in his tent, just starting to doze off. He'd tried writing another letter to Maria, but it lay on his chest unfinished. His pen had slid from his hand and onto the floor. The nights were starting to get a little chilly, and in his slumber, he pulled the blanket up to his chin, crumpling the half-written note.

Suddenly, he was jolted awake by the sound of gunfire. *Rat, tat, tat. Rat, tat, tat.*

The door to his tent shook as someone hammered on it with their fist. "Donovan! Donovan! Help, we need you right away!"

Max clambered out of bed, strapped on his Beretta, and bolted from his tent. It was dark and cold. He sprinted in the direction of the gunfire. It seemed to be coming from inside the medical tents where the operating rooms were. Max could hear screaming and the trampling of boots hitting the ground.

Just as he approached the door . . . *Whoomph!* Max was blown to the ground. An explosive had blown the door off and pieces of it had come to rest on top of him. He lay on his back, stunned, his ears ringing. At first, he hadn't realized what had happened. He tried to open his eyes, but they burned. Smoke filled his lungs as he gasped for air. Pain shot down his right side as he struggled under the debris of the door. His pounding head raced between confused visions of his childhood and the present. Of his mother. Of Sam and Maria. How they would cry for him like they had cried for his father.

Rat, tat, tat. Rat, tat, tat.

The sound of the ongoing gunfire snapped Max back. Something was happening. He needed to help. He staggered to his feet, tossing the bits of broken door to the side, and ran into the triage area. As he approached the operating rooms, he saw Asadi standing in the doorway firing his carbine into the room where Max had shown Asalah around. He had a wild, crazed look in his eyes.

"Where are you?" he shouted. "Where are you?"

Max froze. Blood was splattered along the walls. Body parts were scattered about the floor. Max started toward Asadi but began to stumble. He looked down and saw blood pouring down his arms, his shirt soaked in blood. Searing pain ripped through his chest with each breath. His vision began to blur, but he knew he needed to stop Asadi. He gathered all his remaining strength and charged.

Asadi turned the gun in his direction. Max could see the anguish in his eyes. He could have pulled the trigger, but hesitated. Just before Max reached him, Asadi turned the gun on himself. Max tackled him as his body fell limp to the floor.

~ ~ ~

The Present

"Says here in the report your bravery in confronting the enemy resulted in the saving of dozens in the surrounding rooms."

"Maybe, I guess."

"And you had shrapnel. Let's see. Lodged in your right chest with a pretty nasty chest wound by the look of this photograph."

Max sat quietly as he listened to Dr. Simkins shuffle more papers.

"Lucky to be alive. Why do you think he didn't shoot you? Looks like he could have."

"I don't know."

"Why do you think he did it?"

"Beats me. Who knows what goes through the mind of someone over there? Years of war. Anything can make you crack, I guess."

"Did you know the results of his toxicology report?"

Max sat up. "Toxicology report? I didn't know they did one on him."

"Said he had traces of methamphetamine and fentanyl in his blood."

"Really? How the hell did he get access to that? Opium is everywhere, but those are synthetic."

"Don't know. I did a little snooping around on my own. I have some friends still in the service. Looks like there was someone in the unit possibly supplying drugs to some of the Afghan troops. Never caught anyone, though. Once your MASH unit packed up, the problem went away."

Max sat on the edge of the couch with his head in his hands. "You mean he was high when all that happened?"

"Maybe. Can't really tell from this report. Just indicates that he'd used."

"Huh. Maybe that's why he always seemed so mellow when the shit was hitting the fan. But that night something was different. He was upset. Crazy, like I'd never seen him before." Max shook his head. "He was a friend. A really nice guy. Good father. Just could never figure it out."

"Have you ever dreamt of that night?"

Max turned and looked Simkins in the eye. "Yes. All the time. Keep seeing the bodies strewn across the floor. The sounds, the smell. Blood and dirt. All of it."

"Do you think that could be contributing to your anxiety?"

"I'm not anxious. I don't have anxiety."

"Maybe not what you would think of as anxiety, but do you think it has negatively influenced anything you've done since coming home?"

Max reached down and rubbed his knee. He thought of his recent misadventures. They scared him. Then again, he'd been running scared ever since coming home. Ever since he saw how evil he could be. How his impulsiveness had led to an unforgivable crime—one that would never allow him to be clean again. To ever rest. How it would've been better if he'd never returned at all from that hellhole.

"No, not really. Just trouble sleeping."

"Whatever happened to Asalah? Did you ever see her again?"

"I was flown back to Kabul that night with some of the other casualties." Max leaned over and stared at his dirty clogs. "No, never saw her again." He rubbed his nose on his sleeve. "All things considered, back then we were not too far apart in age. Of course I thought she was a kid, but I was barely twenty. Now she would be old enough to be a doctor. In practice many years, maybe."

"Have you ever tried to find her?"

"No, never crossed my mind." Max lay back on the couch. "I guess it would be interesting to know what happened to her."

"Well, Max, I think we made some progress today, don't you?" Dr. Simkins straightened his papers and slipped them into a manila folder.

Max knew that was the sign that his time was up. "Sure. Great time rehashing some past trauma. Thanks."

"Don't be so cynical." Dr. Simkins walked around to his desk and sat down. "It's good to get this all out and for me to know what may trigger your anxiety."

"Okay, if you say so."

Dr. Simkins wrote him another script for sleeping pills. "Only giving you enough until next visit. Don't want you getting hooked on these things."

That would be the least of my problems, Max thought as he shoved the prescription in his pocket. It was time to go home and sleep. He wouldn't be working for a few days, and he wanted to rest. He had to admit he did feel a little better now that someone else in this world knew about that night.

Chapter 18

The Present

Max lay on his back staring at the ceiling fan as it slowly creaked its way around in wobbly circles. He tried to close his eyes but was too agitated to sleep.

What the hell really happened back in Afghanistan?

Dr. Simkins had read to him what he already knew. He was a little surprised about the drugs found in Asadi, but that didn't explain anything.

"Ruined my whole damn life," he mumbled.

He finally got up from the bed and walked out to the living room and up to the credenza. He picked up the picture of Maria holding her stuffed elephant and dusted it, then gently placed it back next to the one of Sam with their big fish. He slowly opened the top drawer and pulled out a bundle of letters wrapped in a rubber band and walked back to the sofa and sat down. He took the band off and removed the top letter, delicately placing the others on the coffee table.

"Last one you ever sent me," he whispered.

He held it up to his nose and tried to smell her perfume. Just the slightest fragment of her remained.

Max struggled to remember what had made him so angry. So hard to be around. So full of rage.

He slowly read the letter, studying each line, every curve of her beautiful cursive handwriting.

Dearest Max,

I have not heard from you in so long now. I hope you're recovering well. They tell me you may be transferred back to the military hospital in San Antonio soon. I bet it will be nice to be back in Texas again.

It is very hard for me to write this. The paper is crinkled because of my tears. But I can't take this kind of love from you. I need someone. Someone that will be there for me. Even when you've been back, you have not been here.

I have found someone that is here physically and emotionally. I'm sorry. I wish you well.

Love,

Maria

Max ran his fingers over the crinkles in the paper. He slowly folded the letter and placed it back in its envelope and laid it on top of the others. He fell back into the sofa and sighed.

Such a long time ago now.

He started to drift off to sleep as he tried to remember how she felt.

~ ~ ~

2004

Sam sat next to Maria on the porch swing. Winter had turned to summer, and the heat wave that smothered Katy was one for the record books. Max was still gone, but Sam was happy that Maria continued to come over every evening and have dinner. He'd gotten a job as a cashier at the local grocery and liked the fact that he was bringing home money to help.

When Max left, Maria had decided to delay going to a four-year college and was taking a few classes at the community college while working at a local restaurant as a receptionist. "Are they treating you okay at work, Sam?"

"Yes, the management is good to me." Sam swatted a fly off his bad arm. The sun was still high in the sky, even though it was getting late. The humidity was starting to abate and made sitting on the porch tolerable. It would have been much more comfortable sitting inside, but his mother was on the sofa watching the television, and they preferred to be alone.

"No one picking on you?"

"No. The occasional customer will look at me kinda funny and not want me to pack their bags." Sam looked down and kicked a dead wood roach with his foot. "That's nothing new. I've dealt with that since I was old enough to know something was wrong with me."

Maria leaned in and squeezed his bad arm. "There's nothing really wrong with you. Do you feel up to a walk in Peckham Park?"

Sam smiled. "Sure. I can do that."

They climbed into Maria's truck for the short drive to the community park. She parked close to the trail that led around a small lake. The lake was surrounded by tall pines and oaks. Fields with low, rolling hills stretched out to the single-story houses that bordered the park. Several egrets and a great blue heron paced back and forth along the water's edge. A mallard and her young chicks waddled quietly along in the grass by the edge of the trail.

Sam got out and stretched his back. He was going to keep up. "Let's see if we can get over to the fishing platform."

"Sure, mister adventurous." Maria smiled, her black eyes crinkling around the edges.

The covered platform was about two hundred yards up the trail and protruded into the middle of the lake. Several young boys leaned over the rail, dangling their lines in the water, hoping to catch some of the rainbow trout the park service had stocked in the lake.

"I love fishing."

"I know. All you and Max ever talked about when I first met you two was the huge whale you pulled out of the Gulf."

"Yeah, I'll never forget that."

Sam's foot dragged, leaving a serpentine trail in the gravel path as they slowly progressed toward the fishing platform. He twisted, pivoted, planted, then twisted again, all the way to the rail overlooking the water. Sweat soaked through his shirt and dripped down his forehead, but Maria never changed her slow but steady pace or asked if he needed a rest. He wouldn't have wanted it any other way. It was the way his father would have wanted it.

Maria smiled at a young boy as he jiggled his rod, hoping for a bite. "Catch anything yet?"

"No, ma'am. Nothin'. Not quite time yet, but soon I betcha they be bite'n."

Sam leaned over the rail and looked into the murky water. It was still as glass except for the occasional ripple from a fishing line. Off to his right was a large flock of young turkey vultures hopping about in the dust by the water's edge.

"Beautiful creatures aren't they?" he said.

"Beautiful? Really?"

"Yeah, really," Sam replied as he tried to straighten up to get a better look at the flock. "Almost hunted out of existence because of their looks and association with death. Fact is, they're beautiful in the air." Sam turned and pressed up against the rail with his back, trying to release a cramp. "They only eat what's already dead, and if it weren't for them, who would clean up all the mess?"

"Guess you're right." Maria leaned against the rail next to him.

Sam kept looking away at the vultures. "Heard from Max lately?"

Maria stared down at her feet. "I write him almost every day, but I guess he's not a good writer; a lot of guys aren't."

"Well, it was nice when we got to talk with him. Sounds hot over there."

"Yeah, I guess."

"I'll be a senior in August," Sam said, still not looking at Maria. "Not planning on joining the special forces when I graduate."

"You're so funny. I've decided to stay in town and go to the University of Houston. I can get all my prerequisites there for nursing school."

Sam couldn't hide his happiness. "That's great!"

Now it was Maria who couldn't look at Sam. "I'll be moving out of my house and getting a place with one of my girlfriends."

Sam turned and looked into her eyes. "Has it gotten that bad?"

Tears started streaming down Maria's face. "Could I sleep on your sofa until we get the apartment, Sam?"

Sam wrapped his arm around her. She buried her head in his shoulder and started to cry.

"I like the sofa," he said. "It's better for my back. The room is yours as long as you need it."

Maria kissed him on the cheek and let him go. "Thank you, Sam. You're such a good man."

Sam held onto her hand, his voice shaking. "I can take care of you. I want to take care of you."

Maria blushed and turned away.

"Why can't you see how much I love you?"

"Please Sam, no."

She tried to pull her hand away, but Sam held tight. "Maria, I can't stand it. You're all I think about. You are the only one that makes me feel like a man, not a cripple. The only one that makes my shitty life feel like it's worth something."

Sam tried to pull her closer, but she released his hand and turned away. She placed her face in her hands and started to weep. "I can't Sam.

Max is over there alone. We can't do this to him. Please don't make me." She turned to Sam, her face puffy and streaked with tears. "Please."

Sam leaned in and kissed her on the cheek. "Ok," he whispered. "I love Max too."

They both turned and slowly walked arm in arm from the fishing platform and headed back to the truck. This time Sam walked slowly, pulling Maria close with his good arm. Their heads leaning in almost touching. He breathed in her presence while trying to block out all thoughts of betrayal of his absent brother.

Chapter 19

The Present

Max lay back on the leather couch and waited for Dr. Simkins to say something. He was no longer bothered by the ruffle of papers or the occasional sigh of disapproval.

"Where shall we begin today, Max?"

"I don't know, Doc. You have the file. Tell me what interests you."

"Says after you were injured, you were transferred to Brooke Army Medical Center in San Antonio." The papers rustled. "Must have been nice being closer to home."

"It was different."

"Tell me about your mother. Sounds like she had a breakdown when she heard you were injured."

"My mother or my brother? I guess they both weren't doing too well right about then."

~ ~ ~

2004

Sam sat gently rocking back and forth barefoot on the front porch swing, the toes of his good foot curling with each push. The calluses on the outside of his bad foot scraped the dust into small piles. His mother was gone most of the day working extra shifts. Maria had decided to go to Galveston for a few days with some friends. Max had been gone for over a year now. He seemed to have left and not looked back. His calls were short and did little to fill in for his absence.

Sam felt a darkness within himself that he'd not felt before. The shock of his father's death was starting to settle in. Instead of getting better with time, it seemed more permanent, more oppressive. Maybe if Max were around, he could have filled the void. With his father's death, all that had supported him, all that had made him able to tolerate his deformity and his feelings of inadequacy, seemed to have been taken away. He always knew that one day he was going to have to rely on himself. That was what his father would have wanted anyway.

But not just yet. Not at barely twenty. To make things worse, the only person who brought him any semblance of joy was Maria. Yet she was his brother's girlfriend, not his despite their growing feeling for each other. And she had made that fact very clear to him.

It was early October. The afternoon heat was still oppressive and should have forced him inside, but he couldn't stand to be alone in the house. As he tried to swat an annoying black fly that found the sweat dripping down his forehead a good place to get a drink, he noticed his old friend Logan slowly walking up the street. He'd not seen him since the night of Max's big game. He had mysteriously disappeared. He'd stopped showing up for classes and had not returned Sam's calls. Sam hadn't thought much of it. He'd been so distracted with all that had been going on that worrying about a classmate was the last thing on his mind. Anyway, as depressed and lonely as he currently felt, seeing an old friend was just what he needed.

"Sup, Sam?"

"Logan. Where the hell have you been?" Sam was shocked by his appearance. His acne was much worse. He had grown his hair, and it looked as if he hadn't washed in a while.

Logan slowly climbed the front steps and sat down on the swing. His clothes reeked of sweat with an undertone of dirt. "Been away for a while, Sammy boy," he replied. He pulled out a cigarette from his shirt pocket. His hand trembled ever so slightly as he placed it between his lips then struggled to pull a lighter from his pants pocket.

"Where ya been?"

"Been on a different plane, sort of."

"Huh?"

The cigarette slipped from his lips and fell to his lap. "Like you, Sammy. Been a little depressed. Found a way to be happy. They say I went a little too far, but I think I'm just fine."

"How do you know I'm depressed?"

Logan tried to smile. "Look at you and me. If I'm depressed, damn well know you're depressed." He leaned over to grab the cigarette, but it fell to the floor. "Fuck it. Didn't want that anyway." He turned to Sam. "Brother, I want to make you happy. Happier than you've ever felt."

"You're a nutter, Logan."

Logan once again dug deep into his pocket. This time, he pulled out a small glass pipe. "You say that now, but you don't know. This life sucks for guys like us. I realized that. So screw it. Have fun when you can."

Sam tried to look away as Logan placed a small, crystalized rock into the bowl of the pipe and lit it with his lighter. He took a deep breath as the rock crackled in the flame. He closed his eyes and smiled. "You were always my best friend, Sam. Nice to sit here with you again and feel so good." Logan kept his eyes closed as he reached across to Sam and held out the pipe. "Take it, man. Let it chase your blues away."

Sam looked around at the empty street. The empty house. The emptiness he felt inside. "Logan, you're a devil."

"Maybe going to hell, but sure feels good."

Sam's eyes teared as his trembling hand reached for the pipe. "Would be nice to feel good for once."

~~~
~~~

It had taken only a few visits by Logan to get Sam hooked. Now he woke every morning with cravings. The little money he'd saved from his summer job at the grocery was gone. He felt Logan must have taken half of the money to buy crack for himself because the amount he brought over daily seemed smaller and smaller. His first hit had been incredible. Nothing hurt. He felt so good. Now he was just chasing it. Trying to get that feeling again.

The paranoia had been terrible. He'd locked the door to his room that first night when his mother came home.

"Are you all right, Sam?" she'd asked sweetly as she tried to open the door.

"Okay, just want to be alone for a bit."

"All right, baby. See you in the morning."

He'd slept in the next morning and again had the door shut that evening. He'd missed several shifts at work, and Logan was now a regular when his mother wasn't home.

The real trouble started when Maria came back. Sam had forgotten when she was returning. His days had become obsessed with waiting for Logan. He'd developed the habit of sitting on the front porch, punching his right thigh with his fist repeatedly as he looked up and down the street for his supplier. When Maria pulled up in her truck instead of Logan, he panicked. She was going to get in the way! She would know!

"Hey, Sam. Miss me?" She sprang up the steps and sat on the swing next to him.

"Hi, Maria," he replied flatly.

She sat sideways, looking at him. Her smile faded. His eyes darted from her to the street and back as he continued to punch his thigh with his fist.

"Sam?"

He looked away. He couldn't stand her staring at him.

"Sam! What is happening here?"

"Nothing! What's wrong with you?" Sam started to sweat profusely. "You leave me alone here, then show up out of the blue and start pestering me about what's going on. Huh? Nothing!"

"I was only gone a little over a week, and you look like shit." She turned her body to him and placed her hand on his sweaty forehead. "You're hot, and your pulse is racing. Are you sick?"

"Nothing. Nothing is wrong with me, all right?" Out of the corner of his eye, Sam spotted Logan heading down the street for their daily session. He turned to Maria. "You should go. I'm busy this afternoon."

"Sam! What's wrong with you?" Then she saw Logan. She turned back to Sam, her mouth half-open. "Oh no. Sam, no."

"Hey, Maria." Logan slowly clomped up the steps.

"What did you do, Logan? How could you do this to your friend?" She stood up and placed herself in front of Sam. "You were supposed to be going into rehab, the last I heard."

"You know what they say, Maria. Rehab is for quitters." He tried to move around her and sit on the swing.

"No, Logan. You know I love you, but you need to leave."

"No, Maria. *You* need to leave." Sam tried to stand but fell back down on the swing. "Logan, I need my stuff now."

"No!" Maria grabbed Logan by the arm and spun him around. She reached into his pocket while he was off-balance and pulled out his pipe and a small plastic bag with the drugs.

"Hey, woman, what're you doing? I paid for that."

She threw the pipe into the bushes that ran along the side of the house. She then emptied the bag and threw the contents across the yard.

"What the hell!" Logan shouted as he took a halfhearted swing at Maria.

Sam winced as Maria easily sidestepped the attempted blow, then grabbed Logan again by the arm and led him down the steps. "The drugs are gone, and so is your smoking buddy. Go home."

Logan frowned and looked down at the ground. "Wish I could, Maria, wish I could." He turned and looked up at Sam. As their eyes met, Sam could see the pain in his old friend's face. "Okay, my friend. Next time when the wife ain't around."

"No, wait, please."

"Sam!" Maria shouted. "Get in the house."

Sam reluctantly stood, then opened the screen door and went inside. The noise of the slamming door made Logan jump. Sam turned and waited just inside and watched as Maria stood on the top step of the porch, her arms folded across her chest.

Logan staggered down the street. When he'd finally turned the corner, Sam knew for sure he wasn't coming back that day, and he started to panic. He moved to the sofa and lay on his side. He buried his face in the pillow and started to cry. His clothes were soaked with sweat, and he found it impossible to stop shaking.

He heard Maria enter the room and gently close the door. As she approached, he groaned.

"Sam?"

"My side is in spasm." He started to writhe in pain.

Maria knelt down and started rubbing his back. She stretched out his arm and leaned hard into the knot that was forming between his shoulder blades. "Take your shirt off."

He struggled with his shirt as she reached into the drawer of the side table and pulled out his mother's massage oil. When he settled back down, she poured it on his back, then slowly moved her hands up and down his distorted spine. His breathing slowed as the sensation of her hands on his skin made his muscles relax.

He kept crying quietly as she worked his lower back, then down his crippled leg. "Please don't let my mom know," he whispered. "No one can know."

"Be quiet now, Sam."

"I've been so depressed with everyone gone."

"I know."

"I was out of control. It happened so fast."

"Don't worry. I'll get you through this."

Maria took a towel from the kitchen and moistened it with cool water, using it to wipe the oil off his back. When she was done, he lay motionless. He could sense her standing by the sofa, silently looking down on him. The ceiling fan above them creaked in slow, lazy circles. Flies bounced off the screen door as they tried to get out of the heat.

Sam heard her sigh, then the soft pop of her buttons as she took off her blouse. He froze when she slid onto the sofa and pressed her naked chest up against his.

Gently, she kissed him on the ear. "It's going to be all right."

They spent the rest of the day wrapped in each other's arms. The ceiling fan provided just enough breeze to keep them comfortable. Sam said nothing as Maria rubbed his back whenever she felt a spasm starting. He closed his eyes and tried to stay calm. He didn't want to do anything that would make her leave, his cravings and paranoia checked only by the sweet smell of her body pressed against his.

Chapter 20

2004

Sam woke when he heard his mother's car pull up to the side of the house. The living room was dark, and he realized they'd spent the entire day together just lying in each other's arms. The cool of the evening made him shiver.

Maria stood and quickly dressed. She took a throw blanket and covered Sam, then went into the kitchen. He rolled over and watched as she turned on a small light over the stove and took a seat at the dining-room table, the dim light barely outlining her figure as she waited.

Sally Donovan came through the front door and turned on the living-room light. "Oh, Sam darling, sorry." She quickly turned off the light and moved into the kitchen, placing her purse on the counter.

"Hello, Mrs. Donovan."

Sally jumped. "For God's sake, Maria. You nearly scared me to death. I didn't see you sitting there."

"Sam's not feeling well. I think he's getting a cold. I was just keeping an eye on him."

"You're so good to us, Maria. Thank goodness we have you."

Maria sat quietly as Sam's mother moved around the kitchen. She put some water on the stove to boil, then took her bag and went into the bedroom to change out of her work clothes.

Sam jumped when the phone rang.

"Maria, honey, can you get that?" Sally shouted from her bedroom.

Maria stepped across the room and picked up the phone. "Hello?"

A gruff voice on the other end of the line asked if Sally Donovan was there.

"Mrs. Donovan, they want to talk to you."

Sally came quickly. She was now dressed in shorts and a T-shirt with the face of a beaver on it. "Hello, Sally Donovan. How can I help you?"

Sam watched his mother through half closed eyes. He noticed the color drain from her face as she listened to the voice on the phone.

"When? How bad is it? Thank you. Please keep me updated." She slowly put the phone down and turned to Maria, her eyes wet with tears. "Max has been wounded. They're airlifting him to Kabul."

"Oh no!"

Maria stood just as Sally's knees buckled. Her head struck the kitchen counter on her way to the floor. Blood started to pool by her head as Maria grabbed a towel and tried to apply pressure to the large gash on her scalp.

"Sam!" she screamed. "Sam! Call 911!"

Sam struggled to his feet and twisted and pivoted his way to the phone. He quickly dialed 911. His heart was pounding. He could hardly catch his breath as he looked down on his mother, the pool of blood creeping toward his feet. "Help, please, she's not moving!" he screamed. He watched helplessly as Maria frantically tried to stem the bleeding from the large cut.

The paramedics arrived just as his mother was regaining consciousness.

"Not Max!" she whispered. "Please, not Max too."

Sam pressed himself against the wall as the paramedics lifted her off the floor and onto the stretcher. He had to look away as Maria took several more towels and tried to mop up the pool of blood. He twisted and pivoted as best he could across the room and got to the front door just in time to see them load his mother into the back of the ambulance.

He jumped when Maria touched him on the arm. "Come on, Sam. Let's go."

Sam turned and slowly limped back to the sofa. "I . . . I can't."

"Sam, this is your mother. We need to go."

"I'm sorry, but I just can't go the way I am right now. Please go and take care of her."

"Sam!"

Sam couldn't look Maria in the eyes and buried his head in his lap. He'd had to deal with that look of disgust all his life, but now he couldn't take it from her too.

"No one comes in here," she snapped. "Do you hear me? No one. Especially Logan."

Sam kept his head down until he heard her lock the door and her truck pull away. He took a deep breath, stood up, and slowly twisted his way across the room. He stood looking out the front window at the dark, quiet street. The neighbors had all gone back inside, and he was once again alone.

What happened to Max? His heart ached. Guilt raged through him as he thought about how nice it had felt lying next to Maria all afternoon.

~ ~ ~

The Present

"Yes, Dr. Simkins. My mother took it very badly. Was in the hospital for a while."

"And your brother?"

"He didn't come out of the house for a week or two. Only person who had contact with him was my old girlfriend, Maria. Apparently, he got pretty sick. Not a good week for the Donovan family."

"And how were you doing all this time?"

"Well, they left the chest tubes in until they flew me stateside. Didn't realize at the time how bad I was. Flail chest with a whole mess of busted ribs. That door exploding in front of me did a lot of damage." Max shifted uncomfortably on the sofa as he remembered the pain. He reached up and started rubbing the right side of his chest.

"Amazing that you were able to disarm the gunman with that kind of trauma."

"It is, isn't it?" Max took a deep breath. He could still feel some of his ribs pop. "Strange. I felt it was just something I had to do despite the pain. At the time, I didn't think twice about trying to stop him. And by the way, I didn't disarm him. He shot himself."

"All the same, if you hadn't done what you did, there could have been many more lives lost."

"Funny, that sounds good, but it doesn't make me feel any better. He was a good man. I liked him."

"Well, obviously he fooled you. He must've been a plant there or was recruited by the Taliban. Something made him do it."

"No, not him. He wasn't political. He was happy that we were there. He had a daughter he loved. He had everything to live for. No one just does that without a good reason."

"What happened when you arrived back in San Antonio?"

"Don't know. Seems like when I got injured, everything I had at home got blown apart as well. Don't really know what happened there."

Dr. Simkins sat quietly. Max stared at the ceiling, still gently rubbing a bump on one of his ribs. He heard the ruffle of papers as Dr. Simkins closed his chart.

"Max, you really have been through a lot. This injury obviously was a turning point in your life. I get the feeling that you've never let go trying to find out why he did what he did."

"You may be right."

"Do you ever feel anger or rage when you think about it?"

Max smiled. He wondered what Simkins would think if he knew he drove around at night with a pig mask and a baseball bat looking for trouble.

"What's so funny?"

"Oh, just thought how difficult it would be to do my job if I stormed around all day raging."

"Lots of surgeons do, by the way, but that's not your reputation." Dr. Simkins stood up and went to his desk. "Do you need more sleeping pills, Max?"

Max stood and buttoned his white coat. "No. I still have a lot left from last time, thanks."

Chapter 21

The Present

When Rosa woke, there was a tray of food by her bed. She never saw anyone bring it. Never heard a noise. She assumed it was morning, but the blacked-out window gave no clue as to the time of day. She really didn't even know what day it was. How many days had she been on the road or asleep in this place? How many days since her sixteenth birthday? That day that would always be remembered as the day she was grabbed off the street and her life was changed forever.

A television had appeared on a rolling stand along with the food. She turned it on and found that only Spanish-language stations were available. Nothing local to give her any idea of her location. The reality had set in that she was not getting rescued.

She decided that she was going to find a way out, a way back home. The threat implied by the photograph was not going to stop her from trying. Her mother would have expected her to fight. Her father would have wanted her back at any cost. Life for her in Nuevo Laredo had been relatively good, but she'd heard the stories. The kidnappings. The murders. The only ones that survived were the ones that took control and made their escape. She was going to be one of those survivors. She knew that. She had to make a plan.

She smelled the food and took a small taste before eating everything on the plate. She knew that someone must be putting something in the food because she'd slept so soundly. But she had to eat, and obviously whoever it was keeping her wanted her up and eating. The man who took her seemed so kind and reassuring. How could he do this to her?

When she'd finished, she got up and tried the door again. There were no visible hinges, and the door handle wouldn't budge. She kicked the door with her foot, then moved to the window. There had to be a way. She peered behind the long drapes for any sign of a crack in the window frame, but it was tightly sealed. She pounded her fists on the glass and shouted for help, but the glass seemed so thick that she felt as though she were screaming inside a glass bottle.

In her frustration, she moved to the television and placed both hands on top and started to shove it toward the window. Just before it smashed into the glass, she heard a deep monotone voice fill the room.

"Stop!"

Rosa froze. It was the voice of the man who had brought her to the house.

"Let me go!"

"Do not break the TV or you won't be given anything else to watch."

Rosa looked around the room to see if she could find the speaker, but the voice seemed to be coming from every direction. "Let me go!" She grabbed the television again and pushed it as hard as she could, slamming it into the window. It simply bounced off the stand and crashed to the floor.

"That was not very smart, young lady."

"I don't care. Let me go!" Rosa looked about the room for anything that she could use to help her escape. She gave a good hard pull on the drapes, but they were solidly affixed to the wall. She looked under the bed and found that it was no more than a wooden box lying flush against the floor. She looked in the bathroom, under the sink, everywhere for some kind of weakness in this cage she was trapped in.

She stared at the large mirror for a few moments, then climbed up on the sink and pressed her face against the glass. Nothing. She walked across the countertop and tried to turn off the light, but the switch didn't work. She cupped her hands around her face and pressed up against the glass one more time. She squinted and tried to block out all the light from the bathroom. As her eyes slowly adjusted, she started to make out the faint outline of a figure. He was sitting at a desk in front of a microphone, staring back at her. He was bathed in a faint red glow, his face expressionless.

"There you are," she whispered.

He sat motionless as a black shade slowly descended and blocked her view. She sat down on the counter and pulled her knees up to her chest. *It's the man who brought me to his house.* "Why?" she shouted. "Why me?"

The speakers crackled to life, and the man's voice filled the suite. "What a stupid question."

"What did I ever do to deserve this?"

Rosa could tell that the man had pressed his mouth close to the microphone, the talk switch on. She could hear his breathing and the squeak of his chair as he squirmed in his little dark room. "Really, you have to ask why? You appeared to me, right from the outset, to be a very intelligent girl."

Rosa started to sob. "I've done nothing wrong. I'm a good person. Why is this happening to me?"

"That's exactly why you're here."

Rosa stopped crying and turned to face the blacked-out mirror. "I'm being punished because I'm a good person?"

"You're old enough to know the rules of this world. It's simple. There's good. There's evil. We live in between. The battle has raged since Adam and Eve."

"So what does that have to do with me?"

"You're good. Evil people don't understand you. They get excited by you. Long ago, I realized that I could do pretty well for myself by being . . . how would you put it? An intermediary between people like you and people like them."

"You're a sick, evil man."

Rosa heard a loud thump as if someone had punched the mirror. "I'm not sick! I've done a lot of good in my life. Relieved a lot of suffering."

"What do you call this, you sick pervert? Let me go!"

"I call this modern media. I call this no different than the millions of viewers every day who watch stories of murder and rape on cable and network television. Oh, they never bat an eye at the fake violence and horror. The influence of evil in their daily lives, so subtle, so acceptable. Maybe even an Emmy for the actors who make it seem really real." He paused. She could hear his heavy breathing, his mouth pressed close to the microphone. "I market reality TV, young lady. The same stuff that nets them millions, and I'm a psycho?"

Rosa placed her head back on her knees. "Please, let me go."

"Sorry, sweetheart. I tried making money the legit way. Got me nowhere. You're going to do your part in this little show until I've made enough to call it a successful season and move on to another sequel. The evil shits in this world have a lot of money, and I intend to take as much of it as I can."

Rosa heard the microphone click off and realized their little conversation was over. She couldn't tell from what he'd said whether he was going to let her go when he was done or if she was going to die like in those murder shows. At least now she knew the game he was playing. That was a step in the right direction.

Chapter 22

The Present

There was no reason this time. Or maybe there was one, but he didn't know what it was. Maybe it was sifting through Maria's old letters that had set him off. Maybe it was Dr. Simkins asking about his mother and Sam. Didn't matter. There was no gunshot victim he wanted to avenge. No drug overdose he wanted to reverse. He was just angry.

He climbed into the Nova and tossed the bat in the back with the pig mask. He squealed the tires as he backed out of the garage. It was midnight and the air was still, as if in anticipation of something bad about to happen.

Max felt like going back to Dr. Jernigan's clinic. Scout out the neighborhood. Something he didn't like about the place. All those people waiting. The dingy clinic with his old captain hiding in the back.

He headed out of West University and got on Route 59 and headed north. He exited into the Fifth Ward and meandered through the poorly lit roads, looking down back alleyways between rows of shotgun houses raised on bricks and in need of paint. Many of them boarded up and interspersed with vacant overgrown lots. It had once been prosperous but that was long before anyone could remember. Now it was occupied by a racial mix of the poor with high cancer rates and a remarkably high concentration of ex-felons. No one was about. Most of the ward was sleeping, getting ready for another hard day of trying to make a living.

When Max rounded the corner facing Jernigan's little strip mall clinic, he was surprised to see several cars in the parking lot. He could feel the low thump of bass, and as he got closer, he saw that the music was coming from a dropped metallic-orange Cadillac DeVille. The trunk was open, and in it he could just make out the silhouette of an oversized speaker outlined in neon light. Several young men were pacing back and forth in front of the clinic door. A solitary light in the waiting room shone through the dirty glass.

On the corner, standing alone as if waiting for a bus, was a girl. She was pretty and young, though made up to look much older. She rolled her ankles back and forth in her red stiletto heels as if she were not used to wearing such uncomfortable shoes.

Max slowed as he drove past. She gazed at him with a helpless look in her eyes. She took a step off the curb but stopped when Max continued to cruise down the street.

Once out of sight, he parked the car and leaned back in his seat. "Bad idea," he whispered. He slipped his Beretta into the small of his back and got out of the car.

He walked back toward the strip mall, pausing in the shadows just at the edge of the parking lot. He saw two men leaning on the Cadillac and one lounging behind the wheel. The girl slowly walking up and down the sidewalk.

Max was at a loss. He'd always gone out with a purpose before. Now he just stood and watched. He wasn't after anyone. He had no plan. He looked across the lot and just didn't like what he saw. The poor girl was a prostitute. Someone in the group probably her pimp.

Max turned away and looked at his car. He knew he should have just walked away and driven home, but he couldn't. The helpless girl on the corner. The people hanging around late at the captain's place. His gut told him something was wrong. He wanted to do something about it, but what?

"You looking for some action, white boy?"

Max froze. He'd been so lost in thought that he hadn't noticed someone come up from behind.

"No need to turn around." The voice was deep and raspy, full of intent. "For some reason, you don't look like the kind of guy that should be on this side of town."

"Just looking for some excitement," Max replied as he continued to look forward. He could feel the firm muzzle of a pistol pressing up against his flank.

"You look more like a cop to me."

"No, definitely not a cop."

"You like the girl?"

"A little too young for my tastes."

"How about you pay for her anyway?" While still holding the gun against his side, the man reached around to Max's front pocket and pulled out his wallet. He opened it with one hand, pulled the cash and cards out, and tossed the wallet to the gutter. "Thanks. I hope she was worth it."

Max couldn't stand feeling so helpless. He ran through multiple scenarios in his head. *Go for my Beretta? I'm dead. Go for his gun? I'm dead. Call for help from his buddies in the lot? I'm dead.* "Yeah, your sister was worth it, you motherfucker," he said through gritted teeth.

He felt a sharp blow to the back of his head as his mystery assailant pistol-whipped him. The boys from the lot must have joined in, because the kicks seemed to come from every direction. Eventually, everything went black.

Chapter 23

The Present

When Max woke, he found himself lying facedown in an overgrown lot. He rolled onto his back and groaned. There was a stabbing pain in his chest when he tried to take a deep breath.

God, they broke my ribs again.

Max struggled to his feet. Once he'd wiped the sweat and dried blood from his eyes, he could see it was early morning and that he was not far from where he'd been assaulted. He walked through the knee-high weeds and into the street. He was surprised to see his wallet still in the gutter. He picked it up and flipped through it. Everything was there except his cash and credit cards.

"Well, I guess I deserved this," he mumbled as he shoved the wallet in his front pocket.

He reached down and slid his finger into his boot and felt the folded edge of the twenty-dollar bill he always kept there in case of an emergency. His father had always taught him to be prepared and to have something extra at all times.

Max walked in the direction of the strip mall. Several cars were still in the lot, and a line was already starting to form on the walk in front of the clinic. Max knew he must have looked like hell, but he decided to go see if Nick Jernigan was in anyway. Maybe he had some antiseptic he could put on his scraped-up face. He really didn't care if he asked what happened and why he was around there last night. Max would think of some smart response, and that would be that.

Max pushed his way through to the front desk. "I'm here to see Dr. Jernigan, please," he said to the young, sleepy-eyed receptionist.

She was pretty in a rough kind of way. She looked as though she'd just left the clubs and come straight to work. She was wearing a skintight, off-the-shoulder black tube dress and long, dangling earrings in the shape of marijuana leaves. Through the gap in the window, he saw a pair of blue high heels placed on the floor beside her chair.

"He doesn't come in until later." She looked him up and down. "We only take cash, and we don't do emergency room work." Her mouth chomped on a large piece of pink bubblegum. "Looks like you need an emergency room."

"No, don't need an emergency room."

"Well, he isn't in."

"What do you do here?"

She looked down at her phone, distracted by some chat she was intently engaged in. "Pain management."

Max looked around the dingy clinic front room. The hangers-on outside. "Pain management?"

"Yeah, you got pain, we manage it."

Max pushed the frosted-glass window open a little more so he could lean in over the counter. "You look like a smart woman. How could I get a little pain management? I'm beat-up pretty bad. Can't really wait all day for the doc, know what I mean?"

She looked up from her phone and gave him a blank stare.

"Come on now," he said as he reached down and pulled out his emergency twenty. "Show a little love. Look at me."

She looked around the room and turned to look over her shoulder. "You know the boss is the only one that gives out the meds, right?"

"Sure, I know, but come on. I got to go, and he's not here."

"You're not a cop, are you?"

Max chuckled. That was the second time he'd been asked that question in the past twenty-four hours. He knew he must look like hell from the expression on her face when he walked in. "Look at me, sweetheart. Do I look like a cop?"

She put down her phone. "What do you want?"

"What do you have?"

"Twenty bucks will get you a bag of smack."

Max slid the twenty across the counter. She quickly took it and proceeded to pull open a drawer by her feet. She shuffled around some papers, then pulled out a small lunch baggie containing the heroin and slid it toward him. "Okay, now you can leave. If you need anything more, you'll have to come back when the doctor is in."

Max took the bag and slipped it into his pocket. "I owe you one," he said with a wink, then turned and headed out the door.

It was now bright out, and he squinted as he tried to make out who was in the lot. He could feel how puffy his right eye was, and the bridge of his nose hurt. He placed both hands on either side of his nose and gave it a good squeeze. He felt a pop. He rubbed his hand along the bridge to make sure it was straight. He smiled, pleased with his makeshift plastic surgery. He was still a pretty bastard.

Max slowly walked across the lot and scanned the crowd for the ones who had roughed him up. His eyes eventually settled on the dropped Cadillac DeVille by the edge of the lot. Two men were leaning against the back. The loudspeaker in the trunk blared Tejano music. A large, bald, muscular man covered in tattoos sat behind the wheel. They smiled as Max walked by. The bald man puckered his lips and blew him a kiss. Max nodded. He got a good look at their faces as he made his way to the street and down to where his car was parked. He wanted to make sure that if he saw those three again, he would remind them of last night.

The ride back to his house was uncomfortable. He threw the heroin out the window once he got to the highway. His chest hurt with each breath, but it was nothing like before. That was real pain. This was just a nuisance.

So what the hell is going on at that clinic? Did Jernigan know what the mice were doing while the cat was away working at County? Max decided to tell him the next time he was at work. For now, he needed a shower and to get some rest.

Chapter 24

The Present

Max walked into Dr. Simkins's front office and smiled at the receptionist. "You know, I never caught your name."

"Lucy, Dr. Donovan. My name's Lucy."

Something about getting his head kicked in seemed to have put him in a good mood. "That's a nice name, Lucy."

Max was surprised that he'd never noticed how attractive she was before. Her broad, perfect smile was comforting, and the sparkle in her big green eyes made him relax. Probably why Simkins hired her. She just had that natural way about her that put anxious people at ease.

"Is the boss ready for me?"

"He's just finishing up with something right now. You can take a seat if you like."

Max sat on the leather sofa that was squeezed between two end tables piled high with magazines.

"Would you like something to drink, Dr. Donovan? You don't look well."

Max knew his face was still a little puffy, but twenty-four hours of ice packs and ibuprofen had improved things quite a bit. The black eye was going to take a while to go away, though. "Sure, Lucy. That would be great."

Lucy went into a side room just off the reception area and returned with a glass of water with lemon. "Here you are, Doctor."

"Thank you." Max stared as she sauntered back to her desk, her long brown hair falling neatly across her shoulders. "Lucy, how long have you worked for Dr. Simkins?"

"A little over ten years."

"Are you married?"

Lucy blushed. "No, Dr. Donovan." She crossed her long legs and turned away, looking awkwardly down at the paperwork on her desk.

"How about Dr. Simkins? Wife? Kids?"

"Ex-wife, I believe. No kids. Why?"

"Oh, just curious about the man who picks my brain every week, that's all." Max looked at her over the edge of his glass. "You two ever dated, you know, had drinks or something?"

Lucy shuffled uncomfortably in her chair. "Dr. Simkins and I've never had a relationship. He's very private. I've never seen him after work. Ever."

"Why not? He seems like a nice guy. He could be shy, though. Maybe you should ask him out."

Lucy opened her mouth to say something, then closed it and gave him an appraising look that included a quick glance at his left hand.

Checking for a ring? He wasn't sure.

Just as she seemed ready to respond to his suggestion, her intercom buzzed.

"Your turn, Dr. Donovan." She stood and reached for the door.

"You should do it," he whispered with a wink.

A moment later he was on the leather couch. "How's it going, Doctor?"

"Better than it looks like for you. What happened to your face?"

"Got mugged. No big deal. I'll recover."

"I always knew it was unsafe around County at night." Simkins opened his file.

Max actually felt comforted by the rustle of papers behind his head. "What disturbing things from my past are you going to remind me about today, Doctor?"

"I see in one of your reports, prior to being transferred back stateside, you kept asking about Asadi's daughter."

Max's initial feelings of comfort and playfulness disappeared. "Apparently so."

"Why is that?"

"Why is what?"

"Why were you so interested in his daughter? Did you have a relationship with her?"

Max now cringed when he heard the papers rustle.

"At one of our last sessions, you mentioned how attractive she was and how close in age you two probably were."

"I didn't exactly put it that way. But yes, I'm curious as to what happened to her. I can't imagine her father just going off and shooting up the place for nothing."

"But you've never tried to find her?"

Max paused. He hadn't, and maybe that was why he felt a little guilty. Not until his recent behavior had he even thought about doing anything about his past except burying himself in work. Now all he had to do was look in the mirror to see that his past was catching up with him. His frustrations could no longer be buried in twenty-four-hour shifts and operating until he could no longer think straight. "No, I never looked for her after I got back."

"Have you ever heard from her? Any sign that she may still be alive?"

Max hesitated, then said, "You know, I got the strangest letter the other day."

"Really, what was strange about it?"

"It was an Islamic prayer for peace. No return address. I thought it was sent to the wrong address."

"Was it?"

"I don't know. For some strange reason, I thought maybe it was from Asalah."

"How did it make you feel?"

Max thought about that, then gave himself a mental shrug. "I don't know."

"Did it make you feel happy, anxious, angry?"

"I guess a little of everything. I tossed it on the pile of mail and haven't looked at it since."

"A strange letter like that just out of the blue, and you simply tossed it?"

There was an uncomfortable silence as Max lay quietly staring at the ceiling. Dr. Simkins seemed unsatisfied with his answer and rapidly tapped the chart with his pen as he waited for more, but Max remained silent.

"All right then. What happened when you returned to San Antonio? Doesn't look like you were hospitalized for very long. Did you go back home?"

"Yeah, I didn't stay too long at Brooke. They just got me back on my feet. There were a lot of guys there that were sicker than me."

"How did that make you feel? They treated you like a hero, I understand."

"Like I said before, I was no hero. Those guys were blown to bits. They were out in the field. I just had a door blow up in my face."

"Your family, did they come and visit you?"

"Yeah, they came."

~~~
~~~

2005

"Come on, Mrs. Donovan, just one more step."

Maria helped her down from the porch. Sam waited at the bottom with a walker. Her head hitting the counter had caused a small amount of bleeding in her brain. Maria had told Sam that the neurosurgeon was confident she would make a full recovery, but it would take some time. For now, they were taking her to physical therapy several days a week.

"Come on, Mom. If I can do it, so can you." Sam smiled, but his heart was breaking. When his mother needed him most, he hadn't been there. He failed her because he was withdrawing while she was recovering. Max was hurt. His mother was hurt. They hadn't done anything wrong. They hadn't done it to themselves, but he had.

His mother tried to smile, but the corner of her mouth still drooped a little. It was definitely better but still noticeable.

Sam positioned the walker in front of her, and they slowly moved around to the passenger side of Maria's truck. "Sure you're up to the trip to San Antonio?"

"I need to see Max." A small sliver of spittle rolled down the corner of her mouth. Sam pulled a tissue from his pocket and wiped it away.

They all crammed together onto the bench seat of Maria's truck and headed west down I-10 on the two-and-a-half-hour drive to San Antonio. They didn't talk much on the trip, each lost in their own thoughts. Sam didn't know what to expect, and if he'd been honest with himself, he would've admitted that he didn't want to go. He didn't want to see how damaged Max was. Worse yet, he didn't want to hurt him anymore. He didn't know how Max was going to respond when he found out that he and Maria were together.

Brooke was a massive hospital, its imposing brick towers housing over four hundred beds. Sam looked up at the huge structure and knew that somewhere deep inside was his brother. Battered and broken. Different.

It took quite a while for them to get from where they'd parked to Max's room. They stopped at every bench and rested, knowing that soon things would never be the same. When they finally made it to his room, they hesitated before entering. Sam knew that he was all right. The nurse at the desk said he was fantastic and should be going home as soon as they removed the tubes from his chest. But they all knew it would be different when they walked through that door. The Max that had left to be a hero was back, but nothing was the same.

Sam's mother clacked into the room first, pushing the curtain open with her walker. Sam was close behind, with Maria a few paces back.

At first glance, Sam thought the nurse had lied. Max didn't look fine. As he lay in his hospital bed sleeping, he had two large plastic tubes coming out of his chest. They were connected to a water-filled box on the floor that seemed to bubble every now and again when he took a deep breath. A bag of fluid hanging on a pole by the head of the bed was connected to a catheter in his arm. A monitor on the wall slowly traced out his heartbeat. He was much thinner. His skin was tan, and his hair showed the slightest hints of gray.

His mother quietly moved to his side and touched him on the arm. Max's eyes suddenly opened as he sat bolt upright. He jerked his hand back and started gasping for air. His eyes looked wildly about as he tried to make sense of his surroundings.

"Nurse!" Maria ran out into the hallway and screamed. "Nurse!"

Several nurses stormed into the room as Sam and his mother tried to move to the side. Max stared at them as if he'd never seen them before. He reached across with his left hand and started to pull at his chest tubes just as the first nurse reached him. She grabbed his hand and held it down. Two other nurses grabbed him by the shoulders and gently pushed him back down into the bed. "Come now, Private, you don't want to do that, do you? You were just dreaming."

As Max's eyes focused on the nurse's face, he seemed to settle down. "Just dreaming?" he mumbled, his voice raspy and weak. "Just dreaming, right?"

"Yes, Private." The nurse let his hand go. "Now look who's here to see you."

His gaze shifted from the nurse's face to the faces around the bed. Max smiled weakly. "Hi, Mom. Sam."

Maria still hid by the door.

His mother moved back to his side, bent down, and gave him a kiss.

Sam did his best to move to the other side of the bed, lean in, and give him a hug. "You look like shit."

Max's eyes lit up. "So do you, you damn cripple."

Maria stepped from behind the curtain. "Hi, Max." She leaned over and gave him a kiss on the cheek.

The nurses left the room, and the three of them remained standing by the bed.

"What's with the tubes?" Sam asked.

Max slowly turned his head and looked down at his chest. Then he slowly looked back at Sam. His face held an expression of horror and confusion. "Got a hole blown in my chest, I guess."

"Does it hurt?"

"Not much anymore."

Their mother started to cry as drool dribbled down from the corner of her mouth. Maria put her arm around her and led her to a chair near the foot of the bed. She pulled out a tissue and wiped the side of her face.

Max looked back to Sam. "What happened to Mom?"

"She fell in the kitchen and cracked her head. She's slowly getting better."

They sat around the bed silently for a time. Sam felt like he did when they had sat in a circle listening to how their father had died and realizing he wasn't coming back. Max wasn't coming back. The happy, football-loving boy was now a damaged man. Almost unrecognizable, lying in bed with tubes poking through his chest.

Sam looked over at Maria. She sat with her shoulders rolled as if she wanted to curl up in a ball and hide.

Max stared at her. "I missed you," he whispered.

Maria looked away. "You didn't write."

"I know."

Sam felt his chest tighten as if someone had placed a belt around it and had their foot in the middle of his back. He stood and tried to stretch. He didn't know whether he was having a spasm or whether his heart was ripping in two. Maria had been his. Even with his recent failings, she'd been with him. Not Max. Not his idol. Not the man he loved more than anyone on earth. "I've got to get some air." Sam twisted and pivoted his way around the bed and into the hallway. He leaned against the wall and tried to straighten up. He closed his eyes and took several deep breaths.

When his eyes opened, Maria was standing inches from his face, her beautiful dark eyes staring into his. "Are you okay?"

"No. Are you?"

Maria looked down at her feet to hide her tears. "He needs us, Sam. We both love him. He needs us now more than ever."

Sam knew she was right, but he couldn't help himself. He couldn't lose her. She was all he had. She was probably all he would ever have. "But I love you."

"Sam." She paused, her voice quivering. "Not now, Sam."

"Well, when?"

Maria turned her head and looked down the long, empty corridor. "Not now."

This time it was Sam who turned away. He twisted his body off the wall. He couldn't look at her.

They quietly made their way back into the room and retook their seats. Max and his mother were talking about Katy Lakes football and how their record was not so good this year. Max seemed more relaxed. Happy to be talking about the old days.

They sat for another hour before Max started to close his eyes. "Sorry, just really weak and tired. Don't seem to have much strength lately."

"We'll let you sleep," their mother said as she rose to her feet and grabbed onto the walker.

They said their goodbyes and headed to the nurses' station.

Sam's mother made her way up to the charge nurse. "How much longer is he going to stay?"

"They may take out his chest tubes tomorrow if the chest x-ray is better. Then home in a few days."

Sally nodded her approval, then motioned for them to leave. They took their time, stopping at every bench along the way out to the truck.

That night, they stayed at a Motel 6, his mother and Maria taking one room and Sam a room by himself. He lay awake, staring at the ceiling, at a loss for what to do. By dawn, he'd come to the decision that Max came first, even if it meant losing Maria. Max was his brother. His twin. His blood.

~ ~ ~

The Present

"I don't really understand what happened." Max lay on his back, staring at the cracks in Dr. Simkins's ceiling. "They came but acted so differently. I knew I looked like hell, but I didn't think I was that different. Maybe I was. I don't know. A lot of it was a blur at the time. Pain meds. Sleeping most of the day. You know, ICU craziness." Max let out a sigh. His voice cracked ever so slightly. "It was just a long, long time ago. I think that probably hurts the most. So long ago and yet still so painful."

"Says you were honorably discharged after that."

"Yeah. Went home. Back to school on the GI Bill. Made me the great surgeon I am today."

"Well, from your reputation as a surgeon, we all thank you. I understand you're quite talented."

Dr. Simkins stuffed his notes into the file, and Max knew it was time to go.

He stood up and started for the door.

"Next time, Max, I want to talk about Sam."

Max paused. It felt as if all the air had been sucked from his lungs. He tried hard to take a deep breath and to keep walking. "Sure, Doc, whatever you say." He didn't acknowledge Lucy as he bolted from the office.

Chapter 25

The Present

Max wandered around the hospital, moving from floor to floor. The surgeon's walk. Steady. Purposeful. The walk of someone who's walked the halls at all times of the day and night for years.

And yet that night, he had no purpose. He'd checked on all his patients. The emergency room was quiet. The residents were trying to get a few minutes of sleep. But Max couldn't sleep. Simkins had opened very old wounds, and now they were bleeding. Like boils that had to be lanced. He knew it. But the pain was supposed to get better once lanced. It seemed to be getting worse. When he had purpose, he didn't think. When he hyper-focused on righting a wrong, punishing a punk, or plugging a gunshot wound, he was calm. Now he had nothing to do but dwell on Simkins and his damn charts.

Max found himself standing in the middle of the hallway running the length of the operating rooms. During the day, it was controlled chaos. Patients being rolled into one operating room and out another. There was a hum of nervous energy. Now, in the middle of the night, there were only ghosts.

Max closed his eyes. He could smell the blood, the burning flesh. When he opened them, he could see Asadi standing in front of him, carbine in hand, screaming and firing into the operating room. Max saw his face. The anguish. The fear. Max took a step forward, but the vision disappeared as he heard a noise coming from one of the rooms.

He gave himself a good shake, then headed down the hallway to see who was about. He was surprised to see Dr. Jernigan sitting in the operating room, hunched over by the anesthesia machine. "Nick, what are you doing here?"

"Oh, hi, Max." Dr. Jernigan chuckled. "Just like Afghanistan, you always seem to come in when I'm checking things. You know how I don't like to be caught flat-footed. Got to be prepared for the next big onslaught of trauma."

Max slowly walked around the room. "Yeah, does remind me of the war." He stopped in the middle of the room and examined a loose wire that was dangling from one of the operating-room lights. "Was out to your place the other day looking for you."

"Why, is your knee still bothering you?" He turned his body so he could look at Max straight on. "Your face looks like hell."

"No, just had a headache, kind of. Some guys on the street wanted to give me a beauty makeover. Your staff was pretty forthcoming in selling me some heroin, though."

Nick squinted. "You have a problem, Max? You using that stuff?"

"Me? No. Passionately hate the stuff. Just thought you should know what they're doing when you aren't there."

"Well, I really appreciate that." Nick furrowed his brow. "Who was it, if you don't mind me asking?"

"A young lady at the front window."

"Debbie." He put his papers down on the anesthesia machine. "Will have a talk with her. Probably will have to let her go if she's doing that sort of thing. Really appreciate you letting me know."

"No problem." Max pulled up a stool. "Do you remember that night over there?"

"What night over where?"

"The night I got wounded."

"Oh, that night." Nick slowly nodded his head. "Yeah, what about it?"

"Do you remember what happened?"

"I remember cleaning up the mess. I was way across the camp when the shooting started."

Max bowed his head and rested his elbows on his knees. "I ran toward the shooting."

Nick chuckled as he looked at Max over the top of his reading glasses. "Yeah, that's the difference between anesthesia and surgery. We sit back and make the money and you run ahead and get all covered in blood."

"Any idea why he did it?"

"Not a clue. Probably just some fanatic who hated us."

Max looked sideways at Nick. "I'm not so sure. He didn't seem like one."

"Funny, after all these years, we've never talked much about the war. Why now? That was so long ago for us."

"Guess I never really got over it."

Dr. Jernigan picked up his clipboard. "Well, it's time you forgot all about Asadi and his breakdown. Get on with your life. I've moved on. The war is all in my past."

Max stood and started to leave. "You're right. Need to move on."

Jernigan smiled. "By the way, thanks for the tip about my office staff. Can't tolerate that kind of activity if I'm going to run a business."

Chapter 26

The Present

Rosa now knew what her captor had planned for her. He was probably never going to let her go. She was purely there for his profit. There would be no appealing to his humanity, of which she concluded he had none. Her mother had told her about men like him. The heads in the streets. The boys murdered in front of their families. She knew. She'd grown up around men like him.

But even at her young age, she knew how to deal with his type. Take away what they want. Don't make it easy.

She lay in bed staring at the ceiling. The lights were bright. If she closed her eyes, she saw spots. She had nothing to do but think about how to get out. The television lay smashed on the floor. She figured his play was to bore her to death until she asked for something. The television was the first thing. He'd warned her another wouldn't be coming if she broke it.

The day seemed endless. She occasionally got up and paced the room. Every so often, she would check the door handle. As much as she tried, she couldn't see around whatever was covering the window. It would have been nice to know if it was day or night outside. She kicked the bed and tried to lift off the mattress, but it was fixed in place. She knew she was being watched. She knew there were sick people out there just sitting in their rooms watching her walk about, finding pleasure in her captivity. She knew it would help if she could find the cameras, but she couldn't see anything that looked like one. All she knew was that the creep lived behind the bathroom mirror, and now she really had to use the toilet.

She went into the bathroom and stared at the glass. "I refuse to give your little friends a show." She looked around for a towel or anything to cover herself, but there was nothing. "All right, then. How about this?" She leaned into the shower and turned on the hot water. She closed the bathroom door and smiled as the room slowly filled with steam. She turned and looked straight into the mirror now covered with condensation and raised her middle finger to the glass. She then went and sat on the toilet, exposing as little of herself as she could.

Rosa could hear the latch on the bathroom door lock. Then she heard the door to her room open, then close a minute later. She got up and washed her hands and turned off the shower. She tried the bathroom door handle, but it was still locked.

"Open the door!" she shouted.

The door latch clacked open. She turned the handle and entered the bedroom. She was surprised to see a tray of food on her bed. Next to the tray was a skimpy schoolgirl's dress. She was starving and had thought he wasn't going to feed her again that day.

The hidden speakers crackled to life. The man breathed heavily into the microphone. "Put on the dress, and you can have more food. Don't, and this will be your last meal for a while."

Rosa looked around the room as she clenched her fists. She quietly sat on the bed and started to eat. When she'd finished, she sat staring at the dress, trying to decide what to do.

"Put it on now!"

"Okay." Rosa picked up the dress and walked over to the vanity. She held it up in front of herself as she looked in the mirror and cringed. Then a smile came to her face. She stretched the tiny dress over her shirt and jeans. She walked into the bathroom and looked at herself in the mirror. "*Bien.*" She laughed. She climbed up on the counter and started banging on the mirror with her fists. "Look at the pretty *payaso*! Do your sick friends like it?"

The microphone was still live, and Rosa heard a crash as if something had been thrown against the wall. She crouched down on the countertop and sat quietly as the speakers continued to crackle.

She heard the man's voice again. This time, it was distant, as if he'd stepped away from the hot mic and was talking to someone else. "So you think that will work?" she heard the faint voice say. "Okay, you're the psych expert. I'll try it."

Chapter 27

The Present

Max lay on the couch waiting for the question he knew was coming. He thought he was prepared for it, but he wasn't. He'd even considered not returning to see Dr. Simkins, dodging it altogether. Working and venting his anger as he had for years. But for some reason, here he was. Lying on his back with someone out of his line of sight, someone holding a big folder highlighting all of Max's problems.

"Tell me about your brother, Max. What happened to him?"

Max took a deep breath. "Well, Maria and I started going out late. She would always come when everyone else was sleeping. She'd started taking classes at the University of Houston. I got an honorable discharge and was trying to decide what to do."

~ ~ ~

2005

Maria sat on the edge of Sam's bed. "He'll be coming home soon."

Sam reached out and gently touched her naked back. "You're going to tell him then, right? When he comes home, you're going to tell him about us."

Maria said nothing. She stood and slowly dressed.

He struggled to sit upright. "Why won't you tell him?"

She turned and looked down at Sam as he lay half-naked, covered by a sheet. "Why?" she said, the word coming out with a sigh. "Because I think I still love him."

Sam said nothing as she leaned down and kissed him. She then quietly left, leaving him cold and alone. Sam looked around the small room. Max's trophies still lined the walls. Clippings of articles about Katy Lakes football and their star quarterback were hung in small, dusty frames. Max was everywhere.

When he heard the front door close, he reached across and turned off the light. He pulled the sheet up over his head and began to shake. He didn't know which was worse: when he'd felt so alone when Maria and Max were gone and he'd fallen prey to Logan's temptations, or now, when everyone was coming back.

That night he lay awake, staring into the darkness. He saw his future with Maria coming apart. He could never compete with Max. He didn't even want to. He loved Max. Who couldn't love Max? He just loved Maria. And the thought of a life without her by his side was crushing.

When the sun rose the next day, he was exhausted. He finally fell asleep and only woke at noon when his mother came in to check on him. She was doing better every day and was now motoring around with the walker like it was a baby stroller.

"Sam, I know you need your sleep, but it's already the afternoon. Time to get up."

Sam grudgingly crawled out from under the sheets and struggled to the bathroom. He stood in front of the mirror and stared at his crippled frame. His spastic arm hung by his side. His twisted spine making him several inches shorter than his twin, his rival. "Who could ever love me?" he whispered.

~ ~ ~

A nurse pushed Max's wheelchair through the long, bright hallways of Brooke and out to the patient pickup circle. "Here you are, Private. Time to get on home."

Max smiled as he stood and shuffled to the waiting car.

Holding open the passenger door was a massive African American man.

"Hey, Boomer."

"Come on, Max, get a move on." Boomer winked at the nurse. "No more babying. Back in the real world now."

Boomer was Max's recruiter, and he'd volunteered to pick him up and bring him back home. His real name was Dalton, but he would only answer to Boomer. Apparently, he got the name after tossing a grenade into a building that contained a big arms cache. After that, he was just Boomer.

Max slid into the passenger seat and waited as Boomer closed the door. He halfheartedly waved to the nurse as Boomer squeezed into the driver's seat. Max looked enviously at Boomer's thick, muscular arms. His legs were almost too large to fit under the steering wheel. "Looks like you need to go on a diet, you fat ass," Max chided.

Boomer looked at him and laughed hard. His thick head looked like it had been molded inside an army helmet. It bobbled back and forth as his body shook. "Listen, you son of a bitch. When you get settled back at home, I'm going to take you out and buy you some real food. Looks like they starved you in there."

Max looked down at his withered body. He'd lost a lot since his injury and was only a shadow of his peak football weight. "Good. I think I need a few steaks."

They pulled away from the hospital and soon were on I-10 and the straight shot east to Katy. Max watched Boomer as he maneuvered the Ford Taurus through traffic. He'd realized it was the same make of car that had brought the handsomely dressed officers to his front door to tell them that his father had died. Now, as he looked at Boomer's face, he sensed a certain sadness in his eyes. Max knew he wasn't the first soldier that Boomer had convinced to join up that he'd driven home battered and broken. The endless war had left its scars on more than one family.

Most of the drive back they spent in silence. Max didn't want to talk about what had happened, and Boomer didn't ask. There was a mutual understanding. When the time came, and that time could be years down the road, then they would talk.

As the car left the highway and started down the tree-lined streets of old Katy, Max's heart started to race. All things considered, he'd not been away that long, but he was finding coming back a little overwhelming. He had changed, but Katy looked the same.

"Could you pull over for a minute, Boomer?"

Boomer pulled over on the shoulder of a quiet side street a block from Max's house. He reached across with his massive mitt of a hand and gently touched him on the arm. "You gonna be okay, buddy?"

"Yeah, just need to catch my breath." Max took several slow, deep breaths, holding his chest with his hand as he did. He looked around at his old neighborhood. The streets he used to run down. The backyards he'd played in. No, it wasn't Asadi's town. That was a world away but forever burned into his memory.

"Okay, I think I'm ready."

Boomer slowly drove away from the curb and turned the corner onto Max's street. When they pulled up to the house, Max saw that there was a welcome home banner stretched across the front porch.

"You ready, buddy?"

"Yeah, I'm ready."

Boomer climbed out and moved around the front of the car and helped Max from his seat. By the time he got out, Sam and their mother were making their way down the porch steps. She was no longer using her walker, and the droop to her lip was gone. She slowly made her way up to her son.

"Welcome home, Max!" She smiled as she wrapped her arms tightly around his chest.

Max winced, kissed her on the cheek, then gently removed her arms from his sore ribs.

Sam pivoted and twisted and made it to the side of the car just behind her. He put his good arm around Max's shoulder. "The Nova is all washed. I put a new coat of wax on her."

"Good. We need to take it out for a spin."

Max looked around, expecting to see Maria, but there was no one else.

"Come on in. We brought some barbecue home from your favorite place." Their mother turned to Boomer. "You're welcome to stay, if you like. There's plenty of food," she said coldly.

Max knew that she'd never forgiven Boomer for taking her son away. He nodded to Boomer, signaling that it was okay, but he declined.

"Thank you, ma'am, but I must get back." He opened the trunk and removed Max's duffel. He briskly ran up the steps and placed it by the door. Then, with a nod to Max, he climbed back in the car and was gone.

All three of them slowly moved up the stairs and into the living room. For once, Sam was not left behind. They had set up the sofa as a bed.

Their mother gently held him by the arm. "Sam's going to sleep out here for a while," she said as she led him to the dining room table that was set for three.

On the kitchen stovetop was an aluminum tray filled with barbecue. Max took a seat by the window. She brought him a plate piled high with brisket and sausage with a side of potato salad.

"You need to eat. Didn't they feed you over there?"

Max smiled weakly. "Where's Maria?"

She and Sam exchanged nervous glances. "She said she would be around later."

"So what happened?" Sam asked, his mouth full of potato salad. "Who blew you up?"

Max stopped eating and looked out the window. The park had changed little since he'd left. They were playing basketball on the same court where he'd tackled Maria's assailant. Off in the distance, a baseball game was in session. People were walking their dogs. Children were playing on the jungle gym. Nothing seemed out of the ordinary, except him.

"Guy went nuts and started shooting up the hospital." Max turned back to his plate and stabbed a piece of brisket with his fork and drowned it in barbecue sauce. He placed it in his mouth and slowly chewed as if he were trying to rediscover something from his past. "Must have tossed a grenade behind the door. Blew up in my face. Ripped a big hole in my chest."

"Really, wow!" Sam looked down at his plate and pushed his food around with his fork.

Their mother sat staring at her boy. Max could see her trying to hold back her tears. She said nothing and tried to focus on eating. They never asked him again about it. It was what it was. It happened. They accepted it as a matter of fact, just as they'd grown to accept that their father and husband was never coming back. Now it was time to get on with things.

When dinner ended, Max went to his room and lay down. Sam struggled with his duffel but was able to drag it across the house and into the bedroom.

Max lay staring at the ceiling and didn't acknowledge Sam's heroic effort with the bag. "I got a letter from Maria saying that she'd found a new guy."

Sam looked away.

"Know who it is?"

"Yeah."

"Who?"

Sam turned his back to Max and slowly made his way to the door. "I love her, Max. And I hope she loves me back."

"You sleeping with her?"

"Yes."

Max didn't take his eyes off the ceiling. Sam turned and looked at him, then slowly walked out of the room and closed the door.

~ ~ ~

It was late when Sam heard Maria letting herself in. The living room was softly lit by light spilling in from the kitchen. He was lying on the sofa, his eyes closed. She quietly crossed the room and stopped in front of Max's door.

Sam rose to his feet and stood at the end of the hallway, looking at her. The light from Max's room seeped through the cracks in the doorframe, highlighting her in a golden silhouette.

He sighed as she placed her hand on the doorknob. She turned, and their eyes met. He could see her anguish and his loss. His heart ripped from his chest as she looked away, slowly opened the door, and went inside.

Chapter 28

2005

Sam walked across the stage as a member of the class of 2005. He smiled for the camera as he reached for his diploma. His years at Katy Lakes High School were officially over. From where Max and his mother were seated in the cavernous arena, Sam probably looked like no more than a small, distorted speck. He heard a few distant screams he assumed were from Max and his mother, but they were quickly drowned out by the cheers for the track star who decided to moonwalk his way across the stage.

For the most part, Sam's labored transit across the stage was ignored by the majority of the class. Just the crippled guy. Not a star athlete. Not president of the class, newspaper editor, or top-ten GPA. Just another kid leaving school to enter the real world. His fellow students traded funny faces with their friends as they watched him fight the stairs in his descent to the stadium floor. Once down, they hurriedly moved around him and raced to their seats.

Maria wasn't there. She said she had an afternoon class and would be around to the house later. He knew she was avoiding him. They had not spoken much since that night.

As he stood in his row listening to the principal say a few last words, he wondered where he was going to go from here. He hadn't spent much time thinking about anything other than a future with Maria, and now that seemed to be gone forever.

Suddenly, the room erupted as a thousand students cheered and threw their caps into the air. Sam held tightly to his. He wanted it as a memento of his years of struggle. If he tossed it, there was no way he could scramble to get it back.

When the convocation ended, the class filed out of the building and into the parking lot, where throngs of excited families pushed and shoved their way to their loved ones. Sam stood by the edge of the door leading to the lot, overwhelmed by the chaos. He was terrified of stepping into the tempest and falling. As more and more people flooded through the doors, he was pushed deeper into the corner. He desperately searched the crowd for a familiar face. Finally, just as he was starting to panic, a hand reached out and grabbed him by the arm.

"There you are." Max pulled him in close and wrapped his arms around him like a shield. He kept his elbows out as if he were running a block through the defensive line and guided Sam through the crowd to the edge of the parking lot where their mother was waiting.

"I'm so proud of you," she said as she squeezed him tightly.

Sam was panting and dripping with sweat from his short trip across the lot. "Mom, I can't breathe."

"Come on, boys, stand next to each other. I need a picture."

Sam straightened himself up as much as he could but still looked small next to his twin.

"Smile."

She grabbed a passerby and had them take multiple pictures of the three of them as they stood perfectly still in the stifling heat.

"Thank you," she said as she took back the camera. "Okay, now where would you like to go?"

"Can we go home?" Sam said. "I'm tired."

Their mother seemed too overwhelmed with the excitement of the evening to want to go home. She'd made a dramatic recovery, and only a trained eye could tell that she had any deficits at all after her brain injury. "No, not now. I have two boys that have graduated from high school, and I want to celebrate."

"Anywhere's fine," Max said.

"Okay, then it's my call." She climbed into the back of the Nova. "Let's go to Red Lobster. Your father always loved that place." She paused as her voiced cracked. "If he can't be here in person to see his two beautiful sons and celebrate this great achievement, at least we know his spirit is here and he would love to be sitting with us."

They all nodded and headed in the direction of the Katy Lakes Mall. The Red Lobster was already filling up with after-graduation families when they arrived. They were lucky enough to get a seat on the bench next to the lobster tank as they waited for their names to be called.

Sam stared into the tank at the doomed. Their claws were wrapped in bands so they wouldn't harm each other. Sam noticed one of them had lost a claw and was smaller than the others. It seemed to cower in the corner as its bigger rivals moved freely about the tank.

"You're the smart one, you cripple," he whispered. "You're eventually going to get eaten, too, but the big ones are going to get grabbed first."

When their names were finally called, they were led to a four-top at the far side of the restaurant. Sam twisted and pivoted between the rows of tables packed with celebrating families. Grandparents sat next to babies in highchairs. Former students still wearing their caps flipped their tassels in the faces of their siblings. As Sam passed, they paused to watch him struggle. Once he was seated, they forgot about him and went back to their dinners.

"What will it be, boys?" their mother asked as she slid two menus across the table. She opened hers and scanned the offerings.

Sam watched as her expression changed and she gently put the menu down. "What's wrong?"

"Your father and I always used to share the admiral's feast." She reached for a napkin and wiped a tear from her eye. "Don't know what I was thinking when I said we should come here."

Max reached across the table and placed his hand on her arm. "I'll share one with you. Let's just order two dinners. That should be enough for the three of us."

She nodded and put the napkin on her lap. "You two are all I have." She placed her hand on top of Max's. "By the grace of God, at least you made it back, Max. Maybe a little beat-up but you're here. We should be thankful for that."

"Amen to that," Max whispered.

Sam looked down at the table. He felt guilty as thoughts ran through his head of how life would be if Max hadn't come back. How Maria would be his. "Yes, amen to that. Well, let's order then. Two feasts." Sam slid the menus to the edge of the table, and soon, the three of them were eating their seafood with the thought of their father's spirit sitting by their sides.

"So you are happy going to the University of Houston next year?" their mother said.

Max nodded. "Yes. I'm ready to get away from the Katy Lakes crowd."

"You really need to decide what you're going to do."

Sam watched as Max leaned on his elbows and looked around the restaurant. "Thinking of medicine. Maybe a surgeon."

"Well, that would be wonderful." Her face glowed at the thought of one of her children becoming a doctor. "How about you, Sam? Any ideas?"

Sam cringed at the thought of working in a hospital. He'd been in and out of the hospital a good part of his youth. He'd had several surgeries on his limbs and going back into that environment where he'd been so scared did not sound appealing. "Not medicine, I can tell you that. Law, maybe. I can do that without having to walk too much."

"My goodness wouldn't Luther be proud if we had a doctor and a lawyer in the family. He only wanted the best for you two."

"Yes, that would be something," Max said.

Their mother appeared happy for the rest of the meal. Sam would catch her looking up from her plate and staring at her two sons, a smile on her face.

When the meal was done, Sam turned to Max. "Can I have the car keys? My big night. I want to drive."

Max smiled. "You know it's going to be Mom in the back seat, not Maria this time. Think you can behave?"

Sam laughed. "Maybe."

Chapter 29

2005

Max gently grabbed Sam by the shoulders and gave him a shake. "Come on, get up. I got a surprise for you."

"What time is it?" Sam struggled to sit up. "It's still dark outside."

"Yeah. That's the point. Get your lazy ass up."

Max had the urge to grab him and hoist him to his feet like he had done most of their lives. He put an arm under his shoulder and started to pull but immediately realized they'd both changed. His ribs screamed in pain with the effort. Sam rolled his shoulders back and gently pushed him away.

"Don't need your help. I'm not a child."

Max stood up and twisted his back as he tried to undo the spasms. He took a few deep breaths blinking his eyes hard several times as the pain shot though his body. "Ok, well get the hell up. We'll eat on the road."

Max sat behind the wheel of the Nova with the engine running. He had a thermos full of coffee on the floor. Several egg and chorizo tacos wrapped in paper towel were on the dash. He'd fried them up while Sam lay snoring on the sofa. As he watched Sam make his way down the front porch steps, he could see the difference two years had make. Sam appeared taller than he remembered. He'd put on a few pounds which was a good thing. He was starting to look less fragile. Max's hand trembled as he adjusted the rearview mirror. "I've changed too," he whispered.

Sam swung open the passenger side door and slid into his seat. "So, what's up?"

Max reached up and grabbed a taco and handed it to Sam. "Going fishing."

Sam took the taco and excitedly unwrapped it. "Really?"

"Yup. Got a cooler and the rods in the trunk. Boat rental waiting for us down in Galveston." Max reached down and grabbed the thermos off the floor and poured Sam some coffee into a plastic cup. "Hardest part of this trip was getting your ass up."

Max could see egg stuck between Sam's teeth as he smiled. "You should have let me know. I could've helped."

"Then there'd be no surprise," Max said as he placed his hand on Sam's back and gave him a squeeze. "Let's have some fun today."

Max shifted into first and slowly pulled the Nova away from the house making sure not to jerk the car and have Sam spill his coffee. Traffic was light that time of the morning. They both didn't say much as they raced south toward the island. Max was lost in thoughts of the last time they had gone with their dad. He assumed Sam did the same.

"Maria? Is she meeting us there?"

"No Sam. Just you and me. Thought we could just have a guy's day out."

Sam's disappointment was palpable, but Max said nothing. He kept focused on the goal of the day. They'd lost that bond they'd had before he left. He wanted their relationship back. Not only had he been unable to write to Maria, but he'd neglected Sam as well. The occasional video chat was good enough to show that both worlds still existed but not much more than that.

Max looked out the window at Galveston Bay as they drove across the long causeway that led to the sleepy island. The sun had just cracked the horizon and rays of orange light radiated through gaps in towering clouds that stretched to the up to the heavens. A few boats were already on the water. The long white tails of their wakes disturbing the calm of bay.

Max turned east when they hit the island and headed towards the marina. The island was still. Many of the century old buildings off the Strand were empty, still trying to recover from years of neglect in one of the nation's largest per capita welfare communities. Several cars were pulling into the parking lot of the marina when they arrived. A breeze was starting to blow from the southwest.

"Gonna be a little choppy out there today. You up for it?" Max said as he got out of the car. He popped the trunk and started grabbing the rods.

Sam twisted and pivoted his way to the back of the car. "Don't worry about me. Just worry about how many more fish I'm going to catch than you, looser!"

Max laughed as he handed him his pole. "Not a chance you're catching more than me."

"Bet?"

"Sure. What will it be? You buy the beers?"

"I drive home."

Max stared at Sam. It was hard to believe they were the same age. Yes, he had grown and yes, he seemed much more mature than when he left. Definitely more mature. But in his mind, he'd always been his little brother. Not an equal. He was someone Max had to take care of and protect. The idea that he was someone who could take care of himself seemed foreign. Sam expecting to drive home should not have been a shock and yet it was. Sam being with Maria was suddenly more than just his handicapped sibling with a crush on his girl. It was a real threat.

"Sure. Of course," he said as he looked away toward the waterfront. "You drive home anyway. It's as much your car as it is mine."

With a smile Sam grabbed his tackle box and hooked it on his bad left hand and grabbed his pole with his right. "Then looser cleans the fish and cooks."

"Deal," Max replied as he locked the car.

They slowly made their way to the cay and found their boat. It was an old 23-foot center console Boston Whaler. It looked well used but sturdy. In it was a gray-haired sun-bleached man who looked as though he lived on the beach. His clothes were well worn, and he smelled of body odor mixed with fish.

He climbed out of the boat and extended his massive, calloused hand to Max. "Curtis Boudreaux."

Max hesitated slightly before putting down his gear and grabbing his hand. His grip was powerful and as Max pulled away, he could feel a thin film of fish oil on his hand.

"I'm Max and this is my brother Sam."

Curtis looked over at Sam. He turned away and tossed two life vests on the deck then looked back at him again. This time with a long knowing look. "You boys've been here before, haven't you?"

"Long time ago, but yeah."

"Thought I recognized the name when you booked. Only clicked when I saw you two."

Curtis walked to the back of the cay and returned a minute later with two large buckets of foul-smelling chum. He stepped carefully over the gunwale and kicked open a bait box towards the back of the boat and poured them in.

"Smells like hell but the fish love it." He bent down and started washing out the buckets with a hose. "Was that your Papa that was with you last time?"

"Yes," Sam replied.

"I remember him. Thought what a damn good job he was doing getting you two out here considering you're a cripple."

Sam turned abruptly away and swung his tackle box and pole over the gunwale. He then pivoted and climbed onto the deck without a word. Max knew he was angry. Sam no longer seemed to cower when confronted with his handicap. He was different now. He just powered through it.

"Is he going to be coming, your Pa I mean?"

"He's dead."

"Oh," he grunted uncomfortably. "Let's just get you boys started then."

Max climbed in the boat and placed his gear in a corner near Sam's.

Curtis untied the moorings and tossed the rope onto the deck and gave the boat a good shove to get her away from the dock and gave them a wave. "You know its one-hundred bucks if you mess up the prop. Make sure you lift the engine if you're in the shallows."

Max nodded in is his direction as he started up the engine and slowly pulled the boat out into the marina channel. Sam had placed himself on the bow and sat looking down at the water. "Let's head out to the jetty. That's where we had good luck last time." Sam gave him a weak smile then turned his head back to the water.

Max kept looking up at the sky. Dark clouds were forming in the south. The sea was gray, and he could already see white caps forming in the distance. To his left a flock of brown pelicans skimmed the waves. Laughing gulls called to each other as they followed the boat hoping for a scrap. The spray felt good as it kicked up from the bow. He watched Sam sit motionless as the water soaked his expressionless face. The jetty would be a good spot, he thought. It was almost 7 miles long and shot straight out into the gulf. If it got too rough at least they would have a little shelter and there the fishing was usually good.

Max followed the jetty for about twenty-five minutes keeping it about two-hundred yards off to his right. He found a spot several hundred yards away from some other boats and cut the engine. "Sam, drop the anchor," he shouted over the rising wind.

Sam struggle to his feet on the rocking boat and released the anchor. He then headed to the back of the boat and sat down as he reached for his pole. Max sat next to him and took out a large hook from the box and attached it to his line. "Big hook for big fish," he said with a smile. He reached into the chum bucket and pulled out a fish head and stuck it on the hook. "Go get'em bro," he said as he patted him on the back.

"You're definitely cleaning the fish," Sam replied as he struggled to his feet almost dropping the pole.

Max sat motionless as he watched Sam tuck the pole under his left arm. He proceeded across the rocking deck, grabbing the rail and pulling his useless left leg behind. He eventually got to the bow by shear will if by nothing else.

Max affixed bait to his line then walked to the bow and stood by Sam. Sam had seated himself on the bench and had the pole resting on the gunwale lodged between his foot and his good right arm. He cast his line then looked down on Sam.

"It was right about here that we caught that Red, remember?"

Sam smiled but said nothing.

"Ya might want to jiggle that line or something. Fish ain't going to bite if it's just sitting dead on the bottom."

"I know how to fish. Worry about your own damn line."

Max reeled in his line then sent it flying again in the direction of the jetty. A wave smacked the side of the boat sending spray across the deck as they both struggled to hold their positions.

"What's with the attitude, Sam?"

Sam slowly reeled in his line, checked to see that the bait was still on the hook then lowered it back over the side. "No attitude. Just let the crippled kid do his thing alright."

"Don't let that old shithead get to you. You're not just that crippled kid."

Sam glared back at Max, "says the football star, war hero. What the hell do you know."

"Now you're being a jerk. Forget about that guy and fish."

Sam tried to stand up as another wave hit the side of the boat and knocked him back down onto the bench.

Max cast his line again. "You can't spend your whole life getting upset with guys like that. He knows no better. You need to look to the future. Think about the positives and not that negative shit."

Max looked down and through the sea spray could see tears welling up in Sam's eyes.

"Future?" Sam stammered. "What future?" He turned his head away and looked across the water. "I had a glimpse of a future. I had some hope before you came home."

Max felt as though a knife had ripped through his heart. He felt lightheaded and had to lean his pole against the gunwale and sit. "So, you'd rather I died in that godforsaken place?"

Sam turned and looked him in the eyes, his face flushed red. "That was your choice. You left me…left us. The impulsive hero couldn't think through to the damage he was leaving behind."

"I had to go Sam. It was something I felt I needed to do. And I sent home money. Didn't that help?"

"No!" Sam shouted. "No, it didn't fucking help. Not the kind of help I needed!"

The boat started to drag on the anchor as the wind increased. Max looked up and noticed that they were being pushed in the direction of the jetty.

Sam struggled to his feet and stood staring down at Max. "And I love Maria. You left her as well. You left the both of us and you have no right to take her back!"

Max rose to his feet on the rocking boat and pressed his face in close to his brothers. Neither of them had noticed that all the other boats had headed back to shore and that the dark clouds that started the day far to the south were now directly overhead. Lightning streaked from one cloud to the next. The waves slapped against the boat pushing it ever closer to the rocks.

The mention of Maria now made him angry. He had noticed the changes with her when he'd returned. The glances over at Sam. The occasional sighs when he'd been too lost in thought to pay attention to her. How simple conversations were becoming a struggle.

"I didn't take her back. She came back. Maybe she'd had enough of fucking a cripple and wanted a real man!"

"I am a real man!" he shouted. He clenched his teeth and pivoted hard on his left leg. He spun his body around with all his might and struck Max hard across the face knocking him to the deck. As Max lay on his back stunned, Sam's pole started ripping along the rail. Max reached up and grabbed it just before it flew overboard.

"Sam! Fish on!" he shouted as he struggled to his feet. He handed the pole to Sam. "It's your fish. Don't lose it."

Sam grabbed the pole and slid into his corner and braced himself against the side of the boat. "Damn, it's a big one he shouted. Get the net!"

Max raced to the back of the boat and grabbed the net. By the time he had got back to the bow, Sam had reeled it in close to the side. He was laughing and rocking back and forth just as he had done that night when he floored the Nova and almost got them a ticket.

Max leaned over the edge and could see the beast just below the surface. "God, Sam, it's a huge Red! It won't fit in the net."

"Go get the baling hook!"

Max stumbled along the rail to the back of the boat again and as he reached down to pick up the hook the boat was hit with a huge wave. Max was thrown into the corner as the bow kicked straight up in the air. "Holey shit," he whispered. When he finally was able to get back on his feet, he looked to the front of the boat but there was no Sam!

"Sam!" he shouted as he raced to the bow. "Sam!"

When he leaned over the edge, he saw Sam floating just below the surface where the fish once was. He was not struggling. He just looked up at Max expressionless as he quietly slipped deeper into the dark churning water. Max jumped in and blindly thrashed about until he felt Sam's limp body. He grabbed him by the arm and pulled him to the surface. Sam gasped for air and started to flail about.

"Sam stop fighting or you'll drag us both down!"

"No Max. Let me go!" cried Sam.

Max put both arms around his torso and lifted him higher out of the water. "Never brother," he whispered in his ear.

As Sam relaxed Max realized there was no way he could get them both back into the boat. They had been foolish not to put on the life jackets and had already drifted quite a distance away. The jetty was closer now and he decided to try to reach it. At least there they wouldn't drown. He floated on his back keeping Sam's head elevated on his chest. His lungs burned and his ribs screamed in pain as he kicked hard with his legs in the direction of the jetty. He felt as though he deserved the pain. Sam was right. He had just gone. Left everyone he cared about without a plan, without asking if there was another way. Then just dropped back into their lives expecting everything to be the same. How could it ever be the same?

Max dragged Sam's body up on the rocks of the jetty and away from the crashing waves. Sam lay silently on his back gasping for air and staring unblinkingly up at the dark sky. Max placed his burning arms over his head and reached for heaven as he tried to break his muscle spasms. He then squatted down next to Sam and looked out across the water.

"How are we going to get home now?" Sam asked, still staring up at the sky.

Max saw their boat in the distance being battered by the waves. It was slowly being pushed toward the rocks.

"Do you really wish I'd died over there?"

Sam shook all over as he started to sob. The waves crashing on the rocks threw water over them both. It rolled into Sam's mouth making him gag but he continued lying on his back crying uncontrollably.

"Come on Sam, you just can't lie here and drown. Sit up." Max placed his hands under his head and lifted it up as Sam spit out the salty sea water.

"No," he gasped as he sat up and placed his head on his knees. "But I love Maria. She's the only good thing that's ever happened to me. She doesn't see me as some damn cripple. She sees me."

Max sat quietly with his arm around Sam as he watched the boat moving ever closer. He didn't know what to say. He just looked out across the dark water, the salt spray burning his face. There was no answer. Nothing could be said.

When the boat was about twenty yards from the rocks Max plunged back into the sea. The warm muddy water seemed to want to suck him under. For a moment he thought that might not be so bad. Drift downward and rest on the sticky brown bottom. Letting the ocean swallow him up, never to be seen or heard from again. That would allow everyone to get back on with their lives like they had when he was away. They all seemed better off. He stopped swimming and let his muscles relax. As his head started to sink below the water a wave lifted him up and spun him around. He saw Sam sitting alone on the rocks like a bent and twisted piece of driftwood. He couldn't die. Not today.

Max swam to the boat and pulled himself over the side. He went to the bow and pulled up the anchor that had dragged along the muddy channel bottom. He then made his way back to the console and started the engine and slowly maneuvered the boat close to the jetty. Sam sat motionless, his head on his knees. When Max was close enough, he grabbed the bow rope and jumped back into the water and swam the few feet to the rocks. He climbed up and shook Sam. Come on, let's go. Max pulled the boat in close and helped Sam wade the few feet to the boat then hoisted him over the side. Sam just slid onto the deck and lay there motionless. Max pulled himself back into the boat then went to the controls and started the engine.

Bang! Bang! Bang!

"Shit!" He turned the engine off and flipped the lever for the engine lift. He looked over the edge of the boat and saw that the propeller had been badly mangled on the rocks. He grabbed the bow rope again and jumped overboard into the shallows and gave the boat a good shove. Once he was sure it was clear of the rocks he swam back and climbed in. Sam still lay on the deck staring up at the sky. When Max restarted the engine he heard a disturbing wobbling sound, but at least they were moving.

The trip back to the marina was longer than he'd remembered. Sam eventually got up and sat in his spot by the bow. No fish had been caught and the bonds that he'd been trying to rekindle may have been permanently severed. Either way they both were going to live and that was not a certainty a short time ago.

Curtis was waiting when they finally crept up to the dock. Max could see immediately that he was not happy. The noise from the engine was not something they could hide. Curtis jumped on board the second they tied up and went to the stern and looked over the edge of the boat as he raised the engine.

"Goddamn! I told you two to watch out for the prop in the shallows!"

Sam climbed over the gunwale and started slowly making his way back to the car. Max stayed behind on the boat collecting their poles and tackle boxes.

Curtis grabbed him by the arm. "If this is more than just the propeller, you're going to pay a lot more than a hundred bucks! Shit. What did you do? Let that little cripple drive my boat up on the rocks!"

Max dropped his gear and lunged at Curtis. He grabbed him by the shirt and with a sweep of his leg kicked Curtis' legs out from under him, slamming him to the deck. He straddled him and place one hand on his throat while cocking his right fist high in the air. Curtis was stunned. The big man did nothing but try to cover his face from the expected blow. Max trembled. What was he doing? He lowered his fist and reached into his pocket and pulled two-hundred dollars out of his wallet and stuffed it into Curtis' shirt.

"This is all I got," he said as he stood. "Should cover whatever I busted." He gathered up his gear and left Curtis still lying on the deck. He didn't look back as he made his way to the car where Sam was waiting for him.

"Did he say anything about the prop?"

"No. I paid him though and gave him a tip. We should be alright."

The trip home was silent. When they pulled up to the house Max could see Maria sitting on the porch swing. She rose from her seat and stood at the top of the stair and looked down on them as they got out of the car. He could see that her eyes first looked over to Sam then to him.

"What the hell happened to you two? You're both soaking wet and look like hell."

"Just went fishing, that's all," Sam said quietly.

"Yea, just fishing."

Chapter 30

2005

Maria stopped coming around during the day. She would usually arrive after the house was asleep, then she and Max would go out and cruise around old Katy.

"Please be quiet, Max. I don't want to wake Sam."

Sally Donovan had left for the week to go visit a sick friend in Richmond and had prepared enough food for the boys so they wouldn't have to cook.

Max watched Maria look over her shoulder at Sam lying on the sofa as he pulled the front door closed. That night, they'd decided to drive down to Galveston in Maria's truck. Max had been home for six months now, and felt that since his return, she and Sam had barely spoken. At least not in his presence.

The lights of the refineries along Route 45 south toward Galveston were so bright that it appeared as if the sun would rise at any moment, their light only dimming in the distance as Max and Maria drove farther south through the wetlands bordering Galveston Bay. The causeway was empty as they crossed onto the island and headed through the quiet, dimly lit streets to the beach. The heat and humidity were overwhelming despite the gentle sea breeze. Little moved. Even during the day, most of the activity seemed to be concentrated along the beachfront. The grand old Victorian mansions that lined the boulevards leading to the beach hadn't seen glory since before the great hurricane of 1900 that killed thousands. At night, even the beachfront activity that kept the island alive was absent.

Max felt happy with Maria by his side. He still hadn't been able to open up to her, and most of their conversations were one-sided, but that didn't bother him. It was comforting just hearing her talk. He hadn't noticed how hard she'd been trying to get him to say something. Anything to let her know that he wanted to be a part of her life.

They drove east along the seawall that protected the island from the hurricanes that routinely ripped through the Gulf of Mexico. At the easternmost tip of the island, they came to a narrow, twisting road that led through high dunes and scattered scrub that in places encroached onto the road.

Max slowed the truck to a crawl as the headlights illuminated the gates blocking off East Beach. He placed the truck in low gear and maneuvered onto the soft sand and around the gates. They slowly made their way across the beach and parked near the water's edge. He turned the engine off and rolled down the windows. The cool sea breeze kept away the mosquitos that had swarmed the truck as they'd passed through the dunes.

Maria slid up next to Max and placed her head on his shoulder. He pulled her in close and sat quietly looking out at the gulf. To his left, the dark hulk of a giant oil tanker silently made its way into the Houston ship channel. Before him lay the expanse of the Gulf of Mexico. Out in the darkness, the lights from oil rigs lit the horizon like small candles.

They sat in silence. Max was happy. He closed his eyes and tried to think of nothing except the smell of Maria's hair and the warmth of her body pressed up next to his.

Maria moved under his arm to get more comfortable and inadvertently hit him in the ribs with her shoulder. Max took a sudden breath in and winced in pain.

"Sorry. Are you all right?"

"Yes. Don't worry." Max sat up and tried to stretch. "Give me a minute." He opened the door and slid out of the driver's seat and onto the sand. He kicked off his boots and socks and placed them by the side of the truck, then stretched his arms over his head. He could feel his ribs popping as he twisted back and forth. He closed his eyes as he took in a deep breath of the salty sea air. A warm gust of wind struck him in the face. He trembled as his mind shot back to Afghanistan. He felt the heat of the door exploding in his face. Saw body parts scattered across the floor. "Ahh!" Max jumped as Maria gently touched him on the arm.

"You okay?"

"Yeah. Just the ribs are still a little sore, that's all."

She stood holding on to his arm as they looked out at the ocean. She gently pulled on his hand. "Let's go for a walk."

They made their way along the edge of the surf until they came to a lifeguard station.

The tanker had slid effortlessly into the channel and was just a shadow off to their left as another giant beast lined up to follow it in. Max was desperate to say something. To say how he was starting to feel like he was home again. How he wanted to forget his nightmares and start living. But he didn't.

They climbed up into a lifeguard's box and sat on the floor, resting their backs against the wooden siding. They kept their eyes trained on the churning sea before them, neither saying anything. Maria eventually fell asleep. Max stared at the lights twinkling on the edge of the ocean all night while she curled up next to him.

When the sun came up, he gently woke her. "Come on, Maria. Sun's up. Don't want the rangers to give us a ticket."

They got back in the truck and started the long drive back to Katy.

"Max, I'm done," Maria whispered as they got closer to home. "Sam loves me, and I love him. I thought I loved you and that we could be as we were, but you're different. I'm different."

Max kept his eyes on the road as he maneuvered the truck through the midmorning traffic. In his mind he was screaming, but he said nothing. It was as if the muscles that controlled his mouth were frozen. He was so overwhelmed with emotion that he could do nothing more than run. Run away from the woman he loved. Just keep moving and somehow it would work out. Keep running and the clouds of fear and self-doubt, terror and emotional heartbreak, would clear and he would be able to make rational decisions. Tell her that he loved her. Stop dwelling on his past and look to the future. Be the man that she needed. But in that moment he failed and remained silent.

As they pulled up to the house, she touched him on the arm. "We're done. I love you, but this is it. I want to be with Sam."

Max killed the engine and handed her the keys, then opened the door and walked toward the house without saying a word.

Maria stepped out of the truck and came around to the front. "Max, wait. Not like this, please. Say something. Anything." She bent down and picked up a handful of gravel from the road and threw it pelting him on the back. Her voice trembled as she screamed, "tell me you want me to stay!"

Suddenly, Logan burst through the front door in a panic. When he saw them, he stopped. Tears were streaming down his face. "I'm sorry. I didn't mean to do it. They're on their way. I'm so sorry."

"Logan, what did you do?" Maria screamed.

"I'm sorry. They're on their way."

Logan staggered off the porch and down the street. Maria raced past Max and burst into the house. Sam was not on the sofa. Max pushed past her and into his bedroom. There he found Sam lying in bed motionless, his face blue, a syringe dangling from his crippled arm.

"Sam!" Maria screamed.

Max shook him hard. "Sam, wake up! Sam!" He dragged him off the bed and onto the floor, tilted his head back, and started mouth-to-mouth resuscitation. Maria started chest compressions. Tears streamed down both their faces as they desperately tried to breathe life back into their loved one. Over Maria's sobs, Max could hear the sirens coming closer and eventually stopping in front of the house.

Soon, they were surrounded by paramedics who took over the effort. Max and Maria stood in the corner holding each other tightly as the paramedics inserted a breathing tube and lifted Sam onto a stretcher. They rushed him through the living room, knocking over a table lamp as they went, and out to the waiting ambulance. A medic continued with the chest compressions as they loaded him on board.

Max and Maria rushed to the front porch, then stood frozen as the ambulance drove away.

Max felt a smothering tightness in his chest like he'd felt on the helicopter flight back to Kabul. He looked around and could only see a yellow haze as the world around him started to spin. "Maria!" he mumbled as he fell to the ground.

Chapter 31

The Present

Max found himself standing beside the couch, panting, his scrubs drenched in sweat.

"Max, are you okay?" Simkins's voice was jubilant. "Why don't you sit back down for a bit?"

Max looked wildly around the room. His ribs ached as he hyperventilated. "No. I have to get out of here."

Simkins stood and grabbed him by the elbow. "Max, I really think you should try to relax. Have a seat."

Max jerked his arm away. He was surprised by the delighted expression on Dr. Simkins's face. "No, Jack. I'm fine. Just need to get out of here." He pulled his white coat tightly around himself, bowed his head, and stormed from the room. He didn't acknowledge Lucy as he stumbled into the corridor. He paused briefly and took several deep breaths, then hurried down the crowded corridors of the professional building and out to the parking lot.

Simkins, that bastard, was happy to see me suffer. Was that what he'd been waiting for all these weeks? To see me break down? Is that the way these shrinks work? Rip open every possible wound until you're standing there naked and shaking?

Max raced home. The thought of Sam lying there blue with the needle in his arm had shaken him so deeply he could hardly see to drive. It had brought back memories he had desperately tried to repress. He had hated drugs and their pushers with a passion ever since. He knew it had affected him. It was still affecting him. His uncontrollable violent outbursts against anything he deemed an injustice. His exhaustive work schedule that he used to blunt his memories and guilt. But that was not all.

He pulled into the garage and stormed into the house. Tears streamed down his face as he walked up to the credenza. He stared down at the pictures of his past. Silent. Accusing.

"Stop staring at me!" He shoved the pictures off the credenza. Their glass shattered across the floor. "I've saved thousands of lives, haven't I? Thousands relieved of their suffering! Isn't that enough? Isn't it?"

Max walked across the room, the broken glass crunching beneath his feet. He tore off his clothes and lay naked on his bed. He stared at the ceiling fan.

"So long ago, and yet I still can't get myself clean."

Chapter 32

The Present

Max did something he'd never done before: he called a colleague and asked for coverage. He needed to take a day or two off.

When he eventually dragged himself from bed, it was late morning. He knew he'd taken a few too many sleeping pills, and he still felt a bit groggy. He slipped on a pair of shorts and flip-flops and went into the kitchen, where he grabbed a broom and a dustpan. He went into the living room and picked up the pictures and placed them back on the credenza. He cleaned up the broken glass and dumped it in the kitchen wastebasket.

He went back to the living room and knelt on all fours and looked for any last speck that might be hiding on his wood floor. Just as he was picking up a small shard from behind a leg of the coffee table, he heard the mail slot flip open, followed by the sound of mail scattering across the floor.

He carried his little splinter to the wastebasket, then washed his hands before returning to the front of the house. He picked up the mail and brought it back to the coffee table and began sorting through it.

"Shit, shit, shit," he said each time he picked up a piece of junk mail and tossed it back down on the table.

Suddenly, he saw something that made his heart skip a beat.

"What the hell? You must be kidding."

The envelope he pulled out from under the stack was made from the same thick, cream-colored stationery as the last strange letter he'd received with the Islamic prayer written in it. He carefully opened the envelope and removed the neatly folded letter.

You killed my father. The soldiers in the hospital died because of you. Allah's mercy is infinite, but I will never forgive you.

Asalah

Max sat down on the sofa, his mouth half-open as he stared at the letter. Same watermark as the one he'd received earlier. He grabbed for the envelope and looked at the stamp. It had been posted yesterday from somewhere in Houston.

How could that be? She's alive and in Houston?

Max felt light-headed as he stood and walked to the kitchen and pulled a bottle of Jamaican rum from the shelf. He unscrewed the top and tipped the bottle back and took several large gulps. He sat down at the kitchen table. He took several more swigs of rum. The burning in his throat helped stop him from hyperventilating.

"I've not killed anyone else," he mumbled as he took another drink. "No one innocent at least. Not since that time."

He tipped the bottle back again and didn't stop swallowing until half of it was in his gut. He continued to stare at the letter spread out on the table until his vision started to blur.

She's alive? All these years, and now when Jack Simkins has ripped my world wide open and I'm at my lowest, this comes! And she blames me for the horror of that night. For my injuries. For the deaths of all those innocent soldiers and Asadi, my friend? How cruel to put all that on me.

Max continued to drink until he felt himself sliding from the chair. His head hit hard against the floor as he passed out.

When he woke, he found himself in a pool of vomit. He climbed to his feet and staggered to the sink. He tried to steady himself as he fumbled for the cold-water faucet, then drenched his head as he wiped the vomit from the side of his face. He blindly reached for a kitchen towel and buried his face in it, clawing at the crusted mucus in his eyes.

After tossing the towel in the drying rack, he turned and looked in disgust at the mess on the floor. His head was still spinning from all the alcohol, but his thoughts were getting clearer by the minute. He didn't know how long he'd been out, but the sun had set, and the house was dark. He left the kitchen and switched on several lights, then grabbed the letter off the table and went back into the living room and sat on the sofa.

They died because of me, huh?

Max knew that wasn't true. He knew what he knew, and if he knew anything, it was that he'd had nothing to do with that slaughter. Anyone who was there would know that. Anyone who knew him would know how much that night had affected him. But was Asalah really alive? Did she blame him? How could that be when he'd only met her once?

Max stood up from the sofa and went into his bedroom and pulled open the top drawer of his side table.

"Thought I'd never be calling you again," he mumbled as he pulled out an old, worn business card from under a stack of papers. He looked at his watch: 9:46 p.m.

Hell, call him anyway.

Max dialed the number and waited.

To his surprise, his old friend picked up after one ring. "Hello, this is Boomer."

Max smiled. "Hey, Boomer. This is Max."

"Donovan? You shitting me?"

"How've you been?"

"Goddamn. I thought you were dead or something."

"Nope. Still alive."

"Last I saw you, I was dropping you off at your front doorstep and your mother was shooting daggers at me the entire time."

"That was a long time ago."

"So, what's up, brother? Why the call out of the blue?" Boomer lowered his voice. "You in trouble?"

"Maybe. I don't know. Just needed to talk to someone from the old days. You still in?"

"No, got out a while ago. In long enough to get my pension. Out soon enough to keep my sanity."

"Think we could meet up for a drink?"

Boomer's voice lowered to a whisper. "Sure, bro, but can't stay out too late. The old lady will ride my ass if I come home late, waking up the kids and all. Got work tomorrow."

"Where're you living? I'll come to you."

"Up here in the Heights. Place around the corner called the Potato Head. Open late."

Max winced at the thought of going back to the Heights. He hadn't been back there since he sent those two dealers to the hospital. "Sure. I'll find it on my GPS. Be there in thirty."

Max wiped up the mess on the kitchen floor, then jumped in the shower. He still felt a little drunk but definitely could pass a sobriety test, as long as they didn't breathalyze him. He put on a pair of jeans, T-shirt, and a pair of boots, then grabbed the keys to the Nova.

He pulled the car out of the garage and headed toward Rice University. The streets were empty. There was a slight chill in the air as autumn was finally approaching after a dreadfully hot summer. He looked in the windows of the homes as he drove by. All the good people were tucking their kids in bed for the night and locking their doors against whatever was roaming the streets. Max was roaming the streets. He thought about his life. No kids. No wife. No reason for him to lock the doors really. Just stuck in a vicious cycle that had started with an unthinkable act so many years ago.

Max turned up Kirby Drive, then headed north toward the Heights. The GPS on his phone directed him to an old, industrialized part of the Heights that had recently seen some trendy renovation. As he drove through the poorly lit streets, he was surprised to see nice new condo complexes interspersed between derelict warehouses.

He found the bar on the corner of a strip center across the street from a microbrewery. A freight train covered in graffiti passed behind it. In the distance, the Houston skyline shone through the darkness.

Max backed the Nova into a parking spot in front of the bar. He stepped out and looked around for his old recruiter.

Out of a dark corner stepped Boomer. "You're still driving that piece of shit car."

Max smiled. Boomer hadn't changed. He was the same solid rock of a man he remembered from so many years ago. He slapped him on the shoulder. "It's a classic."

"Damn, man, you smell like you've already had a drink or two without me. What the hell is going on, Max?"

"You're right. Don't need another drink. Mind if we just sit out here for a bit?"

"Sure, brother."

They walked around to the side of the building and sat on a low retaining wall facing the train tracks. Another freight train passed by in the other direction, most likely heading down to the ship channel to get another load.

"So what's going on, man? Haven't seen you since the day I dropped you off at the house. You disappeared."

"Been around."

"You working here in town?" Boomer picked up a stone and threw it in the direction of the train. "Looking for a job? That why you called me? Lots of vets call me looking for some kind of help."

"No, got a job."

"Really? To be honest, man, you don't look too well."

Max looked down at his feet. The swelling in his face was finally going away, but he knew he must have looked rough. His lack of sleep, his recent binge, it was all taking a toll on him. "Wanted to ask you some questions about Afghanistan."

"Dude, that was a long time ago for you."

"I know, but I got some unresolved stuff going on I still need to work out."

"You and everyone else. Got a lot of guys calling to talk about what happened over there."

Max stood up and started to pace back and forth. "You saw my file, didn't you? When I got back, you saw what happened, right?"

"Yeah, I saw it. Wanted to put you up for a Bronze Star, but you wouldn't hear of it."

"You know who the guy was that shot up the place? Asadi. Afghani guard."

"Yeah, what of it?"

Max stopped pacing and turned to face Boomer. "I got a letter from his daughter today."

"What?"

"Actually, it was the second letter I got from her."

"Max, what are you talking about?"

"I'm talking about the gunman that slaughtered half the medical unit had a daughter, and she just sent me a letter. Says I'm responsible for all that death and destruction. For my own injuries. The whole lot."

Boomer looked confused. "I thought the guy only had one daughter."

"He did. Asalah. That's who sent me the letter."

"Bro, that's not possible."

"Believe me, I'm just as surprised. Really messed with my head today."

"No, I believe you when you say you got a letter, but it's not possible that it came from her."

Max raised an eyebrow. "Why?"

"Because she's dead."

"What?"

"She's dead, bro. I thought you knew."

"How would I know? I was blown apart and shipped home."

"Sorry, I just assumed you got a rundown on what'd happened. She stepped out in front of a bus and killed herself."

Max suddenly felt lightheaded and had to sit back down on the retaining wall. He bent over and placed his head between his knees.

"Man, it's all in the report on what happened. When I looked into getting you a commendation, I got the rundown on the whole thing."

"Why didn't you tell me?"

"I did, dude. I told you when you arrived at Brooke." Boomer tossed another stone. "Maybe you were still too out of it to remember. They did have you pretty drugged up while you were there. Always trying to pull your tubes out and run out of the place. Never occurred to me that you didn't remember what I was telling you."

Max straightened up. "So, tell me now. What the hell happened?"

"Well, looks like someone was supplying Asadi with drugs. Got him pretty damn hooked, apparently. When whoever it was found out he had a daughter, he raped her."

"What? How the hell did they find that out?"

"Big attack like that doesn't go uninvestigated. They went to the house. His wife was obviously distraught. Lost a husband and a daughter."

"So she told them all this?"

"Not really. Of course, she didn't want to disgrace the memory of her daughter in the village." He shook his head. "It's crazy; they're all related, you know." He dug his shoe in the dirt and picked up another stone. He threw it hard, and they watched as it clanked off the steel rail of the train track. "She felt someone had been slipping her husband drugs from the hospital for a while. He'd been acting erratically for some time, and she didn't know why. Then her daughter told Asadi something just before he went off in a rage. When they went through her stuff, they found some notes suggesting that someone had gotten to her. Mom spun the whole attack as a patriotic act against the infidels to save face."

"What happened to the mother?"

"Funny, she was right. She was taken care of. If it got out that her daughter had been raped by a soldier, she'd have been shunned."

"So who the hell sent me these letters? Obviously not her."

"Don't know, brother. Maybe someone who likes messing with people's heads. But it wasn't her."

"Shit." Max stood and walked down to the edge of the train tracks. Another train was headed in his direction.

Boomer stood and jogged the few steps it took to catch up to Max. He grabbed him by the upper arm and held him firmly as they watched the train pass feet from their faces.

Max continued to stare into the darkness long after the train had moved on. Boomer eventually let go of his arm and stood silently by his side.

"Thanks, Boomer," he said as he turned away from the darkness. "I think I know what to do now."

Boomer frowned at him. "You're not going to do anything stupid, are you?"

"I'm always doing stupid, impulsive things. Seems to be my curse. Just this time, I think I have a little direction."

"You have my number, Max. You know you can call me anytime."

"I know. It's been a long time, but you're still a good friend and I appreciate you."

Boomer placed his arm around Max's shoulder and walked him back to his car. "Get in this piece of shit and get on back home. Get some rest. You had nothing to do with what happened back there. Just some screwed-up psycho messing with you. Let it go and move on."

"Wish I could, but I don't seem to be able to let anything go. I'll sort this out one way or another. It's been really good seeing you again. Now get back to that wife of yours. Remember you have to work tomorrow."

Max climbed back in the Nova and drove off into the dark city streets. Maybe tomorrow he could go sniff around Simkins office and find his file. He'd said he had his record from the VA and the toxicology report on Asadi. Would be nice to see the whole report. Maybe he could move on as Boomer suggested if he could just see what the investigation really said.

Chapter 33

The Present

That night, the lights never went out. At least Rosa assumed it was night. She huddled under the thin sheet that covered the bed. The temperature in the room had plummeted since she'd made fun of the dress her captor had wanted her to wear.

She contemplated her next move. She needed a way to get out of the room. It was obvious that there were no inherent weaknesses in her cell. The door was solid and the window unbreakable. She'd tried chipping at the walls with some of the broken metal parts from the television, but they appeared to be cinder block, and she couldn't make even the slightest dent in them.

Her stomach ached with hunger. She knew it was much easier for her jailer to outlast her, so she needed a different plan. Freezing and starving were not going to get her out. If anything, they might get her killed.

Finally she sat up on the edge of the bed, the sheet wrapped tightly around her shoulders. "All right, you win. Warm the place up and give me some food and I'll entertain your sick friends."

Rosa heard the speakers crackle to life as her captor pressed his mouth close to the microphone. "Good. I'm glad to see you're finally being reasonable." She could hear a chair squeak. "I just turned down the air conditioning. It should be getting warmer soon."

"I'm hungry."

"One thing at a time. I did something for you. Now you need to do something for me."

Rosa cringed, but she knew she had to start playing him if she was going to get out. "Okay, what do your sick friends want me to do?"

Rosa could hear the rustle of papers as if he were reading instructions. "Okay, now go up to the mirror on your vanity and kiss it."

"What?"

"You heard what I said! Kiss the mirror like you're kissing your boyfriend."

"I don't have a boyfriend."

"Even better. Kiss it like your first kiss with your first boyfriend!"

Rosa tossed her sheet to the side and strode to the mirror. She made a pouty face and whispered, "I love you, big boy. You're *muy grande*." She then put her face up to the glass and kissed it with a big, wet kiss.

"That's what I'm talking about. Pure gold."

Rosa returned to the bed and wrapped the sheet around herself. "Now I want my food."

"Please step into the bathroom, and dinner will be served."

Rosa walked into the bathroom. She could hear the door automatically lock as she climbed up on the counter. She pressed her face up to the glass. Once again, she could barely make out the man's image backlit with the red lights. "Now!" she shouted. She could see that she'd startled him.

The black shade slowly lowered once again, blocking her tormentor from view.

Rosa could hear the main door unlock and the food being placed on her bed. She was starving, but if her plan was to work, she knew she couldn't eat that night.

When the bathroom door unlocked, she walked into the main room and tried the door to see if her captor had accidentally left it unlocked.

No such luck. The door was solidly secured as before. She kicked it in frustration, then moved to the bed and sat beside the tray of food. It smelled good, and the pain in her stomach made her want to eat it and just forget the plan and try again tomorrow. But then she saw the photo of her house with the orange front door lying on the floor. It was no longer a threat for her but a reason to keep fighting. She looked up and around the room, knowing that she was being watched. She took a small bite of food and slowly started chewing it.

The lights in the room slowly dimmed. When the room was completely dark, she spit the food out on the far side of the bed away from the door. She scraped the remaining food onto the floor and placed the tray back on the bed. She took her pillow and shoved it under the sheet, then quietly walked to the vanity beside the door, crouched down, and waited. She knew someone came in every night. She just needed to be patient.

To her surprise, she didn't need to wait very long. She heard footsteps outside the door, then the key turn in the lock.

The drugs must normally work quite quickly, she thought.

But tonight, her captor was going to be surprised.

The door swung open, shielding Rosa from view. She saw the man come to the bed and pick up the empty tray. The dim light from the hallway did not reveal the food dumped on the floor on the far side of the bed. She watched as he stared down at the lump under the sheets. She was surprised when he placed the tray back down and sat on the edge of the bed.

Rosa knew this was the time she needed to go, but she hesitated. She couldn't take her eyes off him. She hated what he was doing to her. Hated the anguish he was putting her family through. She watched as he put his hand on the pillow and slowly started to stroke it.

Then he paused. He stood up suddenly, knocking the tray to the floor. With both hands, he reached down and pulled back the sheet, revealing the deception.

Before he could turn, she squeezed around the open door and bolted down the dimly lit narrow corridor.

What confronted her was confusing. This was not the nice house she'd first been taken to. She came to a doorway at the end of the corridor and tried to open it, but it was locked. She started violently kicking the door as the man stepped from the room.

"Help me!" she screamed. "*Ayuda!*"

To her surprise, someone on the other side turned the latch, and the door swung open.

"You okay?" a young, disheveled man asked. "Was just leaning up against the door and heard you kicking. Sorry, didn't see the sign."

Rosa didn't stop to talk. She pushed past him and ran down the hallway in the direction of what she hoped was a way out. Along the way, she jumped over several people lying on the floor. When she burst through the front door, she realized two things: it was late at night, and it was definitely not the nice neighborhood that the man had initially driven her through. Several people were sitting in cars scattered around the parking lot, but none of them took notice of her.

She walked along the front of the building until she came to a corner. Next to the building was a large thicket of bushes and an empty, overgrown lot. She ducked into the bushes and disappeared in the darkness.

Chapter 34

The Present

Max arrived at work the next day, on time and sober. His head still hurt, but that was to be expected. He felt the need to work. Boomer had created more questions than answers about his fateful night in Afghanistan, and work was going to help him sort his head out.

He walked through the emergency room, looking for something to do. As the attending surgeon, his job was to do the big things and let the residents do the minor stuff, but that morning, the place was slow, and he felt like cutting someone. "Margo, what have you got in the rooms today?"

The charge nurse glared at him over the brim of her cup of coffee. She put it down on the desk as she fumbled through her list of patients. "Well, Dr. Donovan, you must be bored if you're asking for work." She squinted as she tried to read the list.

Max smiled. Margo had been an old-timer in the emergency room long before he'd arrived, but she refused to wear her reading glasses. She was frequently heard saying that reading glasses were for old women, and she was not old. Her lipstick was thick and her makeup comical, but she was a good nurse. Knew her stuff, and that was all that mattered.

"Let me see . . . there's a fractured tibia in room seven. Waiting for the orthopedic resident to get down here for that." She paused and took another sip from her lipstick-stained cup. "Room nine has a slipped disc and can't get up. Hum, oh, here's a good one for a big-time surgeon like yourself. Room three has a large buttock abscess. Needs draining, but the general surgery residents are on rounds and said they would be a while."

Max frowned. "Well, I guess it'll be my good deed for the day. Please have the nurse get the minor surgical tray ready with some local anesthetic."

Max pulled the chart from the rack. Rodrigues: diabetes, hypertension. Four-day history of pain. Weight: 375. *Well, probably better I did it anyway. Residents would struggle with this one.*

Max walked across the emergency department and stood in front of the door to room three. He sniffed the air and caught the slightest whiff of dead tissue and infection. He thought it funny how non-surgeons couldn't smell it, but he could. The smell of gangrene—that same smell you get when driving in the car downwind from roadkill.

He took a deep breath, then strode into the room. He found the patient lying on her side on a narrow emergency-room bed. "Ms. Rodrigues, I'm Dr. Donovan, surgeon. I'm here to see you about that boil you've got on your backside."

Ms. Rodrigues tried to turn to see Max, but she was too large and in too much pain to move very much. "*Si, gracias. Mucho dolor.*"

Max noticed a young lady sitting quietly in the corner. "Hello. I'm sorry I didn't see you sitting there. Who are you?"

"She's my daughter, Conchita. She helped me get here today."

Conchita sat quietly looking at her mother. Max gave her a sideways look. There was something very familiar about her, but he just couldn't place where he'd seen her before. She was quite pretty, but the lines on her face and the few streaks of gray in her hair told of a hard life. "Well, Ms. Conchita, are you okay watching while I drain this abscess?"

"Yes, I'm fine."

The nurse brought in the minor surgical tray and placed it on a tray stand.

Max glanced at her. "Please help me retract her buttocks so I can get a better look."

The nurse lifted the patient's gown, and together, they pried apart her buttocks. A large, fluctuant boil lay close to her anus.

"Hurts a lot, I bet."

"*Dios mio!* I've never had such pain. Please make it stop, Doctor."

Max quickly cleaned the area with antiseptic, injected the surrounding skin with local anesthetic, then stabbed the boil with a scalpel. There was an immediate gush of pus that flowed across the bed. The room immediately filled with a ghastly, rancid smell.

"Oh, thank you. I already feel better."

Max cleaned up what he could, then went to the sink to wash his hands.

"Dios mio, is that smell from me?"

"I'm afraid so. That's why you felt so bad. Don't wait so long next time."

"We should have come earlier, but we have no insurance. I was putting Vicks rub on it, but it wouldn't go away."

Max laughed. "Vicks can't cure everything, you know."

"My daughter kept telling me that, but I didn't know what else to do." She sighed. "You know she was going to be a nurse."

"Mama, be quiet."

"No, I won't!" She tried to look over her shoulder at her daughter. "She was good at school. Always got *A*'s."

"Please, Mama, they don't want to hear about all that. Let's just get out of here and go."

Max turned and looked at the two of them. He could see the resemblance, minus a few pounds. "Never too late to try, Conchita. It's a great profession."

Ms. Rodrigues grabbed the nurse by the hand as she pulled the sheet over her torso. "She was really smart, and pretty just like you. All until she met that damn boyfriend of hers."

"You're going to have to find your own way home if you don't stop right now."

"Fine, leave your mother here. That bastard Juan ruined you." She shook her head. "Used you like a piece of meat." She started to cry. "My beautiful daughter; damn piece of meat!"

Max didn't want to get in the middle of their argument. "Ms. Rodrigues, you're going to feel better now that the abscess is drained. I'm going to put you on some antibiotics and send you to the surgical floor. If things are much better tomorrow, I might send you home."

Ms. Rodrigues continued to cry. "*Gracias a Dios* for *El Chancho*. He saved my daughter."

Max was turning to leave, then stopped. A chill ran down his spine. "The what?"

"El Chancho. The pig-man saved my daughter."

Conchita stood to leave. "You've said way too much, Mama."

"He put that *hijo de perra* in the hospital. Should have killed him," she snarled. "But Juan left my daughter alone after that."

Now Max knew where he'd seen Conchita before. She was working the corner when he took a baseball bat to her pimp's ankles. "The pig-man?"

"Si. El Chancho. He wears a pig mask. People are afraid of him."

"People? What people?"

"People on the street." She finally was able to roll over and look at her daughter. "People who are now better off because they come home at night and are going to go back to school."

Conchita looked down at her feet. "Si, Mama. You're right."

Max paused and turned toward Conchita. "Well, maybe it was a sign to get your life back on track. Make the best of it." He walked out of the room and across to the nurse's station to write orders for her admission. *So that's what they call me. El Chancho.* He smiled, while at the same time, he felt terrified. It was a part of what he'd become that he didn't often acknowledge to himself. He was the surgeon. Did his work and went home. What he occasionally did when the horrors of life seemed too much, he desperately tried to suppress. Dr. Simkins was supposed to help him with that. That was why he'd asked Jernigan if he knew a good psychiatrist. The trustworthy respected surgeon in him wanted help stopping El Chancho's rampages.

Max tossed his pen across the desk. What the hell was Simkins really doing? Boomer had told him the truth. Maybe the only person in a long time to tell him something worthwhile about his past. Simkins was just ripping the wounds open and watching him bleed.

Max left the emergency department and stopped in the doctors' lounge to get a cup of coffee. A television hung high on the wall over a row of shelves stacked with worn magazines and discarded coffee cups. Along one wall was a large sofa with a resident sleeping on it. Half a dozen four-top tables scattered about the room were covered with discarded drinks and wrappers. Max hated how lazy some doctors could be. They could work all night saving lives but couldn't pick up their trash and walk it ten feet to the garbage.

He sat down at the only clean table and stared mindlessly at the television. The local news was warning that it was still hurricane season and to be prepared. Max didn't have to worry. He had County, and that was probably the safest place in Houston in a big storm.

His ears perked up when the next story had a strangely familiar ring to it.

"Early this morning, police officers pulled the body of a young female from Buffalo Bayou. She's been identified as Debbie McGuire, resident of the Fifth Ward, who has been missing for several days. Family members had been suspicious of foul play after she didn't return home from work."

Max stared at the picture of the young woman on the screen. It was the girl at the reception desk at Nick Jernigan's place!

What the hell?

He got up and walked over to the television and stood staring at the picture as he sipped his coffee. Soon, the story turned to one of a puppy adoption drive in Pearland, and Max turned away.

So the girl that sold me a little smack ends up floating in the bayou. What do you think of that, Max old boy? There's always been something messed up about Jernigan's little clinic. The people always hanging around. Drugs being dispensed from the front desk.

Max crumpled his now-empty coffee cup. He cringed at the thought of another night prowling as El Chancho, but he couldn't help himself. He knew he wouldn't be able to rest until he had another look at Jernigan's place. This time, he wouldn't let them get the jump on him. But first, he needed to see what was in the report that Simkins said he had.

That evening, the emergency room was quiet for a change. The autumn chill always kept people inside, which meant fewer shootings, stabbings, and generalized mayhem. The hallways were empty except for the occasional resident wandering about looking for a place to sleep.

During a break, Max crossed the skybridge that connected the county hospital to the professional building where Simkins' office was located. He paused to look out the windows at the traffic passing below.

They don't know we're in here just waiting for something bad to happen to them, he thought.

The ones who didn't die were going to need him to put them back together. The idea that he was the one to keep those fortunate enough to make it from a wreck to the hospital alive didn't ease his mind. He would do what needed to be done when the time came, but at that moment, he was focused on Simkins.

As he passed through the silent corridors, a smile came to his face. Just what the doctor ordered. A cleaning cart was crammed in the front door to Simkins's office, propping it open. The cleaning staff were the only ones that had access to all the offices, and Max was hoping that he could catch them before they finished.

"Hola," he said to the young woman as he squeezed past the cart and into the office where she was vacuuming the carpet. "Forgot something in my office."

She smiled the smile of someone who didn't understand and kept going about her business.

Max closed the door to Simkins' office behind him.

"Where the hell do I start?"

He turned on the computer but didn't expect to find much. He knew he wasn't a genius computer hack like you see in the movies, and after putting a few random words and numbers into the password box, he decided to turn it off and look for some old-fashioned tangible clues.

First, he went to the file-room door and tried to open it. Not surprisingly, it was locked. Had to have a key somewhere. He returned to the desk and opened the center top drawer. What he found was not the report he was looking for but something much worse. His mouth fell open as his shaking hand reached in and pulled out a sheet of thick, cream-colored stationery like the one Asalah supposedly had written her letter on.

"Son of a bitch!" He lifted the sheet of paper to the light and saw the familiar scratchy handwriting of Dr Jernigan.

I am sending you a colleague of mine, Max Donovan. A real head case. Don't think you can help this one.

Max was glad he didn't have his bat, because if he had, he'd have destroyed the office. He stood shaking with rage as he stared at the paper.

"Jernigan's been playing me. Screwing with my head."

Max didn't need to see anything else. He knew his past. No need to find his file. What the doc had written in it didn't matter anymore. Boomer had cleared up some of his questions, not Simkins. Why Jernigan was jerking him around he didn't know, but he was going to find out.

Max closed the drawer and slipped out of the office while the cleaning woman was in the adjoining bathroom. He headed back to County and went to his call room and lay down.

The rest of the night, he lay staring at the ceiling, trying hard not to go out into the darkness as El Chancho and do something to Jernigan he would later regret.

Chapter 35

The Present

Rosa crouched in the bushes and watched as the man burst through the door and started shouting orders. The parking lot emptied. Her tormentor looked desperate as he paced back and forth in front of her prison. Through the thick foliage, she could barely make out the figures of men running by. Several cars screeched their tires as they raced from the lot, fanning out in different directions.

She desperately tried to slow her breathing. It was chilly out, but the bugs were still thick in the air, and she tried not to shake as mosquitos buzzed by her ears. She felt that her best chance of getting away was to stay where she was for a little while. They would assume she was running, so that would give her a chance to circle back and go where they wouldn't expect. She had no idea what time of night it was or what part of the city she was in.

Once the lot was empty and she'd seen the man go back inside, she crawled under the thick shrubbery that ran along a broken wooden fence that separated the strip mall from the adjacent overgrown lot. She hated crawling in the dirt. The black soil caked her hands and the knees of her jeans. When she wiped her face, the dirt got in her eyes. Mama would be so upset if she'd known how filthy she was.

Rosa eventually came to a small hollow that abutted the fence. At the base of it was a deep, narrow hole.

Probably the home of an armadillo or raccoon, she thought.

She dared to look out through the bushes to get a better understanding of her surroundings. Just over the tops of the tall grass and weeds, she saw that at the far side of the lot was an abandoned shack, its roof partially collapsed, and the windows and door long gone.

They'll be looking for me in there, she thought.

Better to stay here for a little longer.

As soon as she pulled her head back into the bushes, she saw flashlight beams darting across the lot. She soon heard the trample of feet and the muffled voices of men not happy to be out traipsing through the brush in the middle of the night. As the lights came closer, she slid down into the small hollow and pressed her back hard up against the fence.

Two men came to a stop directly in front of her hiding place. "Damn it," the first one said. "Can't believe we're out in the middle of the night looking for this little bitch."

"Just shut the hell up and find her. I don't want to have to tell the boss that she's gone."

"Fuck the boss."

"Watch what you say." He pulled a cigarette from his pocket and lit it. "You may end up like Debbie."

"Debbie, huh? Well, that was some dumb-ass stunt she pulled."

"She didn't deserve what she got, though."

"You're right about that. The boss can be a bit of a psycho at times."

They stood quietly as the man took a deep drag on his cigarette. Rosa could hardly breathe. She pressed her body deeper into the dirt, trying to keep any bit of herself from showing above the level of the ground.

Suddenly, she noticed something pressing up against her arm. She gasped when she saw a snake come out of the hole and slither alongside her. She put her hand over her mouth and tried not to scream. The snake continued to pass along her side, its head well past her feet when its tail finally emerged from the hole.

"What was that?" asked the man with the cigarette as he pointed his light in Rosa's direction. They both bent down and moved in for a closer look.

"Shit!" shouted the second man as he jumped back. The snake made its way out of the bushes and moved into the deep grass near their feet. "God, I hate snakes, and that was a damn monster! I bet this field is full of them."

"Yeah, you're right. Let's get the hell out of here." They pointed their lights down at the ground as they made their way to the safety of the street.

Rosa finally started to breathe again, and when the voices eventually faded, she poked her head up over the edge of her hiding spot. The sky was just starting to get lighter. Dawn was not too far off, and she needed to move quickly. She looked out across the lot, and now it was much easier to see the abandoned shack. Her gut told her that was not the way to go, but she wanted to get away from the snakes and out of that field. She needed a place to sit and plan her next move.

She crawled along the edge of the fence until she came to a break in the bushes beside the shack. She squatted in the dirt and watched the ruin for any signs of movement. The sun was starting to rise, and the lot was now bathed in an orange glow. She knew that she would easily be seen from the street if she waited much longer. She looked both ways, then bolted from the fence and straight through the doorless entryway and into the crumbling structure.

Inside, it was a mess. The wood floor had rotted, and the floorboards creaked with each step. Several areas had no floor at all, and through the holes, weeds had grown waist high. In one corner, she noticed several rusted gardening tools: a long-handled trowel, a shovel, a rake, some broken clay pots.

Rosa made her way across the unstable floor and squatted down next to the tools, resting her back against the wall. Maybe it had been a mistake not making a run for it and getting as far away as she could while it was still dark. But then again, she had no idea where she was, and all those cars from the lot were out scouring the streets. She probably would've been caught pretty quickly. She rested her head on her knees as she thought about her next move.

The sun was up now, and light filtered in through the collapsed roof and filled the small room with shadows. She raised her head from her knees and stared across the room at the dark far corner. Through the high weeds, she thought she'd seen something move. God, she hoped it wasn't another snake. She hated snakes.

To her horror, a man stood up and stretched his arms over his head. His skin was dark and ruddy, his hair long and sun-bleached gray. A ratty beard dangled from his chin down to the middle of his skinny, naked chest. He walked across the room and stood silently looking out the front door.

Rosa sat motionless as he farted and scratched his backside. She wished she could've disappeared into the wood and found herself pressing her back hard into the wall. Without warning, the long-handled trowel slid from its position beside her and clattered to the floor.

The man jerked his gangly body around and stared directly at Rosa. "Well, well, what do we have here?" he mumbled as he stood blocking the door. "Just what the doctor ordered for breakfast."

Rosa slowly rose to her feet. She kept her eyes fixed on the man as she blindly probed with her hand for one of the gardening tools. Her hand came to rest on the shovel. She gripped it tightly as he started to shamble across the room.

"Don't be afraid, little girl. I won't hurt you. Just want a little hug, that's all. Bobby don't have many friends. Maybe a little kiss, that's all."

Rosa didn't move. He got within a few feet before he raised both arms and lunged for her. She easily sidestepped him as he stumbled face first into the wall.

"Come here, you little whore," he shouted as he regained his balance and turned to face her.

Rosa lifted the shovel over her head and brought it crashing down with all her might onto the side of his face.

"Augh!" He grabbed his face as he stumbled backward, knocking over the clay pots. "You little bitch. Come here!"

She dropped the shovel and bolted for the door and out into the lot. A thin trail ran through the high grass. She darted along it until she came to the edge of the street. Rosa looked up and down the road to see if any of her pursuers were still searching for her. The street was empty.

Across from her was a shotgun shack with peeling white paint. An air conditioner was precariously propped up in the front window, and trash was piled in front by the edge of the street. Burglar bars covered the windows. A car was in the drive, wheelless and lifted up on cinder blocks. Similar houses lined the street, but this one had a light on in one of the front windows.

Behind her, she heard the man stumble out of the shack. "Come back here," he shouted. "I just want a little hug."

Rosa raced across the street and up onto the porch. She started pounding on the front door with both fists. "Ayuda! Help me, please!"

She saw more lights come on, then a clacking sound as if someone had cocked a gun.

"*Por favor!* Help me!"

The door cracked open just enough for her to see the barrel of a shotgun poking through.

"Get the hell away from here or I'll shoot!"

"Please, help me. They're keeping me prisoner across the street. I need to get to the police."

"Who's keeping you where?"

"Those men across the street. They're trying to catch me. I need help. Please let me in."

The door closed briefly. Rosa could hear the door chain being undone, then the door slowly opened. She was greeted by an elderly black man standing barefoot in boxer shorts and a stained sleeveless T-shirt. His gut hung low over his shorts, and his bald head was surrounded by a crown of graying fluff. His face was creased with age, and in his hand dangled a shotgun. Rosa was immediately struck by how tired he looked.

"From across the street, huh? Come on in." He stepped to the side as she entered the front room.

"Please, call the police."

"My, you look a mess. All covered with mud."

"I've been hiding all night."

"Well, don't track all that shit across my floor." He closed the front door and walked toward the back of the house. "Come on, get yourself cleaned up while I make a call." He directed her into the bathroom and closed the door.

Rosa looked at herself in the mirror. Her face was covered with mud, and her hair was matted. She ran the water until it stopped flowing brown, then scrubbed her face with soap. She put her head under the spigot and scrubbed her hair, trying to remove all the clumps of dirt as best she could.

When she finished, she tried the door handle, but the door was locked.

"Hola! The door is stuck." She got no response. She pressed her ear against the door. She could barely hear the old man as he spoke on the phone.

"Hey, I got one of your whores over here at my place. I told you before, I don't want them on my property or in front of my house, you hear. Keep your goddamn business on your side of the street and leave me alone. Yeah, yeah. Get your asses over here now and take care of this shit. I got to get to work."

"What are you doing!" she screamed. "Call the police! They kidnapped me!" Rosa kicked the door and pulled on the handle with all her strength, but it wouldn't budge. She climbed on the toilet above which was a small window. She ripped down the shade and tried to open it, but it wouldn't move. She saw nails hammered into the frame, and on the outside were burglar bars.

As she looked around the small room for any way to escape, she heard the front door open and the sound of footsteps heading toward the bathroom. The door flew open. Rosa screamed as several men pounced on her. They gagged her with duct tape and secured her hands and feet with zip ties. They carried her out the front door and tossed her in the back of a waiting car for the short drive across the street and down to the end of the block.

Rosa heard the old man shouting as her body landed heavily on the back seat. "Keep them bitches of yours on your side of the street. This used to be a nice neighborhood before they started working here."

The ride back to the mall was brief. The car pulled up behind the building, and three men hauled her from the car as she kicked and squirmed as much as she could to make their job more difficult. They carried her through an open back door, and before she knew it, she was back in her cell. They tossed her on the bed like a sack of potatoes, then left her there still bound. The door slammed shut, and once again, she was trapped and alone.

Chapter 36

The Present

Max arrived for his appointment with Dr. Simkins fifteen minutes early. He was clean-shaven and had a pressed white coat and scrubs. He smiled at Lucy and took a seat as he waited for his encounter with the man who was supposed to be helping him.

"I must say, Dr. Donovan, you're looking much better this week," Lucy said with a flirtatious smile. "You must be getting a lot of rest finally."

"Yes. Feeling a lot better about some things. Took a few days off as well."

"It certainly shows. Can I get you something to drink?"

"Sure."

"Coffee?"

"Water would be fine."

Lucy stood and went into the breakroom and returned with a bottle of water. "Here you go, Dr. Donovan." She handed him the bottle and held on to it just a little bit longer than she needed to as he took it from her hand.

Max could tell that she'd dressed for him. She'd looked nice last visit, but today, she was stunning in a tight, short, dark-gray skirt and a loose white blouse opened a little too low for a day at the office. She wore heels that brought her almost up to his height.

"Thank you, Lucy. And please, call me Max."

"Well . . . I'm not sure . . ." She was interrupted by the intercom. She glanced at it, then smiled at him. "Looks like you're up . . . Max." She held the door, gently brushing up against him as he passed.

Always an interesting experience when I come to this office, he thought.

"Good morning, Max," Simkins said. "Have a seat."

"Good morning, Dr. Simkins." Max lay down on the couch.

"Well, Max, how have you been?"

"Good. Sleeping much better."

"I was a little concerned after our last session. You were very upset when you left."

"Yes, I was. But you know, after I let it all out, I felt much better. I've never slept so well."

"Really?"

"Yup. I tossed out all those sleeping pills. Don't need them anymore."

"That's fantastic. I guess we really did have a breakthrough then."

"Yeah. Seeing a lot of things more clearly now."

"How is the stress at work? Handling it better?"

"Work? Not a problem. Took a few days off. Decreased my intensity a bit, and it's made a world of difference."

Max clenched his teeth as he lay on his back listening to the ruffle of papers behind his head. He didn't know why he'd shown up for this visit. What did he expect? It wasn't Simkins who was his problem it was Jernigan. He just couldn't stop thinking about Jernigan sitting behind his machine contemplating ways to mess with him.

"So, Max, any more strange letters?" He turned a page in the file. "You told me at one of our sessions about some Islamic prayer you thought might have come from . . . let's see, her name was Asalah."

"No, never heard another thing." Max crossed his legs and put his hands behind his head. "I guess it was just sent to the wrong address."

"Excellent. I was hoping you would be able to move beyond that. Sometimes we place too much emphasis on coincidences and give them more meaning than they deserve."

Max smiled. "Yeah. Good thing too. That would have really messed with my head if I knew Asalah was still out there trying to get in touch with me."

He remained quiet as Simkins tapped the edge of the chart with his pen. Max finally turned his head to look at Simkins. "Tell me, Doctor, where did you meet Dr. Jernigan?"

The tapping on the chart stopped. "We were in the service together."

"Really? I didn't know you were a vet."

Simkins offered a thin smile. "Well, we're not here to talk about me. It's you I'm here for."

"What do you think of him? Kind of guy you would trust?"

"I don't know him that well. Crossed paths a few times in the officer's mess. Always seemed unhappy. Probably could have used my services if you want to know the truth."

"Do you think he's capable of tormenting someone for the fun of it?"

"That's a strange question."

"I know. But just humor me. Is he capable of that?"

"I don't really know. I would have to sit and examine him. That being said, you know 1% of the population are psychopathic. Very functional. Often in positions of authority. Not the typical one you think about in the movies with bodies buried in the basement but still psychopathic. Total lack of empathy or remorse. Complete disregard of generally accepted standards of morality. People like that often rise high up in the social hierarchy because they are ruthless."

Max shrugged his shoulders and looked down at the floor. "I am feeling better. Don't think I will need to be coming back anytime soon."

"Are you sure? I still get the impression you have a lot of repressed guilt and anger from your past trauma."

"Probably right but let's just leave it on an as needed basis. You okay with that Jack? I have some things I need to sort out and my schedule may be a little irregular in the coming weeks."

"Sure, Max." Dr. Simkins got up from his chair and walked around to his desk and sat down. "You're a very bright man and from what I hear an excellent surgeon. Don't let your past define your future. You have choices."

Max stood and headed for the door. "Unfortunately, some sins of the past can never be erased. They follow you to the grave."

"Well, you know where I work. Come in anytime you feel the need."

Max smiled weakly as he reached for the doorhandle. "Thanks Jack. I will keep you in mind."

He closed the door and struggled to put on a smile for Lucy. "Well, that went great today. He says he doesn't need to see me anymore. I'm a free man."

Lucy smiled and stood up beside her desk. "Well, isn't that wonderful. I never saw a reason for you to be here in the first place." She gently grabbed Max by the hand as she slipped a card into it. "Good luck, and if you need anything, feel free to call me."

Max looked down at the card. It was her personal business card with her cell phone number on it. For a moment he dared to forget all about Jernigan and everything else he'd been struggling with. It'd been so long since he'd been with a woman. So long since he'd had someone to confide in, rely on, be weak with. "Thank you. You'll be the first person I call." Just before turning away, he paused. "By the way, what branch of the service was Simkins in, do you know?"

She smiled. "Special forces. Psyops."

"Lucy, I need you in here right away," crackled the intercom.

Max raised an eyebrow as he turned to look at the closed door leading to Simkins's office. He leaned in close enough to Lucy to smell her sweet neck. "You better get back to work." With that he turned and left, not looking back as he closed the door.

Chapter 37

The Present

Max spent the afternoon sitting on the sofa shirtless, his shredded chest exposed. He stared at the credenza. In his hand rested the remains of the bottle of Jamaican rum. This time, he only sipped it. He didn't want to get drunk. He wanted his wits about him.

As the sun set and the room slowly darkened, he took Lucy's card from his pocket and turned it over and over in his hand. He took another sip, then held the card to his nose. It smelled nice. It was the smell of a beautiful woman. It was the smell of life, of moving on. Of maybe even being happy.

Max was startled by the sudden chirping of his cell phone. The card slipped from his fingers. "Hello, Donovan."

"Hello, Dr. Donovan. I mean Max."

Max closed his eyes as he listened to Lucy's sweet voice. "Hello, Lucy."

She sounded nervous. Her voice shook ever so slightly. "Now that you're no longer a patient, I thought we could maybe, possibly, go get a drink. That is if you're not working or anything."

Max paused. He could have listened to her beautiful voice all night. Forgetting all about Jernigan and his stupid mind games. About the clinic and the thugs out front. He could have just leaned back on the sofa and talked to her about a whole bunch of nothing, just like real lovers do. Maybe even invite her over. Sure would've been a lot better drinking with her than drinking in the dark alone.

Max's eyes moved from the credenza to the coffee table. The edge of the forged Asalah letter stuck out from under the pile of mail. He left Lucy's card on the floor where it had fallen, picked up Jernigan's note, and crumpled it in his hand. "I would love to get together." He paused and took a deep breath. "But tonight, I have something I need to do."

Max could hear the disappointment in her voice. "All right then, but I'm going to hold you to it. You didn't toss my card away, did you?"

"No, I actually have it right her," he replied as he bent down to pick it up. "It smells beautiful like you. How could I lose it."

Lucy laughed. "You have a very curious way of turning a woman down. Please call me when whatever it is that's so important that you make me wait is over."

"Good night, Lucy."

"Good night."

Max leaned back on the sofa. What could be so important? Shit. *One last gig then Lucy I'm yours.*

Max went into his bedroom, where he put on a pair of jeans and a T-shirt. He pulled on his boots, slipped on his knife and Beretta, then walked back out to the living room. He stood silently looking around the room. The credenza with its dusty photographs, the folded American flag, his brother. The rest of the place? Well, the house had come completely furnished. Nothing there was really his. Just what was on the credenza, and that caused him nothing but pain.

He stepped over to the photos and picked up the one of Maria holding the stuffed elephant he'd won for her in Kemah.

You were always right. Always too impulsive. Sorry once again, but I think it's time to kick up a little dust. These people hurt me.

Max took the picture back to his bedroom. He opened the closet door and pulled down an old oak chest with a hinged top from off the shelf and opened it. Inside was a stack of neatly folded soft cloths. He wrapped her picture in one of the cloths, then carefully placed it inside. He carried the chest to the living room and packed it with the photographs, wrapping each one individually with a cloth. Finally, he rested the box containing the flag on top, closed the chest, and latched it.

Max walked out to the garage and opened the trunk of the Nova and placed the chest down on the floor. There was a sudden flash of lightning, followed immediately by a thunderclap that shook the garage. Rain started falling heavily.

Max paused and looked out the garage door as the wind whipped the trees along the street into a frenzy. It was going to be a bad one. He went around to the front of the garage and grabbed the baseball bat. He reached deep inside the dark hole behind the pegboard and pulled out the mask. He slid behind the wheel and laid them down on the back seat. He instinctively reached for his ankle and felt the firm handle of his knife, then reached into the small of his back and removed the Beretta and placed it at his feet. For some reason, he felt he would not be coming back that night the same.

Chapter 38

The Present

Rosa lay face down on the bed for what felt like hours. Her hands were going numb, and the tape over her mouth made it hard to breathe. Finally, the door burst open, and the three men that had dragged her from the house and tossed her in the car stormed into the room.

One of the men, bald, muscular, covered in tattoos, barked at Rosa. "The boss says you can be untied if you behave." He proceeded to pull the tape from around her mouth. She tried to spit the glue out as one of the other men pulled out a knife. She lay motionless as the blade sliced through her bindings. When they were done, the men quickly left and slammed the door shut.

Rosa sat up on the side of the bed and gently rubbed her hands, trying to get some sensation back.

The speakers crackled to life. "Welcome back."

Rosa said nothing.

"I hope you enjoyed your little tour of the neighborhood, but please don't try anything like that again."

Rosa stood and jumped up and down several times as she shook her arms and legs back and forth. She walked around the room as the speakers crackled. She could hear his heavy breathing and the occasional squeak of his chair.

"Any more noncompliance from you, and our little program may have to be abruptly canceled until we have a new cast for next season. Do you understand, young lady?"

Rosa bent down and picked up the crumpled picture of her home from the floor and shoved it in her pocket. She reached up and pulled the locket from underneath her shirt and opened it. She smiled as she looked at her family. Her parents so proud. Little Miguel so much trouble but so sweet. She looked around at her prison. The shattered television still on the floor by the window, its cart broken in several pieces. The vanity. The cold bed.

"Do you understand? You need to behave and do what I ask."

Rosa tilted her head back and screamed at the top of her lungs: "No!" She walked over to the television cart and picked up one of the broken legs from the floor, then went to the vanity mirror and started beating it with the wooden leg until the glass shattered. "Oh, there you are," she said as she pressed her face up to the small, exposed camera. "Do you love me now, big boy? I know just what your little friends find sexy."

Rosa went into the bathroom and climbed up on the counter in front of the large mirror. She pressed her face once again tight up against the glass. She could barely make out her tormentor, backlit in faint red light. Emotionless, staring back. She gasped as out the darkness a second man appeared. He leaned on the desk next to the microphone and stared back at her.

"So how do you like the show?" She pulled down her pants and squatted over the sink and defecated. She stood up and pounded on the glass. "Find that sexy? TV viewership going through the roof?" She reached into the sink and took a handful of shit and started smearing it across the glass. "How about now? How are the ratings? Making any money tonight?"

Rosa heard a heavy sigh come over the speakers. It was the voice of the second man. It was cold, emotionless. "I think it is time for the final episode before this series is canceled. I'm sorry that we've not been able to come to an understanding of what we needed from you. Goodbye."

Rosa continued to bang on the mirror. "Let me go! Let me go!"

She suddenly heard the door to the next room open. In stepped the bald, tattooed man.

Chapter 39

The Present

Max backed out of the garage and headed through the peaceful neighborhood and into the evening rush hour traffic. There was a chill in the air, and the downpour inundating the city was already causing small pools of water to accumulate on the feeder roads.

He drove out of West University and toward the Fifth. The drone of rain on the roof drowned out any apprehension or forethought. He was just going to go. He'd been there before. He knew who was going to be there. He'd gotten a good look at their faces. The faces of those who broke his ribs. The faces of those who watched the young girl as she walked the street corner.

Max also knew who else would most likely be there: Jernigan. His old friend who thought it entertaining to send him a letter to make him think Asalah was still alive and blaming him for the death of her father. The man whose secretary mysteriously ended up floating in the bayou soon after he found out she'd been selling drugs from the front office.

Max thought it was about time Nick explained himself.

Max crossed town and got on Route 59, only to sit and wait as a tow truck lifted a white pickup off the center barrier where it had wrecked. When the truck was finally moved, Max was able to get going again and eventually got off on the side street leading to the clinic. The ponding was starting to get significant, and he plowed through the water of the side streets, not wanting to approach the mall from the main front road.

He slowed his car to a crawl as he peeked its nose around the corner. He leaned over the dash to get a better view through the downpour. There was only one car parked in front: an old green Chevy Impala. From his vantage point, he could see that there was an alley that ran the entire length behind the strip mall.

"What the hell am I doing here?"

Just then, the orange metallic Cadillac DeVille flew through the rain and came to a halt in front of the clinic. Three men bolted from the car and ran inside.

Max knew who those men were, and they owed him. He didn't question himself again. He turned into the alleyway and parked, then reached into the back seat and grabbed the bat and mask. He pulled the mask over his face. It still reeked of the sweat and dirt from the last time he'd worn it. He slipped the Beretta into the small of his back.

"Here we go."

He opened the car door and stepped into the tempest. He jogged along the back of the mall, hugging the wall as he tried to stay as dry as possible. Piles of uncollected trash lined the alleyway, and several rats scurried across his path. When he got to a spot where he suspected it backed up to the clinic, he started trying the multiple doors that exited the mall, but all of them were locked.

Close to one door, he saw a large, strange-looking window that had a black vinyl covering on it. It lined up perfectly with where he would have expected Jernigan's clinic to be. The door beside it was locked.

He pressed his ear up to the glass, but with the sound of the pouring rain, he couldn't hear anything. He pushed on it to see if it would give, but it was solid. He reached down and pulled out his knife, then stuck it under a corner of the material and tried to peel it up. It was surprisingly hard to etch, but he was eventually able to make a cut in it. A bright light shone through the small tear. He continued to dig at it until he was able to peel up a small corner. Then he pressed his eye up to the glass. It took a moment for his eye to adjust to the blinding bright light.

When he could eventually see, he gasped and took a step back.

"Oh, God!"

He pressed his face against the glass again, and this time he came face-to-face with a young girl. She was pounding on the window. He could tell that she was screaming, but he could hear nothing.

He took off the pig mask and looked again. This time he could see that there was a man in the room. He was bald and muscular, covered in tattoos. Max remembered him from the parking lot sitting in the Cadillac with his two buddies. The one who blew him a kiss after he'd bashed his face in the night before. He was one of the men Max had come for. He was taking his shirt off as the girl continued to pound on the glass with her fists.

Max let the mask drop to the ground. He went to the nearest door and tried to force it open with his shoulder, but it wouldn't budge. He kicked the handle, but still nothing. He reached around and pulled out his Beretta and fired two rounds into the lock. He kicked it again, and this time the door burst open.

Max stepped inside and found himself in the back of the clinic. He vaguely remembered the layout and rapidly moved down the hallway in the direction of where he thought the girl should be. He holstered the Beretta and spun the bat in his fingers. He peered around the corner and down the hallway with the door that had the big red sign on it. He noticed that the door was being held open by another one of the men from the Cadillac.

His back was turned to Max, and he was talking with someone who must have been farther down the hallway. "No, you little fucker, I'm next. I'm not following you, you piece of shit."

Max came up behind the man and tapped him on the shoulder.

The man turned. "What the hell!"

Max spun the bat around before he could say another word, striking him across the side of the head. He dropped like a sack of turnips. The second man stood frozen. He was big, but Max had dealt with bigger. His hair was buzz-cut short, a teardrop tattooed under his eye.

Max stepped into the hallway and raised the bat. Just as he was about to bring it crashing down, a door toward the end of the hallway opened and out stepped Jernigan. Max hesitated as their eyes met. Jernigan, his reading glasses dangling from the tip of his nose, his gray hair a shaggy mess, turned and bolted back into the room.

Excruciating pain rippled through Max's jaw as the man's fist connected with his face. Max dropped the bat to the floor as he fell. The man fell on him, pinning him down. He began striking his face viciously. During the fall, Max's leg had crumpled up to his side. He reached down with one hand while trying to block the blows with his other. He pulled out his knife and thrust it deep into the man's flank. The man sat straight up, the pain seeming to paralyze him. Max shoved the knife in further and pushed him off to the side. The man curled up in a ball after Max pulled the knife out and cleaned it against his leg.

He wiped the blood from his eyes, then picked up his bat and raced down the hallway in the direction of Jernigan's room. The door was locked. He tried to kick it open, but it wouldn't budge. He pulled out his gun and was about to shoot the lock as he had done before when he heard the faint screams of the girl coming from the next door over.

He momentarily forgot about Jernigan and stepped over to the next room. Again, the door was locked. He stepped back and fired several rounds into the lock and kicked the door open. When he stepped into the room, he found the young girl standing on one side of a bed. The large man he'd seen through the window was now completely naked. He'd been taken by surprise by the interruption and stood motionless, staring at Max.

Max smiled, puckered his lips, and blew him a kiss. He then swung the bat as hard as he could, bringing it up between the man's legs. He could hear a loud snap as the bat broke his pelvis. The man's face was blue as he crumpled to the ground without a sound.

Max stepped over the writhing body and put out his hand. "Are you okay?"

The girl was shaking. "*Sí.*"

"Come with me."

The girl hesitated. "Are you here to save me?"

"Yes. My name is Max. You can trust me."

"Are you going to call the police?"

"Yes."

"Are you going to get that bad man?"

Max paused. He realized that Jernigan must have seen what had happened. "Yes, but we need to move quickly, or he may get away."

"I want you to get him." She jumped across the bed, and they both headed down the hallway toward the door with the red sign.

Max caught a glimpse of Jernigan's back as he ran through the door. Max sprinted ahead of the girl and saw Jernigan dip into his office. He burst through the office door, only to be greeted by a chair that Jernigan smashed over his back. Max fell to his knees as his gun flew from his back holster and onto the floor. Jernigan raised his foot and kicked Max hard in the ribs. They'd hardly started to heal, and Max felt them snap again. He tried to take a breath but couldn't.

He looked to his side and saw that Jernigan had raised the chair again and was about to bring it crashing down on his head, when suddenly he froze.

Max staggered to his feet to find the girl standing in the doorway, holding his gun and pointing it at Jernigan.

"Now, Rosa, you don't want to do anything stupid with that thing," Jernigan said as he slowly lowered the chair and placed it on the floor.

"It's okay," Max said as he reached for the gun. "We've got him."

Rosa took a step back and waved the gun at Max. "*No se mueva* or I'll shoot!"

"I'm your friend. I'm here to get you away from this creep."

"Do you know him?"

"Yes."

"Weren't you the other man that was just sitting with him in his little hole behind the mirror?"

Max turned and glared at Jernigan. "Who else was here?"

Jernigan said nothing.

"Who was it?" Max was enraged by his silence. He looked at Rosa. "Don't let him move." He stormed out of the room and quickly returned with a large blood pressure cuff. He tossed it at Jernigan. It struck him in the chest and fell to the floor. He then turned to Rosa. "Shoot him."

"Huh?"

"Shoot him!"

Rosa's hand trembled.

Max stepped up to her and snatched the gun from her hand. "Who was here?" he shouted again at Jernigan.

Jernigan, his hunched body turned slightly so he could look directly at Max, stared defiantly back and said nothing.

Max fired three rounds in quick succession into Jernigan's right leg.

He screamed as he crumpled to the floor. A pool of blood accumulated next to his writhing body. "Oh my God, you shot me! I'm bleeding!"

"See that blood pressure cuff? Better put it around your leg and pump it up pretty quickly or you're going to bleed to death."

Jernigan crawled across the floor and picked up the cuff from where it had fallen. His leg was fractured at the knee and twisted awkwardly backward as he struggled to lift the limp extremity. He whimpered in pain. Once the cuff was around his thigh, he pumped it up as quickly as his weakening hands could until it was tight enough to stem the flow of blood.

"Who was here and where did they go?" Max demanded.

"Fuck you, you screwed-up dick of a surgeon. Fuck you."

Max fired another round into the leg with the tourniquet.

Jernigan screamed in pain. "Oh my God!"

"Next few rounds will be in your other leg. And unfortunately, I wasn't able to find another blood pressure cuff. You run this place pretty cheaply. Couldn't get another cuff, Nick? Or maybe you just never took any vitals. This was just all show for your little drug mill you had running here. Right?"

"Damn, this hurts." Jernigan tried to move his remaining good leg away from an easy shot, but he couldn't.

"Well, Nick?" Max raised the gun again.

"Okay, okay, for God's sake, don't shoot me again." Jernigan grimaced. "So I ran a little pill mill. So what? They wanted it. I supplied it." He gnashed his teeth as he pounded his fist on the floor. "Son of a bitch, this hurts." His eyes darted between Max and Rosa. "Who the hell cares anyway? No one cares about these people. I might as well make a little money off them."

Max took a step closer to Jernigan, this time pointing the gun toward his head. "Who else was here?"

"He chuckled. It was Simkins, your little mental friend."

Max's eyes opened wide, his bloodied nostrils flaring. "My mental friend? You sent me to him, you bastard!"

"Yeah, sorry. My bad. But you were always such a goody-goody. You make me sick. I asked him how to screw with you. The snow-white perfect surgeon. War hero. Girlfriend waiting back at home while I rotted over there." He turned his head away and spit some blood across the floor. "Gave me that cute idea of sending you those little notes from our dead Afghan girl. He really is a good psychiatrist. Didn't expect you to find out about this though."

Max's face, already red from his earlier pummeling, was now glowing with anger. "You don't think what happened to me in Afghanistan was enough, you shit?"

Jernigan groaned. "You know, Max, I think I've lost quite a bit of blood here. Feeling kind of woozy. Maybe you could send for some help?"

"You were there in Afghanistan. You know what I went through."

"Oh, by the way, it was also Simkins that fucked with the head of your buddy, Asadi. Kept slipping him drugs until he got him hooked." Jernigan's eyes started to drift back in his head. "Made him a little unstable, to say the least. Son of a bitch almost got me too. Thank God for that damn thick-ass piece of shit army anesthesia machine I dove behind. Can take a bullet, that's for sure."

Max pulled out his cell phone. "Tell me where Simkins went, and I'll call 911."

Jernigan's head drooped to the side. "Probably went on home. He left just before you came storming in. You missed him by a few minutes."

"Where does he live?" Max walked across the room and snatched a post-it pad off the desk and handed Jernigan a pen. "Write it down."

He scribbled out the address and weakly passed it back to Max. "Go get him. Have fun. Bastard ruined my life as well. Held that deal of me raping that pretty bit of Afghan ass over my head my entire damned life. Made me do this," he said as he pointed his nose in Rosa's direction. "Hate that piece of shit." He slid to the floor, his head resting in the pool of blood that surrounded his body.

Max dialed 911 and gave the dispatcher the address and the number of casualties, as well as a detailed description of their injuries. He then handed the phone to Rosa. "You go and hide until you see the police come in, then tell them your story. Understand?"

Rosa nodded.

"You don't leave with anyone else except the police."

She drew a deep, steadying breath, then nodded again.

Max stepped over to Jernigan and felt for a pulse. It was weak, but he was still alive. Max pumped up the blood pressure cuff some more and made sure there was currently no active bleeding getting through the tourniquet. He turned to Rosa and smiled, then walked out into the hallway and was gone.

Chapter 40

The Present

Rosa stood by the door, shaking. She held the cell phone tightly in her hand as she watched Max leave. She didn't want him to go. He was the only one so far who had really tried to help her. In the distance, she could hear the faint sound of sirens. Her heart raced. Were they good police, or were they paid by her captor and just going to lock her up and use her like the man Max had shot?

"Ah." The man on the floor groaned. His eyes were closed and his breathing shallow. Every so often, his whole body would jerk, then become still once again. His leg was twisted in a way that made it hard for her to look at, but at least the bleeding had stopped.

When Rosa heard the sirens stop, she remembered what Max had told her. *Hide until you're sure it's the police and go only with them.*

She looked around the sparsely furnished room for a place to hide. She didn't want to walk near the man on the floor to get to the desk. To her left was a free-standing closet. She went to it, trying not to step in the pool of blood that was slowly spreading across the floor. Inside, she found a rack of white coats. She slid behind them, then closed the door, leaving it cracked just enough so that she could see what was happening.

For a moment, she thought they'd all left. It was completely silent. She could only hear the sound of her own breathing magnified by her small, smelly confines. Then, suddenly, there was a frenzy of activity as dozens of heavily armed men stormed past the doorway.

One stuck his head in the room and pointed a rifle. "We have one in here," she heard him shout into a radio strapped to his chest. "Need the medic."

She could hear the same things happening up and down the hallway as shouts rang out of "all clear," and "medic, stat!"

The man with the rifle stood to the side as a stretcher rolled into the room. A swarm of people picked up her tormentor and placed him on the stretcher and raced him away. He hadn't moved. Maybe he was dead. She hoped so. He deserved it.

To her horror, the man with the gun approached the closet. She pressed her body into the corner behind the coats that reached all the way to the floor. He opened one of the two doors and looked inside, moving one of the coats only inches from her face. She didn't breathe. It was dark, but she couldn't believe that he hadn't seen her. If he'd opened both doors, she surely would've been discovered. He closed the door and left her in the dark. She finally started to breathe again when she heard his footsteps fade into the distance. She cracked the door and waited.

Rosa pulled her face back when she saw two men stop in front of the room. One was tall, with graying black hair and a long gray moustache. He was thick. Not heavy, just thick. Like a bull squeezed into a dark jacket with *police* written across the back. As he turned to look into the room, Rosa saw that his face was pockmarked. He had sad brown eyes that looked as if they'd seen a lot of bad things. The man he was with was smaller and looked much younger. His face was clean-shaven, and he carried a notepad that he wrote in every time the bigger man said something. She tried to hear what they were saying.

The large man stroked his moustache. "You know, I've seen a lot in my fifteen years on the beat here in the Fifth, but this has to take the cake."

Rosa watched as they stepped into the room to let a stretcher pass. The man on the stretcher lay on his back groaning, his hands clutching his groin. She smiled. That was the man who had tried to attack her in the room.

"Don't know what the hell was going on here, Sergeant Juarez," said the smaller officer as he scribbled notes in his pad. "We found that last guy in the back in what looks like some crazy sex room. He was on the floor, naked, holding his dick."

"What's wrong with his dick?"

The officer chuckled. "He didn't really have one anymore. Balls, everything, just one big, squished mess."

Juarez cringed. "Damn. Find anything else down there?"

"Next room over was full of computer equipment. Looks like they were running some kind of porn site."

"Make sure everything goes to forensics, servers, everything," Juarez said as the junior officer continued to scribble notes.

Rosa shifted to get more comfortable. She cringed as the clothes hangers gently clanked together.

"Do we know anything about the person who called in the tip?"

"No, just a male. Had the details of the casualties down to a T, though."

They moved from the doorway and into the room, stopping right in front of Rosa. "Is this where the doctor was found?"

"Yes."

Juarez looked down at his feet, trying to avoid the blood. He continued to stroke his moustache. "Damn, look at all this. You say this guy was still alive?"

"Yeah. Had a blood pressure cuff around his leg that saved his life."

"With this much blood, I usually see quite a few chalk outlines. Know what I mean?"

"Yes, sir."

"How many did you say there were?"

"We found two in the hallway, one just coming to after what looked like a solid blow to the head. Second guy was a stab wound to the flank. Lot of pain but was pretty stable. Then there was no-nuts, and finally, the doc back here."

"Let's not make any press release on this anytime soon. Need some time to sort through all this stuff before we really know what's going on."

"Got it, Sarge. The flooding is the big story right now anyway. Will be a few days before they start snooping around for some crime headlines and this gets out."

"Good. I don't want to scare off any others who may be involved before we can get to them."

Rosa watched as the big man walked behind Jernigan's desk and bent down to look at a safe that was bolted to the floor. "Where did they find the girl?"

"Girl, sir? What girl?"

Juarez stood up and looked across the room at the officer. "I thought the dispatch said something about a young girl on the premises."

The officer looked down at his feet. "Sorry, boss. You're right. With all the bodies, it just slipped my mind. Didn't see a girl. At least not one beaten to a pulp, shot, or stabbed."

Rosa knew she needed to move now. They were looking for her. They were her last hope. Everything they'd said led her to believe they were there to help. She just had to trust them. She slowly opened the door and stepped into the room. She couldn't stop trembling as she held tightly onto Max's cell phone.

Sergeant Juarez's eyes grew wide as his hand fell away from his moustache. "Call the medics, now!"

The officer pulled out his phone. "We need CPS and another medical team. We have one more person at the scene."

"Are you okay, young lady?" Juarez asked as he approached Rosa. "It's okay; we're here to help you."

Rosa nodded. Then, with tears streaming down her face, she raced across the room and grabbed Juarez around the waist and held tightly. "Help me, please."

"It's going to be all right. You're safe now."

Chapter 41

The Present

Max retraced his steps through the clinic, found the back door, and stepped out into the rain. He looked down and saw the pig mask lying in a pool of water. He hesitated, then bent down and picked it up.

"Your work is not done yet, El Chancho."

He jogged back to his car and slid behind the wheel. In the distance, he could hear the whine of sirens getting closer. He didn't want to be there when they arrived.

He backed out of the alleyway and raced through the flooded streets. The water sprayed up on the windshield, making it hard to see where he was going in the darkness. He swerved just in time before hitting a police car as it came screaming around a corner. Soon, he was back onto main roads and headed to the north side of town.

He looked down at the post-it note.

How the hell does a psychiatrist live in River Oaks, one of the richest communities in the country?

He entered the address in his phone and made his way across town. The traffic had died down significantly. Rush hour was long over, and Houstonians knew to stay indoors when the water started to rise. Max passed several cars that had made the mistake of driving into deep water and sat dead by the side of the road, waiting for a tow.

By the time Max got to Simkins' neighborhood, the streets were completely empty. The giant oaks and pecan trees that arched overhead made the road seem even darker and more ominous. Max could barely make out the occasional light from a mansion set far back from the street and partially hidden behind high fences.

As he pulled up to Simkins's address, he was lucky enough to find the gate slowly closing as if someone had just passed through. He drove the Nova up close to the gate, and it immediately swung open again. He turned off his lights and drove up the long gravel driveway to the main house.

Max's pained jaw dropped when he saw the size of the house. "Holy crap! This guy's got some bling."

A black Mercedes was parked by a side entrance under a bright security light. Max parked the Nova in the shadow of a large crepe myrtle.

He looked out his window and across the driveway at the huge house and remembered what Angel had said to him as he was bartering for his Rolex: "People like you not in my situation and they do much worse." Simkins and Jernigan had good lives. Never in want for food or shelter, and yet look at what he'd found at their little house of horrors. They had the souls of dead men.

Max reached around into the back seat and grabbed the pig mask and held it up in front of his face. He stared into its hollowed-out black eyes, its horrific snout fixed in a perpetual grimace. Then he looked at himself in the rearview mirror as he pulled the wet, smelly mask over his face, only to see his own eyes appear in those hollowed-out sockets. The mask hid his contorted face as he tried to suppress a scream. He was no better than Simkins. No better than Jernigan. He had done the unforgivable. He could never be clean.

Max stepped out of the car and moved toward the house. The gravel of the driveway crunched under his feet as he crouched down beside the Mercedes and crept up to the back door. The rain had weakened to a drizzle, but he was still wet, and the chill of the night air made him shiver.

Max looked in through the glass of the door and saw that it opened into a big kitchen with a large wooden table occupying much of the center of the room. The room was dimly lit by a light over the stove. Beyond the kitchen, the house was dark. Simkins was nowhere to be seen.

He pulled his knife out from his ankle sheath. With the butt of the handle, he punched out one of the panes of glass in the door, then reached inside and unlatched it. The door creaked as he pushed it open, the broken pieces of glass making a scraping sound as they dragged across the stone floor.

He knew where he was. He was in Texas, and at any moment, Simkins could step out of the shadows and shoot him, and no court would find him at fault. Max didn't really care anymore. He'd lost so much over the years that he thought a bullet right now might finally put him at peace.

He crossed the kitchen and into a large, darkened living room. At the far side, light outlined the frame of a closed door.

"There you are," he whispered.

He crossed the room and pressed his ear close to the door. He could hear the shuffle of papers and the occasional grunt of displeasure. Max drew his gun, then pushed the door open and stepped into a large, dimly lit library. The dark wood-paneled walls flickered with light from a fire that burned in a small fireplace to the side of the door.

Max found Simkins sitting behind a large, leather-topped desk with a file open in front of him. His long, spidery fingers gently strummed a Sig Sauer semiautomatic pistol by his side. The flames from the fireplace reflected off the lenses of his wire-framed glasses. A floor-to-ceiling bookcase covered the wall behind the desk. Embedded in it were several security monitors. On one of the screens could clearly be seen the Nova parked behind the crepe myrtle.

"Ah, El Chancho, welcome," Simkins said, his thin lips pulled back into a sardonic smile. His calming voice the same as if they were simply having a counseling session. "Come in."

Max pulled the mask off and continued to point the gun in Simkins's direction. "Max!" he said raising an eyebrow. "I didn't realize the pig was your alter ego until now. El Chancho had a lot of my employees on the street scared. Glad to see he'll not be working any longer." He placed his feet on the desk and leaned back in his chair. "You do realize that when you broke that window, a silent alarm went off. The police should be here soon. River Oaks has its own little security force. Very efficient."

"Is it true?"

Simkins stared at him, his face blank and emotionless. "Is what true, Max?"

"You were behind Asadi's breakdown. Loaded him with drugs until he cracked."

He ran his hands over his bald head and placed them behind his neck. "I'm amazed at how you found all this out. And by the way, how the hell did you find me here?"

"Well?" Max demanded.

Simkins sighed. "I didn't expect him to do what he did to be honest. Was just running a little side hustle to make some money. You know they don't pay psychiatrists very much in the army. But it was your good friend Nick raping his daughter that set Asadi off. I had nothing to do with that. Kind of surprised a father would act that way. Never really understood those kinds of emotions myself."

Simkins strummed his fingers on the back of his neck. "I have nothing personal against you Max. In fact, I think I like you. Went through hell over there. You're a real hero." He took a deep breath in then let it out slowly. "But Jernigan doesn't like you. I helped him a little with you to keep him happy. To keep the business running smoothly."

Max was speechless. He no longer had questions, just rage, blind rage. Through a window across from the desk, he saw flashing lights racing up the drive.

Max raised the gun and pointed it at Simkins's head.

"Don't think you can do it, Max." He put his feet back down on the floor and tapped the chart he'd been reading on the desk. "I know your profile. I followed El Chancho. Granted, I didn't know it was you until now, but he never really killed anyone. Scared the crap out of a lot of people. But kill them in cold blood, sitting behind a desk? No. I put my money on you not pulling that trigger. Just not you, Max."

Max slowly lowered the gun and slipped it into the holster in the small of his back. He walked around the desk and stood directly in front of his tormentor. "You may think you know me, but you don't. No one really knows me."

"I bet the brother you left to die knows you."

Max lunged at Simkins as the kitchen door swung open, slamming hard against the wall. He grabbed Simkins around the throat, dragging him from his chair and throwing him to the floor. He straddled him, squeezing harder and harder as Simkins's face turned blue. Simkins tried in vain to pull Max's hands from his throat.

Max was vaguely aware of the heavy footsteps running through the house, moving quickly from room to room. He looked down at Simkins's face, blue, the vessels on his forehead bulging, drool running down the side of his mouth. "No!" Max screamed as he let Simkins go.

Simkins grabbed his own throat as he gasped for air. As Max stood up from behind the desk, he felt the sting of darts drilling into his back, followed by the excruciating pain of a Taser as he fell paralyzed onto the desk.

Max closed his eyes, and eventually the pain from the Taser stopped. He kept them closed as hands grabbed at him from all directions, dragging him across the desk and slamming him on the floor. He was held down face first as handcuffs were applied. It was all a blur. His head spun . . . lights . . . pain.

Chapter 42

The Present

"**D**r. Donovan. Dr. Donovan. Can you hear me?"

Max opened his eyes. Leaning over him was Nigel, his chief resident's freckled face inches from his own, his red hair sticking wildly out from under his surgeon's cap.

"Are you okay? What happened?"

Max looked around. He was in his own familiar trauma bay, but this time on the wrong side of the bed.

"What am I doing here, Nigel?"

"Good question, sir." Nigel stood and paced by the side of the stretcher. "Ran you through the scanner while you were out."

"How do I look on the inside?"

"To be honest, boss, like shit. But I think you'll survive. You've got a cracked mandible, broken ribs, a small pneumothorax." He paused and looked him in the eyes. "God, how were you still walking?" He started pacing again. "A small subdural hematoma and a tiny liver laceration to round everything out."

Max tried to take a deep breath, but the pain in his ribs was unbearable. "That all? Feels like I got more than that going on."

"I had to put a chest tube in on the right. Hard as hell to do. That side was a mess."

Max turned his head and looked down at the tube running from the side of his chest. He closed his eyes. Just like Afghanistan. Jernigan had really done a job on him. Funny how he hadn't felt too much pain when he was going for Simkins. All that adrenaline. All that rage.

"Can you believe it, Dr. Donovan? They brought Dr. Jernigan in just before you. He's in the operating room now." Nigel wiped sweat from his forehead. "What the hell's going on out there tonight, sir? It's damn stressful working on your bosses like this."

Max looked at his resident. He remembered being a chief. It was a hard job and all-consuming. That's what he'd liked. No time for personal life. No time for thought other than work. No time to dwell on the crushing guilt of past mistakes. He'd crisscrossed the country doing rotations in almost every surgical specialty, trying to find peace. Why the hell had he picked trauma? Probably for the same reason he'd found himself getting closer and closer to Houston with each change of job. To come home and face the unfaceable.

"So how was Jernigan looking? Okay?"

"Lost a lot of blood, but overall, he was good." Nigel went to the sink and started to wash his hands. "He's an amazing guy. Coolheaded enough to place a blood pressure cuff around his own leg to stop the bleeding. I guess you old vets are a pretty tough bunch." Nigel turned back from the sink, then hesitated. "Sir, why are you cuffed to the bed? I asked but was told to do my job and keep my nose out of it."

Max could feel the cold steel of the handcuff around his ankle. "Did Jernigan say what happened?"

"He wasn't saying much. Mumbled something about a break-in at his clinic. You know any place that keeps medications is eventually going to get busted into. I guess he was just unlucky enough to have been there when it happened."

"Is that what the police are saying?"

"No." Nigel stepped forward and leaned over the stretcher. "That's the odd thing. Most of the time, the cops are in here shooting off their mouths about the what, when, and how, but they were pretty tight-lipped this time. I did hear someone mention something about a girl being found there, but they took her to the pediatric side to get checked out."

"And me? Say anything about me?"

Nigel glanced down at the foot of the bed. "No. Just don't uncuff you and make sure you lived."

Max stared at the ceiling.

"Sir, what did you do?"

"What I had to, Nigel. That's all." Max sighed. "Don't worry too much about me. I think everything will work out all right."

A nurse entered the trauma bay. "We've got a bed upstairs ready for you, Dr. Donovan. Time to go." A porter entered behind her and started unlocking the bed and tucking in all the tubes and lines for the transport to the intermediate care unit.

"I'll come and check on you later, Dr. Donovan," Nigel said as he rested his hand on his shoulder. "Anything you need, just let me know."

Chapter 43

The Present

Simkins sat silently at his desk. Several of his morning patients had canceled, and he was left staring at the wall with nothing interesting to do. It had been several days since he'd heard from Jernigan. He'd wanted to know how the conditioning of Rosa had gone, but Max had distracted him so much that he'd hardly thought about anything else. He called the intermediate care unit daily to find out what Max's condition was. Was he still handcuffed to the bed? Was he in a lot of pain?

He placed his feet up on his desk and leaned back. He closed his eyes and tried to remember the sight of Max being strapped to a stretcher and carried from his home. He'd found the whole incident surprisingly exhilarating.

~ ~ ~

Simkins remained lying on his back while they dragged Max across his desk. He took slow, deep breaths as his vision slowly returned. He gently stroked his neck while his mind became clearer. He staggered to his feet just as several officers held Max down and handcuffed his hands behind his back.

"Don't get up, sir, until we've had the medical team check you," one of the officers said as a paramedic rushed to Simkins's side and grabbed him by the arm.

Simkins shook him off. He bent down and picked up his twisted wire-framed glasses from the floor. "I'm fine," he said with a raspy voice. "Never felt better." He straightened the bows of the glasses, then wrapped them around his large ears. He steadied himself by placing his hand on the desk. "Thanks for coming so quickly. You saved my life." He smiled as they loaded Max on the stretcher. He staggered across the room and helped hold the door.

"Sir, you should come with us. You need to be checked at the hospital."

"No, no, I really am fine." He couldn't stop smiling as he looked down on Max, motionless as he passed through his living room and out the kitchen door.

An officer approached him, pad in hand. "Can I get a statement from you about what happened?"

"Certainly," he rasped. "That's Max Donovan. I'm a psychiatrist, and he's a patient of mine." Simkins walked across his library to a wine cabinet he kept along one wall. "Where is that port I've been saving?" he whispered as he looked through the rack of bottles. "There you are." He caressed the bottle and carried it back to his desk. "Would you like a drink, officer? Ne Oublie. You're unlikely to ever get an offer of a better port."

"Sorry, sir. On duty and all."

"Your loss." He pulled a glass off the shelf behind his desk and slowly poured himself a drink. He brought it up to his nose and sniffed the sweet aroma as the officer stood silently staring. He closed his eyes as he took his first sip. After a few moments, he opened them again and was somewhat startled to see the officer still standing there.

"Oh yes. Max Donovan. Patient of mine. Tried to do me in. Thank God you showed up in time."

The officer scribbled on his pad as quickly as he could. "Any reason he wanted to target you?"

"Not really. Just out of his mind I guess."

"Are you willing to come down to the station to make a formal statement?"

Simkins sat in his chair and took another sip. "Certainly. Would love to. Just not right now."

~~~

Simkins had found the whole experience, especially the thrill of Max strangling him, so stimulating that he hadn't been able to sleep that night. Now he was feeling the low. He yearned for the excitement again. As he sat behind the desk in his office, waiting for patients, he felt terribly bored.

His spidery fingers rapped the desk as he looked at the diplomas on the wall. He'd achieved quite a bit. Good reputation. Significant wealth, not exactly by way of medicine, but nevertheless, he'd become very financially secure with his side ventures, to say the least. But it was taking more and more to keep him stimulated. The highs were fewer and further between. Running the business had become boring long ago. Not since Afghanistan had he had such a thrill. Psyops had challenged him. Max had reawakened that desire for confrontation. That life-or-death struggle.

He thumped his fist on the desk. "I'm going to go see Max." The idea of it was so outrageous that he had to do it. He stormed out of his office. "Lucy, cancel the rest of my day. I'll be busy with some important work that just came up."

"Yes, Dr. Simkins," Lucy replied without looking up from her computer.

Simkins was excited as he scurried down the corridor to the pedestrian crossover that led to Harris County Hospital. It had been years since he'd ventured into the place, and the break in his routine stimulated him even more.

He had to ask several times how to get to the intermediate care unit. When he eventually found it, he was reminded why he didn't like hospital practice. The smell of antiseptic in the hallways, the reek of stool, the noise. Not clean and clinical like he preferred. He liked to do
~~~

his work in the comfort of his big, paneled office. This kind of medicine where you actually had to touch someone repulsed him.

As he approached the nurses' station, he was happy to see a familiar face. "Hello, Maggie. How's the family?" He'd treated her husband for depression. The husband eventually killed himself.

Maggie looked surprised. "Dr. Simkins!"

Simkins leaned up against the desk. "Son still in rehab?"

Maggie looked sideways at her fellow nurses and nodded slowly. "I assume you're here to see Dr. Jernigan."

Simkins's brow furrowed. "Dr. Jernigan? Is he here?"

"Oh yes, over in room 312."

"What happened to him?"

"What? I'm surprised you of all people didn't know," Maggie replied sarcastically. "Attacked in his clinic the other night during a break-in. Shot up pretty badly."

Simkins felt a lump in his throat. This was not what he was expecting. He was coming to gloat over Max and maybe prod him a little more about his brother. Seemed to be the trigger that set him off. But Jernigan? What the hell had happened there? Obviously, that was why he hadn't heard from him since the other night during the storm.

"You're in luck; he just woke up a little while ago. The police just finished with him."

The veins on his forehead bulged. "The police?"

"Yes, quite a number have been in and out of his room ever since he got out of surgery the other night. It's been nonstop."

Simkins felt sweat rings forming under his arms. He was no longer interested in confronting Max. He was more worried about what Jernigan was saying. "Thank you. I'll go see him now."

Simkins found 312 and was surprised to see a police officer sitting on a chair in the hallway in front of the room. "Hello. Dr. Simkins to see Nick Jernigan."

The police officer nodded and let him pass. His heart jumped when he saw how bad Jernigan looked. His eyes were partially closed. He appeared pale and wasted. His right leg was wrapped in bandages and surrounded in a large, cage like external bone fixator.

"Nick. How are you doing?"

Jernigan opened his eyes. "What the hell are you doing here?"

"I just found out you were here, and I wanted to see how you were doing."

"Like you have the capacity to care about how I'm doing." Jernigan tried to move to a more comfortable position, but the large fixator made it difficult.

"Come now. No reason to be nasty with me. This is just a friendly visit." Simkins moved in closer and now could see that Jernigan's left foot was handcuffed to the bed rail.

Jernigan winced in pain as he pulled on the cuffed leg and tried to adjust the pillow under his knee.

Simkins frowned. "What's with the police, Nick? Why the cuffs?"

Jernigan glared back at him. "What the hell do you think it's all about, Jack? They came out to my place."

"The nurse said it was some kind of break-in."

"Yeah, a break-in by your buddy Max. Shot the place up, including me."

"So why the cuffs on you?"

"You're one piece of manipulative shit, aren't you, Jackie boy. They came to the clinic! They found all the stuff we had there."

"We? What do you mean *we*? What did you have at your clinic?"

Jernigan rolled his head back on the pillow and laughed. "Your clinic, Jack. The one you took a profit off of. The one you used to visit when you were a little lonely."

"You lost me, Nick. What the hell are you on about?"

"Thought one day you would try to throw me under the bus." Jernigan lifted his head off the pillow and glared at Simkins. His unshaven face contorted in disgust. "Yes, I admit you saved my ass in Afghanistan. Gave me a good alibi. Paid the right people. But I think I've paid you back many times over." Jernigan shifted again in bed, this time grabbing for the big fixator as the pins dug into his skin.

Simkins slowly came closer to the head of the bed as Jernigan tried to get more comfortable. He stood looking at Jernigan's wrecked body.

"Got it all, Jack. Got the documents in my safe. I'm an anesthesiologist; we document everything. I can even tell you what your damn heart rate was the last time you got off with one of your little girls in the back room. Got a video of that too. Tried to make some money with it on the dark web, but you know what? You don't sell very well. Guess your dick's too small for anyone to want to watch."

Simkins clenched his teeth. His eyes narrowed to two dark slits behind his steamed-up glasses. *How dare he do that? Play me like I'm some damn fool.*

Simkins thought he'd anticipated any action like this. All payments had been in cash to a third party. No contracts. And the times he'd been in the room were when there was no one else in the clinic, and he'd made sure that he'd shut down the monitors.

"That's not possible."

"Backup cameras and a secondary server, Doctor. I guess you didn't think I was smart enough to have a backup when you really decided to screw me."

"No, I guess you're right there, Nick. I never thought you were very smart." Simkins stepped over to the nurses' fold-down cabinet while

Jernigan closed his eyes and tried to rest his hunched neck. Simkins took a sixty-milliliter syringe out of the cabinet and put a large-bore needle on it, then held it down at his side as he turned back toward Jernigan.

Jernigan remained lying with his eyes closed. "Do you realize how much pain you've caused me over the years, not including this little episode where Max blew the shit out of my leg?"

Simkins stood by the bedside, looking down at his old accomplice.

"Years of pain. Just so you could make a little side profit."

Simkins suddenly pulled the pillow out from under Jernigan's leg. Then, with all his weight he fell onto him, covering his face with the pillow as he struggled. Simkins stabbed him in the neck with the syringe, injecting a large bolus of air into his carotid.

Within seconds, Jernigan stopped resisting, and his limbs started to shake violently.

Simkins took the pillow off his face and placed it back under his leg. As Jernigan continued to convulse, Simkins placed the syringe in the sharp's container, straightened his white coat, and walked out of the room. He nodded to the police officer, who was just returning to his chair with a cup of coffee.

"You didn't uncuff him, did you, Doc?" he said with a wink.

"No. He was just sleeping the whole time. He's still cuffed to the bed, just like you left him."

Simkins decided to head back to the office before stepping out for some lunch. He felt no emotion as he walked slowly through the crowded hallways of Harris County. Killing Jernigan had been necessary, and anyway, he deserved it. Filming him. Putting it out over the web. Simkins had never really known humiliation, and he didn't feel that emotion now, but he did understand disloyalty and risk. Nick Jernigan was a risk that had just gotten too great. *The autopsy won't be able to determine what happened unless they're really good. Probably they'll think it was an embolism from his broken leg. Real problem is what to do about the police and Max.*

Maybe it was time to leave, time to take up residence in a country that wouldn't bother him as long as he paid the right people. The money was already dispersed where he could access it from anywhere. If anything, he had to admit that life in Houston was getting a little boring. *Traveling might shake things up a bit.*

Simkins pushed open the door to his clinic, only to find Lucy pacing about the room, her big green eyes filled with tears. "Dr. Simkins. They were here. They took everything!"

Simkins stood in the doorway. "Who was here . . . and what do you mean they took everything?"

Lucy threw her hands in the air. "Everything! The police were here. They had a warrant, and a bunch of them came in and took it all."

Simkins barged past her and into his office. His file-room door was open, and all the files were gone. His desk drawers were left half-open, and they had been almost completely cleaned out.

"They can't do this," he said. "This is privileged information."

Lucy came up behind him. "See, they just stormed in and cleared it all out. They even opened a safe you had in the back of the file room and took all the papers out."

Simkins was finally starting to feel the pressure. He took off his glasses and wiped his face with his hand. He'd known he had a limited amount of time to do what he needed to do, but he hadn't expected them to move so fast. Jernigan really had sold him out in a big way.

Still, Simkins had options.

Max had really started all this, though. Jernigan was an idiot, but Max had caused his downfall. Jernigan was gone, and before he fled, Simkins wanted to make sure Max ended up the same way.

Chapter 44

The Present

Max lay on his back, staring at the ceiling. Overall, he felt better. The chest tube hurt, but the good news was that Nigel said he was going to remove it today. His ankle where they'd cuffed him to the bed felt raw, but other than that, the pain meds were keeping things in check.

He'd heard from one of the nurses that Nick Jernigan had died earlier that day from an apparent embolism. Max felt nothing for him. He did not feel that he'd killed him by shooting him in the leg. He'd done it to himself. Evil bastard.

"Good afternoon, Dr. Donovan." Nigel burst into the room with forced enthusiasm.

Max knew how difficult it was to take care of your own boss. Mistakes were often made simply by trying too hard not to make mistakes.

Nigel set up his supplies by the bedside. Suture removal kit, plain gauze, Vaseline gauze, tape. "Chest x-ray looks great today, except for all those busted ribs. Time to get the tube out."

Max closed his eyes.

Nigel tried his best to remove the tape securing the chest tube without pushing too much on his broken ribs. He paused every time Max winced.

"Don't stop, Nigel. Just get on with it."

"Yes, sir." He proceeded to dig out the sutures that had partially cut into Max's skin and cut them with scissors. He placed the Vaseline gauze against the chest where the tube was going to come out, then covered that with regular gauze. "All right, Dr. Donovan, one . . . two . . . three."

Max held his breath as the tube was yanked from his chest. It took a few seconds for the pain to settle. Then he could breathe again.

"Feel okay, boss?"

"Fine, Nigel. Good job."

"Just a follow-up x-ray, and then you can get up and about much easier without the . . ." He paused as he looked down at the cuff still anchoring him to the bed. "Oh, sorry. I mean you should feel better."

"I'm good, Nigel. You did a great job." He pulled his gown across his scarred, muscular chest. "Now, don't you have more rounds to do?"

Nigel was happy for the excuse to leave. "Yes, sir. X-ray will be here in a minute." He bolted from the room.

A few minutes later, the x-ray technician came in and said nothing as he took the x-ray and left.

Soon after, Nigel poked his head in. "All good, boss," he said, and was gone.

Max sat quietly, not really thinking. He knew his tour at Harris County was probably over. Didn't know if he was going to jail or not. Surprisingly, although an officer was stationed outside his door, the police had left him alone.

He sat and watched through the window as the sun slowly set. He didn't turn on the light as the room grew darker. Then he heard the officer outside the door talking on his phone.

"Really? The assistant DA said what? Okay."

Max heard the officer stand up and move his chair before entering the room.

"Told me to take the cuffs off and go home." He bent down and unlocked Max's ankle.

Max bent his leg up and gave it a good shake. "Who said that?"

"Apparently the assistant DA himself. I'm to get out of here and leave you. Good luck, Doc." The officer put the cuffs in his belt, then turned and left.

Max closed his eyes and drifted off to sleep. As he did so, a slender figure of a man slipped into his darkened room and stood silently by his bed.

Chapter 45

The Present

Simkins sat in his office, blankly staring at the walls until the sun went down. He'd sent Lucy home early, and using his cell phone, had booked a private charter flight to Brazil. He knew some people there who could get him comfortable relatively quickly. He had a feeling the police had been knocking on his door at home, and he didn't feel like going there until he was about ready to leave. They obviously were still checking on the things Jernigan had told them before they made their final move. He intended to be long gone by the time they truly came in for the kill. That just left getting even with Max as his final act before disappearing.

He rested with his forearms spread across his desk, his eyes hidden in shadow. His office was dark except for the light from a solitary brass desk lamp. The limited light made the creases from his scowling face even more pronounced.

Suddenly, as if awakening from a trance, he sat up and reached into the back of his top desk drawer.

"Huh, thought so. They didn't take everything."

He pulled out a stiletto that he had taped up under the desk. He'd always had it on him when he was in the military. Stealthy and did what needed to be done if used correctly, and he knew how to use it correctly.

Simkins stood and looked down at the knife as he slowly spun it in his fingers. It was long and thin, perfectly balanced in his hand. The blade was black, and dark leather covered the handle. The cross guard was small and black like the blade. He squinted as he held it close to his face.

"Huh?" He looked closer at the blade, then shrugged and scraped away a small speck of dried blood before slipping the knife into his white coat pocket. He walked out of the office and closed the door, knowing it was probably for the last time. There was really nothing for him to come back to anyway.

How had he been so foolish? He'd relied on an incompetent, and he should've known better. Very sloppy in his older years. In the past, he never would've given so much power to Nick Jernigan, never would have let him take that girl to his own house to confuse her prior to taking her to the clinic. But that was the problem. It was all too easy. People were just too stupid for him, and he'd gotten sloppy out of boredom. Pushing it to the edge. Leaving gaps for people to catch him had made the game a little more interesting. Now within a few days, his comfortable little empire had collapsed. Max had contributed to that collapse. Even though he liked him, things needed to be cleaned up. Then he was going to go to the airport and leave.

The corridors of the hospital were quiet. He remembered now how to get to the intermediate care unit, and as he approached the nurses' station, he saw no one about. He knew the night staff often were off on break. He found Max's room number in the ledger. He was in a corner room away from the view of the main corridor. Perfect.

Simkins paused and looked around the corner and was happy to see that there was no guard at Max's door. He slipped into the dark room.

It took a moment for his eyes to adjust. He went to the sink by the bed and turned on the small light over the mirror. It was just enough to see Max's sleeping face and to highlight his own frame. The room was silent except for Max's heavy breathing.

Simkins slipped the stiletto out of his white coat pocket and stood looking down at his helpless prey. "Time to go, Max," he whispered as he raised his hand.

Simkins paused as he heard the click of a gun being cocked. From a dark corner on the far side of the room came a voice. "Put the knife down."

Simkins squinted his eyes as he tried to see where the voice was coming from. "Who are you?"

"Just put the knife down now, or I'll shoot."

Simkins was furious. Not only had his life been disrupted; now his plans for a clean exit were also not going as he would have liked. He looked back down at Max. He now hated him. Before, he was just a loose end. Now he was the focus of all his rage.

He looked back again toward the voice from the darkness, then lunged at Max with the knife.

BAM! BAM! BAM!

~ ~ ~

Max woke and sat bolt upright. He thought he was having another nightmare until he turned to the side and saw blood splattered across the mirror and Simkins' body slumped on the floor.

He started to panic and tried to scream, but his ribs hurt too much for him to make anything more than a weak, rasping cry for help. Then he heard an old, forgotten sound: the sound of a leg dragging behind a twisting body.

Sam stepped from the darkness and into the light by the bed. "Hello, brother."

Chapter 46

The Present

everal nurses in the breakroom heard the loud bangs coming from Max's room.

The charge nurse rose to her feet and ran in the direction of the noise. "Oh my God!" she screamed as she turned on the light. She stepped back out of the room and screamed at the staff. "Code blue! Call a code blue and get security, stat!"

Max squinted as his eyes adjusted to the bright light. They only had a moment before the room would be full of people. Beside his bed stood Sam. He'd aged. His hair was showing the slightest hints of gray. His eyes had dark circles below them, but they were his twin's eyes. The same clear, dark eyes that had greeted him every day throughout his youth. His tall, thin frame was clad in a dark-gray suit, the left sleeve custom-tailored to fit his distorted arm. He appeared comfortably sophisticated in his pressed white shirt and dark-blue silk tie. His smile was sad.

"Thanks, Sam. I guess you saved me."

The room was once again filled with people. Sam just stood and stared as the cardiac arrest team arrived. Nigel burst into the room in a panic. "Dr. Donovan, are you okay?"

"Yes, Nigel. I'm good."

The cardiac arrest team pronounced Simkins dead just as Slim, the security guard, arrived. He looked at the body and then at Sam. He drew his gun. "Sir, please step away from Dr. Donovan and out into the hallway."

Sam looked at Max and slowly twisted and pivoted out of the room. Nigel and several of the nursing staff unlocked Max's bed and rolled him out into the corridor. Max turned his head to see Sam talking to Slim, whose gun was still drawn. As he entered his new room, he saw several HPD officers arrive and surround him.

Nigel performed a physical exam on Max to see if he'd been hurt. "I'm relieved to say you are just as screwed up as when I last saw you. Nothing new to add."

"Thanks, Nigel."

"Think I may retire after this week, Dr. Donovan."

"No, you're too good. Plus, this will make a great story to tell your residents one day."

Nigel smiled for the first time. "Maybe you're right. Pretty damn intense week."

Once Nigel left, Slim maneuvered his large frame into the room and stood at the foot of his bed. "Doc, that guy says he's your lawyer. That true?"

"If he said it, then I guess it's true."

Slim put his massive hand on his chin. "Said the other doctor was about to stab you and he had to shoot him."

Max drew a breath, then winced as his ribs paid the price. "Yes . . . that's what happened."

Slim shook his head. "Damn, I don't know what the hell is going on here. HPD took him downtown for questioning. I did see a nasty-looking knife in that doctor's hand there on the floor." He reached for the door. "Boy, you must have pissed him off, Doc."

"Seems to be what I do best."

"Don't worry about anybody else coming in. They're putting a guard back on your door." Slim was still shaking his head as he left the room.

A nurse came in and turned the light off. Max was finally left alone. He sat up for hours, staring into the darkness. Jernigan was dead. Simkins was dead. His past was not.

Later that night, the small light flickered on by the door, and a large police officer entered the room. "Dr. Donovan . . . Dr. Donovan?"

Max turned to face the officer. He'd been staring into the darkness for so long, he wasn't sure if the man was real or if he was dreaming. He tried to smile. "Yes, can I help you?"

"Sergeant Juarez. I know it's late, but I'm investigating what happened the other night over in the Fifth. With all that's happened tonight, I thought we should talk. You didn't say much last time, but a lot has changed obviously over the past twenty-four hours."

Max continued to stare at Juarez with an awkwardly fake smile. "Yes?"

Juarez moved his large frame to the bedside, pulled up a chair, and sat down. He put his hand up to his face and started slowly stroking his mustache. "We think we have a good grasp of things now. Just need you to fill in a few gaps if you don't mind."

Max continued to stare.

Juarez pulled out a notepad. "Dr. Jernigan was actually very helpful. Seems like he had a soft spot for Rosa. That's the name of the girl we found in the clinic. And he decided to spill the beans. Said he'd had enough and wanted to come clean." He paused.

Max said nothing.

"Admitted to running a drug mill. Says Simkins was his partner and that they had a sideline in online porn and prostitution." Juarez shook his head. "Thought only the punks on the street did this kind of shit, not docs."

"I didn't kill Jernigan."

Juarez appeared surprised by Max's response. "Yes, we know. Pathologist found a suspicious bruise on the side of his neck. It will be a while before they know for sure, but something strange happened there."

Max turned and looked directly into Juarez's dark eyes. "I killed the boy."

Juarez looked confused. "What boy, Dr. Donovan? There was no boy."

Max turned away and stared at the wall. "How's the girl?"

"Rosa's good. She was taken to the consulate. Her parents flew in this evening." Juarez crossed his legs. "She said you saved her. It was your cell phone we found with her, correct?"

Max nodded.

"I didn't know your brother was Sam Donovan. He's a pretty well-known lawyer in town. I think he was the one who convinced the DA to drop any charges against you. Especially after reviewing some of the footage from the clinic. You know that guy had cameras everywhere." Juarez leaned in. "If you don't mind me saying, you're a goddamn beast. Girl's lucky to be alive. Wouldn't be if it wasn't for you."

Max continued to stare across the room. The corner of his lip quivered ever so slightly.

"All right, Doctor. I can tell you've had quite a shock with all that's happened. How about I come around another time? It's late, and you still need to recover."

Max turned to face him. "Thank you for coming." He returned to staring at the wall.

Juarez stood and quietly left.

Chapter 47

The Present

Max woke late the next morning with the sun streaming through the window. He felt comfortable in its warmth, and for a brief moment, he forgot about yesterday, about the blood on his walls, about Sam. He just smiled at the bright sunshine.

"Good morning, Dr. Donovan."

Max didn't recognize his nurse. She was small and spry, and her bleached blond hair bounced around as if on springs. Her perkiness was amazingly annoying. He thought he knew all the nurses. "Who are you?"

"I'm Rebecca, your nurse for the day."

"I haven't seen you here before."

Her bright expression changed to a serious, all-business look. "Agency nurse, Dr. Donovan."

"Why? Where are all the regulars?"

She came closer to his bed. "Well now, Doctor, with all that's happened here this week, most of the staff called in sick. The ones who showed up are currently in crisis counseling." Her smile returned. "So you have me."

Max flopped back on his pillow as she darted from his room, only to return moments later with a tray of food.

"Breakfast is served." She placed the tray on his bedside table. "Would you like me to feed you, Doctor?"

Max rolled his eyes. "No, thank you. I can feed myself."

She bolted from the room, only to return just as he was swallowing his eggs. "Need a sponge bath, Doctor? Back rub? Walk after breakfast?"

"No, thank you. Just need to eat. Thanks."

She turned and left. Max tried to adjust himself in bed, but the pain from his ribs stopped him. His head hurt. His jaw hurt as he tried to chew. It was cracked, they said, but didn't need anything done. Just a bland, soft diet. He was miserable.

The nurse returned. "Doctor?"

"What?" he snapped.

She froze. For a moment, he thought she was going to cry. "Dr. Donovan, you have a visitor."

Max looked toward the door just as Rosa entered. She had a big smile on her face. Following close behind was a middle-aged woman. She was thin and not much taller than Rosa. Max knew right away that she was her mother. The resemblance was striking. She had the same beautiful mix of Spanish and Indian that made Rosa so attractive. Max could also see the stress on her face, the bags under her eyes from the hours of crying.

"Mister Max, this is my mama, Juanita."

Her mother hesitated at first, then rushed to the side of the bed and knelt down. She grabbed his hand and held it tightly as she started to cry. "Gracias, Doctor, gracias." She wouldn't let go as Rosa moved in closer.

"Mister Max, thank you for saving me."

Max struggled to find the right words to say. "I'm happy you're back with your family."

Rosa's mother finally let go of Max's hand and stood up. She looked as if she were going to collapse at any moment from exhaustion. She whispered something in Rosa's ear.

"My mama thanks you. She's sorry that her English is not good enough to tell you how hard it has been and how much she appreciates what you did. Please come to visit our home whenever you get out of the hospital."

Max smiled and nodded.

Rosa held out her hand and handed Max a small silver locket.

He opened it and saw Rosa standing with her family in front of a house with a strangely out-of-place orange front door.

"Please, Mister Max. Take this. This is my family. Thanks to you, we are together again."

Rosa and her mother awkwardly stared at Max for a few more moments.

Finally, Rosa spoke. "We're leaving today to go home. I hope you get well soon and can spend some time with your family." She gave him a hug. Then they both turned and left.

"Well, that was very nice, Dr. Donovan," the perky nurse said. "And what a nice locket as well. Something you can keep with all your keepsakes."

Max looked at the locket in his hand and the picture of the beautiful family. He clenched his fist and held it tightly.

~ ~ ~

Several days had passed since Rosa's visit, and Max had been making significant progress. Nigel had come in every day and proclaimed continued success. One morning he seemed especially chipper.

"Dr. Donovan, you're going to be discharged today."

Max's heart sank. He'd grown secure in the daily routine of his role as patient. Now he had to get out, go home, and start over.

He dressed in the jeans and T-shirt that he'd come into the hospital with and was taken by wheelchair to an awaiting cab. The short ride home was unremarkable. The same students jogging around Rice University.

The village of West University had not changed since his escapade and hospitalization.

To his surprise, when he arrived home, the Nova was parked in the driveway with Sam seated behind the wheel.

As Max walked up from the street, Sam got out and handed him the keys. "Just got it out of impound. You've taken good care of her."

Max smiled. "You didn't scratch it or anything, did you? You were always a crappy driver."

Sam gave Max a careful hug, mindful of his healing ribs, and helped him to the door. Inside, they sat on the sofa.

Max looked down at Sam's shoe. "Looks like you need a new pair. Worn through again."

"Yeah, you wouldn't believe how many shoes I go through in a year."

Max eased himself off the sofa, went into the kitchen, and got two beers. He handed one to Sam.

Sam looked around the room. "Furnished rental?"

"Yeah."

Sam took a long drink, then placed the bottle down on the coffee table. He leaned back on the sofa. "Why, Max?"

Max leaned back and looked across at the bare-topped credenza.

"You know I looked for you," Sam said. "Almost cornered you in Oklahoma when you were in med school, but you continued to dodge me."

Max sat quietly.

"Sent a guy around to contact you when you were in Montana. Same thing. I finally stopped chasing you. Obviously, you didn't want to be contacted."

Max took another drink. "How's Maria?"

"Good. We have two girls in high school. One says she wants to be a surgeon. Imagine that."

"I guess it's in the genes."

Sam twisted on the sofa to get more comfortable. "Come on, Max, tell me. What happened? You didn't even show up for Mom's funeral."

Max said nothing as he continued to stare across the room.

Sam sighed. "Listen, I want you out to the house this afternoon. The kids will be home, and I would like you to meet them." Sam scribbled his address on a piece of paper and handed it to him. "Can you do that, Max? Can you come out to Katy and visit? It's been years, and I know Maria wants to see you. We all want you back in our lives."

Max stared at the address in his hand and slowly nodded.

"Great. Now I need to get back. Lots to do." Sam called a cab, and they sat quietly drinking their beers until it arrived. Sam stood up from the couch. "It's settled then. See you around two. Got some good barbecue, just the kind you like."

Max walked him to the door. Sam turned and held him tightly. "I love you, Max. Please come out to the house this afternoon."

Max smiled. "I'll try."

Chapter 48

The Present

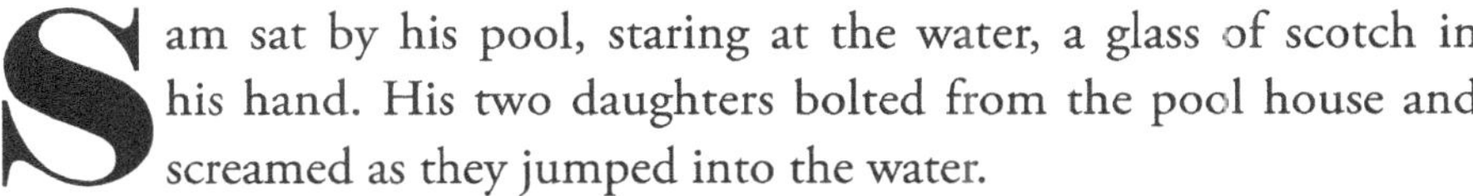

Sam sat by his pool, staring at the water, a glass of scotch in his hand. His two daughters bolted from the pool house and screamed as they jumped into the water.

"Sorry, Dad," shouted his eldest. "Didn't mean to get you wet."

He smiled, then took another sip from his glass.

"Girls, I told you to wait until Uncle Max got here before you got in the pool," Maria said as she walked across the pool deck and sat down beside Sam. "Here, try this cheese. It will go well with your scotch." She held out a small piece of cheese on a cracker and placed it in his mouth.

Sam swallowed, then returned to staring at his two children splashing about in the pool. He looked at his watch, then took another sip.

Maria stood up behind his chair and started massaging his shoulders. "I'm sure he'll come. He said he would, didn't he?"

Sam's body shook. He reached down to the bottle beside his chair and filled his glass again.

"How about you come inside, and I'll massage your back."

Sam said nothing. He just continued to stare at the water.

Maria sat down again and placed her hands on his arm. "Sam, you can't make him do what he doesn't want to do."

"But why, Maria? Why did he run away?"

"I don't know, sweetheart. But at some point, you're going to have to let him go."

"I can't. He's my brother. I can never let him go."

Maria sighed. She ran her hand along his shoulders, then went to the side of the pool. "Five more minutes, girls. Then get dried off and come inside and get ready for your uncle."

Sam looked again at his watch, then returned to staring at the water. A tear trickled down his cheek. *Come on, Max, you can do it. Come on home.*

Chapter 49

The Present

Max waved and watched his twin drive away. He went back to the sofa and sat down. He closed his eyes and rested his head back on the pillow. He tried to forget, but his last time in Katy kept screaming back.

~ ~ ~

2005

Maria helped Max to his feet as the ambulance drove off carrying Sam's still body to the hospital. She walked him to the porch swing and sat him down. "Max, we need to go. I want to follow the ambulance and be there when they arrive."

"It's too late. I think he's gone, Maria. Sam's gone!" Max lowered his head into his hands and started to cry uncontrollably. Visions of the dead young men he'd seen in Afghanistan flashed before his eyes. Asadi. The boy with no legs. All of them now had Sam's face.

"Well, I'm going to be there, dead or not. Are you coming?"

Max looked up at Maria towering over him, then at the lights of the ambulance disappearing off in the distance. "I can't. It's all my fault. Sam's dead."

"Why do I always find myself leaving a Donovan man on the porch when I go off to the hospital? Stay here then. Tell your mother where I am."

Maria turned in disgust and stormed off the porch. Max watched as she slammed her truck door and sped away, hoping to catch up with the ambulance before they unloaded Sam.

~ ~ ~

Sam's eyes darted wildly around the ambulance. The opioid reversal agent had started working while they were putting the breathing tube in, and now he fought against the restraining straps of the stretcher and tried to pull the tube out.

"Calm down, buddy!" the paramedic shouted as he placed his hands on either side of Sam's head to keep him still. "We'll take that tube out when we get you safely to the hospital."

The trip felt like it lasted for hours, even though they were in the emergency room within minutes. When he arrived, a disheveled, unshaven emergency-room doctor walked up to the stretcher, bent down, and looked into Sam's panic-stricken eyes.

"Another overdose, eh, boys?" Sam heard him say to the paramedic giving report. "Damn sick of this shit." He poked and prodded Sam, then took off his gloves and tossed them across the room and into the trash. "He's stable. Let him stay intubated for a few minutes while I finish my coffee. Will be a good lesson for him."

Confused, Sam looked around the room. He'd been in his bedroom the last he remembered, then suddenly in the back of an ambulance. His chest hurt. His lungs hurt. The tube in his throat hurt.

Panic seized him, and he started banging his good arm against the stretcher. He turned his head, pulling on his ventilator tubing, and looked helplessly at a nurse who stood in the doorway staring at him. He started banging his head up and down on the stretcher.

The nurse turned away and shouted toward the nurses' station. "Hey, Doc. Better get the tube out before he hurts himself."

The doctor walked back into the room holding his cup of coffee. "Okay, Mr. Donovan. Let's get this little tube out."

He ripped the tape securing the tube from Sam's face, deflated the balloon in his trachea, and yanked the tube out. Sam started coughing uncontrollably, his hands still strapped down to the stretcher. He watched as the doctor flung the tube against the wall and into the trash.

"The first of many for today," the doctor growled at the paramedic who was watching from the doorway. "How about you guys stop doing such a good job and let these pieces of shit die? They're all trash anyway."

Sam was once again left alone. He stared at the ceiling as he slowly started to remember what had happened. How could he have been so stupid? How could he have risked everything like that? He started to cry.

The nurse returned and untied his arms. "It's okay, Mr. Donovan. You're okay now. We're just going to watch you overnight. Just try to relax." She patted him on the shoulder. "I have a visitor for you."

She left the room and returned with Maria, who rushed to his side and threw her arms around him.

"We thought we'd lost you, Sam," Maria said. "Please never do that again."

Sam wrapped his good arm around her. "I promise you that will never happen again. I swear it."

~ ~ ~

Max's sorrow soon turned to anger.

Logan killed my brother. He did this to him.

The more he thought about it, the more he raged. He raged at the loss of his father. The losses he'd suffered in Afghanistan. His loss of Maria. It now all became Logan's fault.

Max stood up from the swing, ran into the house, and got his car keys. He pulled the Nova out of the driveway and headed to Logan's house.

He parked the car around the corner, then got out and approached the house, staying under the cover of the shrubbery that ran along the fronts of the quiet suburban houses. He looked up and down the street several times to make sure no one saw him before he sprang up the front steps.

He listened at the front door and heard nothing, then gently tried the doorknob. The door was unlocked, and he quietly entered the house. It was very similar to his own, and he crept toward the back, where he could hear sobbing coming from one of the bedrooms. He peered through a crack in the door and saw Logan huddled on the floor next to his bed with his head between his knees, crying.

Max burst into the room.

"Max! I'm sorry, Max. Is he okay?"

"You killed him! You and your damn drugs killed my brother!"

"No, Max. It wasn't like that. He was depressed because of you and Maria. He made me get that stuff. I don't even use that shit."

"No! This was your fault! You killed Sam!" Max stormed across the room and picked him up by the neck.

"Max, stop! Please!"

He dragged Logan across the room, holding him in a headlock with one arm; with the other, he reached under the bed and ripped out a long extension cord from the wall.

"Max, please, stop!"

He wrapped the cord around Logan's neck and squeezed. Logan struggled, his face turning blue as Max tightened his grip, his saliva splattering in Max's face. Panic and sorrow in his eyes. Eventually he stopped moving.

Max dragged the body across the room and tethered it to a hook in the closet, making it look like Logan had hung himself.

Panting and covered in sweat, Max stood in front of the lifeless body. He looked around the room. It was the room of an innocent teenage boy. Sports posters on the wall. Children's books on a shelf. A newspaper clipping of Max winning again for Katy Lakes.

The full realization of what he'd done suddenly overwhelmed him.

"Oh my God! Logan!"

Max ran from the house and jumped in his car. He drove wildly across town, barely able to see the road through his tears. He eventually found himself back in Galveston on the beach, miles away from the scene of his crime and from his brother.

He sat on the sand, then got up and started pacing, wondering what he should do. How could he have done what he did to that poor boy?

That was when he knew his own life was over. He'd destroyed any future that Logan or he would ever have. He would never be able to atone for that horrible act. He would never be clean again.

~ ~ ~

The Present

Max opened his eyes. He looked at his watch and saw that it was one-thirty. If he was going to make it out to Sam's barbecue on time, he would have to leave now.

He went into his bedroom, pulled out a duffel bag, and threw some clothes in it, along with some papers from his drawer. He slung it over his shoulder and left the house through the back door.

He opened the trunk of the Nova and tossed the bag in next to the chest containing his pictures and his father's flag. He climbed behind the wheel and drove out of West University and headed north to the junction with Interstate 10.

When he came to the intersection, there was a sign for I-10 west. He knew where that went. He could stay on it all the way to California, or he could turn off after half an hour's drive and be back home. Home to the scene of his crime. To the place where he'd been foolish and impulsive enough to cut short the life of an innocent boy.

Turn right, and he could take it east, nonstop to Florida.

Max clutched the steering wheel tightly in his sweaty hands. He looked at himself in the rearview mirror. He saw the ugly face of the pig looking back at him. Its hollowed-out eyes. Its grotesque snout. Unforgiving.

Tears streamed down his face as he turned right.

* End *